'Do you wan~~t~~ ~~~~ an inducement?'

Libby thought for a moment. 'No, my lord,' she said, and then added, with a twinkle in her eye, 'But one must be practical.'

'Indeed one must. Some of us more than others, perhaps. In your case, however, your practicality is one of your charms. Incidentally—and I hope you won't mind my mentioning it—I do find this frequent "my lord" a shade trying. My name is Marcus.'

'And you cannot fail to be aware—my lord—that it would be most improper in me to use it!' Libby retorted.

'Not, however, if you were to marry me.'

Stunned, unable to believe her ears and quite sure he must be able to hear her beating heart, Libby stared at him, only looking away when a blush of pure anger suffused her cheeks. She stood up.

'Such a remark may be regarded as an amusing jest to someone in your position, Lord Charlbury, but to someone in mine it is both thoughtless and unkind.'

Previous Titles

FLIGHT FROM THE HAREM
HIGHWAYMAN BRIDE
A CIVIL MARRIAGE

THE
DENMEAD
INHERITANCE

Janet Edmonds

First published in Great Britain 1991 by Mills & Boon Limited

© *Janet Edmonds 1991*

Australian copyright 1991
Philippine copyright 1991
This edition 1991

ISBN 0 263 77375 2

Masquerade is a trademark published by Mills & Boon Limited, Eton House, 18–24 Paradise Road, Richmond, Surrey, TW9 1SR.

Set in Times Roman 10 on 10¼ pt.
04-9108-87726 C

Made and printed in Great Britain

HISTORICAL NOTE

THERE is a tradition drummed into every British child that the last enemy invasion of these islands was in 1066. That isn't quite true. During the Napoleonic Wars a French expeditionary force landed on the Gower Peninsula in South Wales. The legend says that they met a group of Welsh women in their national costume, thought they were witches, and fled. The truth is less dramatic and far less fun. In fact it took the combined efforts of the local yeomanry and militia something like three weeks to defeat them. The events of this novel have therefore a sound historical base.

Nowadays it is hard to imagine the Needles without their lighthouse, but this building was quite a late addition to the landscape, like the fortifications north of Portsmouth—known locally as the Palmerston's Follies—built later in the nineteenth century to protect England from another French invasion which was feared but did not materialise.

Byfield Manor is entirely imaginary, but Chase is loosely based on Cams Hall, near Fareham, in particular in having a north face of stone and a south face of brick. Cams, however, is not an old foundation and has no tower or turret of any kind.

Janet Edmonds

CHAPTER ONE

As THE door closed behind the late Lord Denmead's man of legal affairs, a long silence fell upon the room.

It was broken by a deep, appreciative chuckle from the new Earl, the large, bluff, red-faced younger brother of the deceased. Having, early in life, exhibited no aptitude for either Church or Army but instead a considerable taste for low company, he had been dispatched at as young an age as was decently possible to India, where he had discovered in himself a very considerable commercial acumen and returned to England a veritable Nabob. He surveyed the three men who remained.

The Honourable Max Asthall stood by the empty grate in the library of the vast house in Grosvenor Square, kicking the iron fire-basket with his well-shod foot. His face was pale and his hand clenched the mantelshelf so hard that the knuckles showed through, white and hard.

'It's all very well for you to laugh,' he said, his voice quivering with anger. 'You have the title and that portion of the estates which is entailed—and that's as it should be and as everyone knew it was. But the rest, the bulk of the land and Chase itself... I've worked that land, I've managed those estates, and I've come to regard Chase as mine—and so it would be if there were any justice.'

'Ah, but then, you see, there isn't any justice, nephew. There's one thing I learned early on—nothing is yours until it's signed, sealed and delivered. I'll lay any odds you like you were never promised Chase, for all you think you earned it.'

Max Asthall's pale and angry face took on a sullen edge. '"If I played my cards right", that's what I was told on the only occasion it was discussed.'

6

His uncle gave him a thoughtful look before replying. 'So it would seem you didn't play your cards right—or not entirely. After all, Chase hasn't been taken away from you yet, has it?' The Earl opened a diamond-studded box and took a pinch of snuff, glancing sideways as he did so at the tall figure standing by the window.

Viscount Charlbury was every bit as angry as his brother. Had his back not been turned to the room, his uncle would have seen the tight mouth and clenched jaw which were the only outward signs of the fury seething beneath. He knew he had been the old Earl's favourite relative, and had fully expected to inherit the unentailed part of his uncle's estate, apart, he supposed, from a few reasonable bequests to other members of the family.

Indeed, as the old Earl's health had steadily declined, he had relied more and more on his expectations in that direction to pull him out of the River Tick. He had been fond of the old man and wished him no ill, but there was no denying he had died most fortuitously—or so it had seemed.

Now the Will had been read to the small audience of beneficiaries: to the heir to the title who was to receive only the title and the entailed estates and neither needed nor expected more; to the godson, Lord Wilcote, who received the late Earl's strange and exotic collection of Moghul artefacts, many of them collected by that same brother who now held the title—for Lord Wilcote, despite his youth and a propensity for the tables which he nevertheless kept well under control, was a noted connoisseur; to his late Lordship's younger nephew, Max Asthall, who inherited everything else in the event of his elder brother's failure to comply with the conditions of the Will; and to that elder brother, Lord Charlbury, who had only to comply with certain conditions to acquire an inheritance large enough to settle his immediate problems and insulate him against similar embarrassments for a long time to come, while at the same time leaving his younger brother virtually penniless.

It was not this last aspect of the affair which was provoking Lord Charlbury's anger: he had never been close to Max and had given little thought to the younger man's position, though he supposed he would have made some provision for him, since their uncle had not. It was the terms under which he was to inherit that galled him.

His uncle had referred to him in his Will as his favourite relative and had gone on to castigate him as a reprobate, a rake-hell and a wastrel, descriptions which the Viscount had shrugged off with a wry smile, knowing at least as well as the late Earl just how true they were. The stroke of genius devised by the old man to counter these tendencies—since there was no other conceivable reason for its imposition—was that, in order to inherit, Viscount Charlbury must, within six months of the reading of the Will, marry a 'well-bred, sensible girl of strong character, accustomed to habits of economy'. If he failed to do so, the inheritance would devolve upon the Honourable Max Asthall, his younger brother. It was not a bequest calculated to enhance fraternal goodwill.

Viscount Charlbury could call to mind many well-bred and unmarried females, several of whom had strong characters, but he was doubtful whether any of them could be described as 'sensible', and quite certain that no female of his acquaintance had ever acquired habits of economy—if, indeed, they even knew the word. He could not call to mind one single female of his acquaintance who conformed to all the required stipulations, and he wasn't at all sure he would want to marry her if he did. That his wife must be well-bred went without saying, but he would infinitely prefer someone young and malleable, and he had every intention of controlling the purse-strings himself. In his experience strong-minded females became intolerable once they felt their positions to be secure, and he had an unpleasant suspicion that 'habits of economy' meant boiled mutton every day and no more than three courses on the table.

This dearth of suitable females might have been amusing, had the requirement to marry one been imposed upon someone else, but Marcus Asthall, third Viscount Charlbury, had rarely been thwarted by his doting widowed mother, had resented his trustees' efforts to curtail his recreations and his expenditure, and had, in the fourteen years since coming into his majority, systematically squandered his carefully nurtured patrimony, regardless of advice or admonition. Now, at thirty-five, he felt the firm hand of his mother's brother descend upon him—as it were from the grave—to control his life. True, he could ignore the condition. That freedom at least was left him. But at what a price! He alone knew how desperately he needed that inheritance, but many would guess how much it would gall him to dance to the old man's tune, for he entertained no doubts that the Nabob would pass the word around his clubs.

With admirable self-control he turned to face the others, only a certain extra hardness in his grey eyes betraying any hint of his feelings.

'My dear Max,' he said in the lazy voice he sometimes adopted to wither pretension, 'one can only conclude that you—unlike me—have hidden vices of which our late uncle came to hear.'

Max's pale features flushed with what might have been guilt, but which, thought Lord Wilcote—acutely embarrassed at having been obliged to be present at the reading of so eccentric a Will—was as likely to be fury. Max, with very little money of his own, had lived at Chase and tried to manage the estates efficiently, despite the handicap of his uncle's refusing to countenance any new-fangled methods. It really was too bad of the old Earl to put his nephew in a position where he stood to get nothing. Lord Wilcote did not like Max, and he didn't know anyone who did much like him: there was something indefinable about the young man which put one on one's guard—a certain lack of openness, perhaps. Not that people were precisely enamoured of Marcus. It was true the ladies seemed to find him irresistible, but his arrogant manner and cutting tongue lost him the universal popularity for which many would have hankered.

This did not seem to bother the Viscount unduly. He had a small circle of close friends, of whom Rupert Wilcote was one. They alone saw, just occasionally, the other side of his character: the generosity of which he was capable with both time and money, the loyalty to his friends, and the charm he was capable of exerting—usually, it had to be admitted, when it suited his purpose.

There was, however, no reason for him to needle poor Max. Max could scarcely have been aware of the terms of the bequest—his anger was evidence of that—and, really, one could hardly blame the old man for trying to prevent his fortune going down the same drain that was guzzling the Asthall inheritance, though how the old Earl had imagined that any woman could change Marcus's habits was beyond Lord Wilcote's comprehension. Marcus certainly pandered to the extravagant tastes of the high-fliers with whom he enjoyed a succession of temporary liaisons, but that did not suggest they had any real hold over him. On the contrary, since they inevitably bored him within a few weeks, any liaison was usually very temporary indeed, and it was invariably Marcus who ended the *affaire* with an abruptness which the ladies found disconcerting.

Max removed his foot from the fender and his hand from the mantel, and turned to his brother, his voice quivering with anger as he spoke.

'It's all very well for you,' he said. 'All you have to do is find a suitable woman and I'm left with nothing—nothing.' His voice caught on a strangled sob. 'I only inherit if you fail—and you won't, if only to spite me.'

Lord Charlbury raised his quizzing-glass and contemplated his brother through it, slowly.

'Pray tell me, Max,' he asked silkily, 'when have I previously set out to spite you?'

Max flushed. 'Well, no, not that precisely, I suppose. Only it has seemed like it when I see you spending money like water while I've had to manage on a bare competence.'

'Alas, Max, you really should have arranged to be the elder son, then our positions would have been reversed. Think how joyful you would now be had that been so.'

Max made towards his brother, his fists clenched. Lord Wilcote stepped forward and laid a hand on his arm.

'Don't stop him,' Lord Charlbury protested. 'He's as unlikely to land a punch on me as I am to find a female who fulfils our uncle's specifications. Think on that, young 'un. How many "well-bred, sensible girls of strong character, accustomed to habits of economy" do you think I number among my acquaintance? Believe me, you may inherit yet!'

The palpable truth of this appealed to Max, as did his brother's use of the old, almost-forgotten, familiar soubriquet. In spite of himself, he gave a short laugh.

'What do I do while we wait?' he asked.

'Wait? For what?' his brother replied. 'Oh, I beg your pardon. You mean until I either marry—in accordance with Uncle's wishes, of course—or I don't. May I suggest you return to Chase? After all, you wouldn't wish to see your inheritance diminish by six months' neglect, while I, of course, would prefer to take it over in peak condition. As for what I shall do—nothing could be simpler. Tonight I shall go to White's while Rupert goes ahead to warn his parents that I've accepted his invitation to rusticate at Copthorne. Tomorrow, when I eventually get up, I shall follow him, though I hardly think Copthorne is likely to prepare me for the rigours of life with this unpalatable female.'

Max snorted. 'It's not the sort of place where you'll find one, either,' he said. 'I mean no disrespect to Rupert, but I don't think his sisters qualify.'

The Viscount smiled. 'I'm sure you're right.' He turned to his uncle and bowed. 'Your servant, sir. Rupert?'

The two men left the house together.

CHAPTER TWO

'IT REALLY is too bad,' Lady Somerton expostulated as she entered the darkened drawing-room, a small sheet of paper in her hand.

'It is, indeed,' replied an acid voice from the depths of a day-bed placed in such a way that its occupant was invisible from the door. 'I've told you goodness knows how many times that I like two undisturbed hours after luncheon, and what happens? Rarely half an hour after I've succeeded in making myself comfortable, in you burst like any hoyden. It really is the outside of enough!'

'A thousand pardons, Mama,' answered her daughter-in-law, looking not remotely abashed. 'But I really must let off steam—a vulgar expression but so vivid, don't you think? Libby, dear, draw back the curtains, do.'

'Vividness can't excuse vulgarity and, Libby, don't you dare,' snapped the voice from the day-bed, and its owner immediately sat up, straightening the cap that for comfort replaced her more usual turban. 'One cannot rest save in a darkened room, and I can conceive of no reason why you should need sunlight to enable you to tell me something. Sit down again, Libby.'

The young female thus adjured resumed her seat near the curtained window and took up her embroidery frame.

Lady Somerton allowed herself to be diverted momentarily from her purpose. 'Libby, dear, it can't be good for your eyes to embroider in this light.'

'Rubbish!' snapped the Dowager Countess. 'What do you expect her to do? Read a book? Or twiddle her thumbs?'

'Neither, Mama. If you're asleep there's really no need for her to stay in the room at all. She could then embroider or read—or twiddle, for that matter—in a decent light.'

12

'And get ideas above her station,' retorted the Dowager. 'Libby is my companion, and will do as I require. I like to have a little nap in the afternoon, but I'm an old woman now and I naturally have a great fear that one day I shan't wake up. That is why Libby stays with me.'

The object of these remarks, who seemed not the least put out at hearing herself discussed as if she were absent, paused thoughtfully in her sewing. 'I suppose that would be a situation in which I should be enormously useful,' she said. 'I confess, however, to being somewhat uncertain as to my exact role. Do I, I wonder, exercise my own judgement as to when you are in the process of not waking up and seek to revive you with hartshorn, burnt feathers or a jug of water? Or do I wait until you have failed to wake up and then rouse the household with a display of histrionics? It is, you'll allow, ma'am, a vexed question.'

The old lady, who was neither so aged nor so decrepit as she chose on occasion to make out, cackled. 'Sauciness, my girl, is not becoming. Just you remember it.'

'I'll endeavour to do so,' her companion replied with total composure. 'In the meantime, I can put Lady Somerton's mind at rest. I select all my colours beforehand, and I reserve for these occasions a piece of embroidery which is neither particularly subtle nor closestitched.'

'You see?' announced the Dowager triumphantly. 'Now, Amelia, why have we been subjected to this disturbance?'

'I have a letter here from Rupert, sent in some haste from London.'

'Well, I never. So all that education wasn't wasted—Rupert *can* write!'

'Of course Rupert can write! Please don't be provoking, Mama! Rupert writes that he is coming down tomorrow to Copthorne for a week or two. He had intended to be here yesterday, but was delayed, and hopes I don't mind the short notice—and, indeed, why should

I? It is his home, after all, and therefore quite unnecessary for him to warn me of his arrival.'

The Dowager snorted. '*You* may consider it unnecessary. For my part, I'm delighted that, in addition to being able to write, he exhibits some basic good manners. What mystifies me is why this relatively mundane piece of news warrants interrupting my rest.'

'But that part of his news isn't the point, Mama. Just think—he has invited Charlbury down with him. Says he needs to rusticate.'

'Hm,' said the Dowager. 'You mean the rake?'

'Is there another Charlbury?'

Neither lady noticed that Libby Barton's needle had stopped once more, only this time she was examining her handiwork most intently.

The Dowager stared at her daughter-in-law keenly. 'Charlbury has been here before,' she commented. 'I've met him here. He and Rupert have been good friends for years, despite the disparity in their ages. They seem to pursue the same interests, but you must admit he has never yet led Rupert into the excesses which are said to characterise his own indulgences. So why are you suddenly perturbed?' She permitted herself a smile which an unkind observer might have described as malicious. 'Surely, Amelia, you can't have developed a *tendre* in that direction? Of course, he is said to be irresistible,' she added reflectively, 'but I have to warn you that I've not so far heard that his taste leans towards females of quite your degree of maturity.'

'I believe irresistibility is generally held to be a characteristic of rakes,' her daughter-in-law snapped tartly. 'And that is precisely what alarms me. When he was here last, the girls were still children.'

'They still are! Good heavens, Amelia, Selina is only sixteen, and no rake is going to seduce a well-bred schoolgirl in her own house where he is a guest. Not even Charlbury!'

'I know that, Mama, but both she and Jane—who is, after all, only a year younger—are so steeped in these silly romantic ideas that Selina is quite capable of be-

lieving that all he needs is the Love of a Good Woman
to reform him and that she is destined to be that woman,
even if she won't be out until next season. And then
there's Robert,' she added.

'Oh, come, Amelia—I've heard a great deal about
Charlbury and little of it in his favour, but never in that
context.'

Lady Somerton blushed. 'Mama, please—we're not
alone! That didn't enter my head, as I'm sure you are
perfectly well aware. It's just that Robert is of an age
to be looking for an example upon which to model
himself, and Charlbury lives the sort of life many young
men seek to emulate.'

'Rupert didn't.'

'Rupert is a lot older than Robert.'

'He wasn't when he first became involved with
Charlbury's set. Why should Robert have less sense than
his brother?'

'I don't know why, Mama, and, though I dislike very
much to admit it, the fact remains that he does have less
sense. You've commented upon it yourself. Frequently,'
she added bitterly.

But the Dowager, her afternoon nap forgotten, was
pursuing another line of thought. 'They say Charlbury's
pretty well under the hatches. He could well be hanging
out for a rich wife.'

'But Selina is no heiress, and in any case she's nearly
twenty years his junior!'

'Selina, my dear Amelia, has a very substantial settlement to come on her marriage, and, when Charlbury
had worked his way through it, do you think Somerton
would let him sink? No. Charlbury could be sure his
father-in-law would bail him out. As for the age difference—how wise to have a pliable young innocent for
a wife! Amelia, you were wrong in detail but, upon reflection, I must admit that your instincts weren't at fault.
I fancy a word with Rupert might not come amiss.'

Rightly construing this to be a reference to her husband
and not her eldest son, the Countess took her leave of
her mama-in-law and made her way to the library, where

she knew the Earl—a quiet, scholarly man—would be found. He heard her out with his customary calm.

'You alarm yourself unnecessarily, me dear,' he said quietly. 'I don't for one moment imagine Charlbury has any more precise object in accepting Rupert's invitation than a need to rusticate. As for his intentions towards Selina, I can't imagine he regards her as anything other than a schoolgirl, and I assure you I shall refuse consent to anyone seeking her hand, no matter how worthy, until she has learned some sense.'

'And what if they were to elope?' his wife demanded dramatically.

Her husband raised his eyebrows. 'Charlbury, elope?' he said. 'My dear, can you really imagine his doing anything so uncomfortable? Forgive me, but I can't help suspecting that it isn't only Selina and Jane who have this distressing penchant for novels. Was there anything else, my dear?'

There was not, and his lady left the room feeling unwontedly foolish.

It so happened that Libby was the only person to witness the somewhat untoward arrival of Lord Wilcote and his friend. The Dowager had decided—a decision entirely unconnected with any comments her daughter-in-law might have made, of course—that her companion would be well advised to enjoy some fresh air during the obligatory post-prandial nap, and had accordingly instructed her to go out and cut some flowers from the garden so that the old lady could have several more vases of them about her room.

Fulfilling this apparently simple instruction involved the expenditure of a great deal of tact and diplomacy on Libby's part towards the head gardener, for Framlingham objected strongly to his flowers being cut in the heat of the day, and demanded to know what had been wrong with the ones he had sent up to the house early that morning. Libby appeased him by mendaciously assuring him that they had indeed been so fine that the Dowager Countess had appropriated them all for her own quarters, and had therefore told Libby to find replacements. Naturally, her ladyship would have preferred the task to be handled by Framlingham, but feared that with so much work on his hands it would be adding intolerably to his burden.

Mollified, he indicated to Libby those areas where she might cut at will, and himself returned to the more onerous task of supervising the scything of the South Lawn.

Thus it came about that Libby, a laden trug on her arm, turned the corner by the stable-block as first Lord Wilcote and then Lord Charlbury drew up in their respective curricles. She was at first surprised that they had not alighted at the main entrance, leaving their grooms to bring the teams round to the stables, but one closer look at their dishevelled appearance explained the irregularity. The grooms looked as bad as their masters.

Both Viscount Charlbury and his groom had broken knuckles, and the latter in addition sported the makings of a decidedly superior black eye. Lord Wilcote's groom was without his hat, while his master's cravat looked even more disreputable than did the guest's. All four men were covered with a far greater amount of dust even than was compatible with a long journey in an open carriage.

In short, their appearance was so out of character for both men that Libby dropped her trug and ran forward.

'Good heavens, Lord Wilcote—my lord—what on earth has happened? You look for all the world as if you had been in a brawl!'

'Confound it, Libby,' answered Lord Wilcote. 'What are you doing here? We'd hoped to slip in through the kitchens without anyone's being the wiser. You met Charlbury on a previous visit here, I think. Marcus, Miss Barton, my grandmama's companion. I've a feeling she was here last time you came. My grandmama comes here for most of each summer.'

Lord Charlbury bowed, an elegant gesture at odds with his present appearance. 'Of course. I remember Miss Barton well.'

Libby looked at him speculatively. 'I shouldn't think you do at all,' she said. 'I rather had the impression I was part of the wallpaper—though less of a connoisseur's item than the Chinese papers at Copthorne, perhaps.'

Arrested by this disconcertingly frank reply to what had been a mere conventional pleasantry, and intensely annoyed by its accuracy, Lord Charlbury looked closer at the speaker.

It was difficult to put an age to her—twenty-two or three, perhaps; and he really had never much admired dark-haired women. He preferred them tall, too, and Miss Barton was of less than average height. She had a trim figure, though, and this enabled her to wear her rather plain dress with a certain style which belied the fact that she had almost certainly made it herself. Not for nothing had Lord Charlbury paid the dressmakers' bills for a succession of expensive ladies. Miss Barton had a smooth ivory skin, and though her eyes were dark they did not have that soulful-spaniel look that so often characterised such eyes. In fact, there was a distinctly pert gleam in them which, together with a very decided chin, boded ill, he thought, for the man she married.

He bowed again. 'If you say so, ma'am,' he said coldly.

If he expected her to be disconcerted this time, he was disappointed. She laughed.

'If I were a prime article, I wouldn't be Lady Somerton's companion,' she said.

'If you were a prime article,' retorted that lady's grandson, 'my mother wouldn't let you over the doorstep. Good Lord, Libby, do watch your language. What do you know of prime articles, for goodness' sake?'

'Not a great deal,' she confessed. 'And nothing at all until old Lady Somerton used the expression and I naturally sought enlightenment.'

Lord Wilcote laughed. 'Aye, she would—nothing mealy-mouthed about Grandmama when she sets her mind to it! Now, Libby, be a good girl, please, and let us slip upstairs. The longer we stand here, the more likely we are to be spotted. We'd both be obliged if you'd not say a word about seeing us in our present state. If you do, the questions will be endless.'

'If I'm not asked—and why should I be?—I shan't be obliged to say a word. I must own to considerable curiosity, though. Pray, what *has* happened? Surely you can't *both* have overturned your curricles?'

Lord Wilcote's face took on an expression of pure horror. 'For goodness' sake don't put that story about!' he exclaimed, aghast. 'I don't mind telling *you* because you're the only female I've ever known who doesn't blab, but it would worry my parents if they knew, so not a word.'

'Not a word,' she promised.

'I'd intended to come down yesterday,' he went on, 'and Marcus was going to follow today. In the event, something cropped up and we came together, only we thought it would be more interesting to make a race of it.'

'You *did* overturn your curricles!'

'If you're going to interrupt, I shan't go on.'

'I'm sorry,' she said in a meek voice at variance with the glint in her eyes.

'Marcus was leading by quite a large margin,' he went on. 'In fact, though I hate to admit it, he was out of sight. I came upon him just five miles from here—that spot where the road goes through a thick stretch of woodland—and he was being set upon by four ruffians.'

'Footpads?'

'Attacking a curricle? No, these men had horses and pistols. Fortunately they don't seem to have been very good shots, because they'd discharged their pistols without hitting anyone and Marcus and Fratton were laying about them with fists and not doing at all badly. When Connor and I joined in it evened up the odds and, between the four of us, we sent them packing.'

Libby looked from one to the other, her eyes wide and puzzled. 'What a very good job you delayed your departure! Otherwise there would have been no one to come to his lordship's aid. But what an extraordinary place for highwaymen to choose for an ambuscade; that little lane is a long way from the pike-road and rarely used except by local traffic and drovers.'

'It's certainly the one aspect of the affair that causes one to ponder, Miss Barton,' Viscount Charlbury commented drily. 'However, as Rupert has intimated, that is perhaps the very reason why his parents should not be burdened with the story. I'm sure you agree.'

'Do you know, Lord Charlbury, I really believe that in this matter we're in total accord. How pleasant! Now do forgive me, but the Dowager Countess will wake up soon and expect to see vases of flowers in every unadorned niche.' She paused and looked him up and down dispassionately. 'I dare say that when we shortly meet in the drawing-room you will present a more salubrious aspect.'

The two men watched her pick up her trug and disappear round the stable corner. The Viscount looked enquiringly at his friend.

'Libby? Lord, Marcus, she won't breathe a word. If any hint of this does get out, you can be sure it will be through the kitchen staff—but we can depend upon Connor to square them.'

CHAPTER THREE

THE most notable feature of the next few days was the extreme care taken by Lady Selina's mama to ensure that neither of her two eldest daughters was at any time in the least danger of being alone with Viscount Charlbury. They were chaperoned during their waking hours, which, had Lady Somerton realised it, only heightened their interest in a visitor whom they would otherwise have dismissed as being merely one of Rupert's friends.

Lord Wilcote saw no reason to enlighten either of his parents as to the precise nature of that part of the late Earl of Denmead's estate which concerned Lord Charlbury and his brother. He naturally told them of the bequest to himself, but added that the rest was a complex matter, unlikely to be resolved for some months.

Lady Somerton was, on the whole, quite relieved that Lord Charlbury showed not the slightest interest in Selina or Jane. True, she was very slightly piqued that he seemed not to notice Selina's quite staggering beauty, for he was without doubt a considerable connoisseur in that field, but since he was the last person of her acquaintance whom she would have considered a suitable suitor her common sense told her to give silent thanks that he did nothing to complicate matters by appearing other than indifferent.

The only eligible female for whom no one thought it necessary to suggest a chaperon was the Dowager Countess's companion. Not that Libby had a great deal of spare time in which to need it—the Dowager saw to that. But now that the Dowager had ceased to require her presence after lunch, Libby was free to walk in the gardens or to sew or read indoors or out. Since she liked the fresh air, and the Copthorne gardens were something out of the ordinary, with their terraces, their per-

21

golas, their shrubbery walks and a cunningly contrived cascade that fed a descending series of natural-seeming pools, it was to the gardens that she repaired whenever the weather permitted. Viscount Charlbury found the somnolence that overtook every country house after luncheon decidedly tedious and the restraints of desultory converse in the drawing-room irksome, so whenever he could slip out without his absence appearing discourteous he did so. He would have preferred a good gallop across the fields, but a stroll in the gardens some distance from the house was an adequate, if not entirely satisfactory substitute. Having been greeted on his arrival by Miss Barton in gardening humour, he was not at all surprised occasionally to bump into her on these small excursions.

The first time he had spotted her, his heart had sunk. She had obviously seen him, too, so courtesy precluded his vanishing behind a large bush until he could unobtrusively move elsewhere. He had nothing against Miss Barton. She was an unexceptional female, perhaps not so colourless as he had at first assumed, but there was no denying that females encountered in this sort of situation had a tendency to cling like leeches and expect one to exchange banalities until it was time to return to the house. However, there was no escape, so he inclined his head in greeting.

'Good afternoon, Miss Barton. No trug and no shears this time, I see.' He supposed it must have been his imagination that made her appear hesitant to approach, because there was nothing hesitant about her reply.

'No, my lord. Happily, Lady Somerton has abandoned the pretence that she needed flowers. The gardener wasn't at all happy to have me desecrating his beds every afternoon.'

'Why should she pretend such a thing at all?' he asked, intrigued. 'Surely she has only to ask him to send them to the house?'

'Of course, but that wouldn't give her an excuse to send me out, would it?'

'Does she need such an excuse?'

'Oh, yes. You see, she had always insisted that I stay with her while she had her nap, but, when her daughter-in-law pointed out that my presence made no appreciable difference to the Dowager's well-being, and that the dim light was quite possibly harmful to me—arguments which were irrefutable—the old lady had to find an excuse to send me out at that time, an excuse which she was able to drop once people became accustomed to seeing me about while she was having her nap.'

'I'm surprised you hadn't made a stand before, on your own account.'

'Had it bothered me unduly, I should have done—you mustn't take me for one of these downtrodden little drudges who so often end up as ladies' companions. It didn't bother me unduly, but I'll admit the present arrangement suits me better. You were heading for the Temple of Diana, I think.'

'I was,' he admitted warily. 'Shall you accompany me, or is there somewhere else you would rather go?'

Libby coloured. 'Heavens, no, my lord. I wasn't hinting at any such thing. You came out here for some solitude, I dare say, and a companion to whom you have to make idle chatter will not be what you had in mind.' He opened his mouth to protest, as good manners demanded, that that was not the case at all, but Libby laughed. 'No, my lord, you don't have to be polite—not that polite, at all events. You go your way with your thoughts and I'll go my way with mine. I'm sure we shall both be better suited with that arrangement.'

With these words of dismissal, uttered with an accompanying smile, she turned and walked briskly in the direction that led away from his own destination.

Viscount Charlbury stared after her, decidedly taken aback. It was, he thought, the first time he had ever been given his *congé* by an old woman's dowdy companion. In fact, now he came to think about it, it was the first time he had been given his *congé* by *any* female. The fact that he hadn't wanted her company, and would have hidden to avoid her if he could, was neither here nor there. She had demonstrated very clearly that she

had no wish to hang on his every word or to monopolise
his attention, and there was no denying he was more
than a little piqued. Then the absurdity of the situation
struck him. He shrugged his shoulders and chuckled to
himself. Serve you right to be brought down a peg or
two, he thought. Especially by a nobody. Everyone
should be cut down to size occasionally.

The Temple of Diana was an excellent vantage point
from which to see the gardens, but, broad as was the
vista below him, there was no sign of a small figure in
a nondescript dress.

Libby had been disconcerted to see him also taking
the air. There was no reason why he shouldn't be, of
course, but Libby had got into the habit of expecting to
encounter no one during this hour or two's respite from
the Dowager's demands—a respite for which she silently
blessed her hostess. She was perfectly happy as a companion, but there was no denying she enjoyed the luxury
of a few hours to herself and, apart from the afternoon
of the Viscounts' arrival, her first afternoon of freedom,
she had met no one.

There was more to it than that, of course, and had
she met any other member of the household in the
gardens after luncheon she would have thought nothing
of it. Viscount Charlbury was different. Libby knew she
was being foolish, just as she knew she was wasting her
energy on a hopeless cause. The fact remained that she
had fallen head over ears in love with him almost from
the first moment she had seen him—an infatuation
which, she knew perfectly well, had more place in the
mind of a seventeen-year-old than in a woman of three-
and-twenty.

The last time his visit to Copthorne had coincided with
that of the Dowager he had taken as much notice of
Libby as he had of the furniture. No, that was unfair—
he had never bade the furniture 'Good morning'. His
tall, broad-shouldered figure moved with a deceptively
casual elegance; his voice was deep, with a hint of
harshness in it that was somehow well suited to his lean,
sardonic features. His character was deplorable, though

not so deplorable that Lady Somerton refused to receive him and, whatever might be the general opinion of him, Libby had to admit that his behaviour at Copthorne was everything it should be. Still, the reputation was there, and Libby was old enough and honest enough to accept that it heightened his attractiveness. It was well known that he must marry a rich woman, and Libby was entirely penniless, thereby rendering herself totally ineligible even had he shown the slightest interest in her. And if I weren't penniless, she thought, I wouldn't have been forced to become a companion and would probably be happily married to someone else by now and never have come across Lord Charlbury in the first place.

Nevertheless, the speculation, the ifs and buts, continued. Although she couldn't claim quite such high-born affiliations as his lordship, she was none the less respectably bred, the Bartons having been a far older family than the Asthalls. But she was its last remnant, both her mother and her grandmother having been, like her, only children. Her father, too, an ineffective weakling with no notion of how to hold house, had been an only child, and Libby knew of no relatives at all on either side. Her mother had struggled valiantly to bring her up after her father's untimely demise but had herself died of the smallpox when Libby was sixteen.

The Dowager Countess of Somerton, who had been acquainted with Libby's grandmother, had heard of the orphan's plight and, assessing her as a sensible, practical girl, had offered her the post of companion when her education had been completed—at the Dowager's expense. She paid her a sensible salary and proceeded to get good value for her money. The younger Lady Somerton felt that Libby was in an invidious position: the Dowager was a formidable old woman who could wither pretension with a word and had already disposed of two paid companions by the simple expedient of sending them weeping from the house. In fact, despite the huge disparity in their ages, the two women hit it off remarkably well: Libby was unperturbed by the old lady's acid tongue, occasionally demonstrating her own ability to respond in kind, and the Dowager liked her for it. On their frequent visits to Copthorne, Libby was treated by the Wilcote household as one of the family, but she made sure never to behave like one and thus be accused of 'encroaching ways'.

She supposed it was odd that her visit and Lord Charlbury's had only coincided once before, though perhaps it was for the best, since whenever she caught sight of him she felt herself blush and her heart beat so much faster that she was surprised no one remarked upon it. This day was no different and since, having seen the Viscount and having obviously been seen by him, she could hardly turn her back on him and walk in the opposite direction, she took herself very strongly under control and greeted him in what she hoped was a sufficiently matter-of-fact manner as to betray no hint of her deeper feelings.

She was glad she had done so because it made the occasional future encounter much easier, and furthermore established the fact that neither of them expected to hang upon the words of the other. The initial talk of his visit's lasting a week or two was soon dropped and it became obvious that his stay would be of indefinite duration. Libby was unsure whether to rejoice in so many additional opportunities to see him or to regret that every opportunity merely served to underline the hopelessness of her carefully concealed feelings for him. It was at least some small comfort that he didn't seem to find her company tedious, and she could certainly not have accused him this time of regarding her in much the same way as he regarded the wallpaper. Happily, his behaviour was exemplary, whether they met in company in the drawing-room or came across each other in the solitude of the gardens. No one could have accused him of flirting, despite his reputation. Indeed, thought Libby, it was hard to see in him the ramshackle individual he was reputed to be.

Despite the hopelessness of the overwhelming attraction she felt for the disreputable Viscount, she treasured every word, every moment, and stored up in her mind every gesture, every rare smile that touched those sardonic lips. For whatever reason he chose to sit with her and walk with her she was grateful, even if deep down she suspected it might be due to boredom, to the fact that she was a different face, a different voice. She was therefore quite taken aback when he came to her side at the tea-table one evening and helped her dispense the tea that was always served when the gentlemen had rejoined the ladies after dinner. It was a task she had always taken unobtrusively upon herself, a task entirely fitting for a companion, and she could imagine no reason why he should have come forward to assist her. The whole family was present, so it certainly wasn't for lack of people with whom to converse. Lady Somerton was full of fascinating gossip, and the Dowager's acerbic comments were scarcely dull.

Neither was the Dowager's eye. It did not escape her notice that Lord Charlbury was being rather more attentive to her companion than that young woman's situation warranted, and so, in the privacy of her boudoir that evening, she dismissed her maid with instructions to ask Miss Barton to attend her before she retired. She came straight to the point.

'Charlbury was being rather attentive this evening, Libby. You should warn him off.'

Libby blushed. 'I think not, ma'am. He only assisted at the tea-table.'

'Precisely. I think you'll find that is not a practice of which he makes a habit—a fact which lends it a certain particularity, you'll allow.'

'As to that, Lady Somerton, I couldn't say; I'm not sufficiently acquainted with his lordship.'

'No, my girl, you're not—and, if you take my advice, you'll keep it that way.'

She looked at Libby's heightened colour and downcast eyes in silence for a few moments, and when she spoke again her voice had softened slightly.

'So that's the way the wind blows! Lord, Libby, you're not for him! If he needs anything, it's a rich wife, and that's something you'll never be. You'd be better ad-

vised to set your cap at a country parson—you'd make
a good clergyman's wife.'

Libby raised her eyes. 'Lord Charlbury may have appeared attentive, ma'am, but in fairness you can hardly
accuse me of setting my cap at him.'

'No, you were all propriety. I pay you the compliment
of suspecting that you wouldn't know how to set a cap.
Nevertheless, be warned. He's a dangerous man. You're
a sensible girl—it's what I like in you—and I'm sure you
won't take advice amiss. Avoid him, Libby. He can only
be amusing himself, and you'll be lucky to escape with
nothing more serious than a broken heart. Charlbury's
a rake, remember, and a past master at breaking hearts.'

In the privacy of her own room, Libby acknowledged
it. The Dowager's counsel was well meant and soundly
based. All Libby's practical common sense told her she
should follow the Dowager's advice. But common sense
played no part in her feelings for the Viscount. She knew
she had no hope, and no one could fairly accuse Lord
Charlbury of offering her any encouragement. That
being so, the pleasure of his occasional company would
have to be enough, and she did not feel inclined to forgo
it so long as it was being offered. It was perhaps a good
thing that the Dowager had not been aware of those other
occasions when he had sought her company—occasions
when there had been no chaperon. Libby's heart quailed
at the thought of the interpretation her employer might
put upon them if word reached her ears.

These unsatisfactory thoughts caused Libby to toss and
turn restlessly long into the night, interspersed with wild
schemes by which she might be transformed overnight
into an heiress, and thereby make her eligible for a
viscountess's coronet. Even as she dreamed up one im-
plausible idea after another, the back of her very practical mind asked her if she really wanted to marry a man
whose sole interest in her was the size of her fortune.
Her common sense shouted 'No', but her heart qualified
it with 'But if it were Charlbury...'

It was hardly surprising, therefore, that she awoke with
a punishing headache. She forced herself to ignore this

while she attended the Dowager, but as soon as that lady lay down for her daily nap Libby forwent her daily stroll—and its accompanying chance of meeting Charlbury—and, like her employer, lay down in a darkened room. This time she awoke somewhat refreshed, but as the afternoon wore on her apprehension increased, for she knew the old lady would be watching her especially closely.

In the event, the old lady's vigilance was unrewarded. As Libby descended the stairs before dinner, alone because the Dowager was not yet ready and had told her to go on ahead, she encountered the Viscount emerging from the library.

He bowed. 'I gather you were indisposed this afternoon,' he said. 'I was sorry to hear it.'

'A headache, my lord, nothing more. It's gone now.'

'I'm glad.' He stood aside for her to pass into the drawing-room, and no more converse passed between them.

The ordeal of the tea-table, as Libby now thought of it, passed without incident, the Viscount dividing himself between the Honourable Robert Wilcote, who sought enlightenment as to the relative merits of Cleveland and Yorkshire coach-horses, and Lady Somerton, who wished to ascertain if the story about her dear friend, Lady Noke, was really true.

When Libby went to bed that night it was with a mixture of relief that the Dowager had seen nothing to which she could possibly object, and regret that that was so.

The following afternoon being fine and sunny, Libby took herself for a quiet walk by the lake. The lake at Copthorne was unusual in that it was a natural one and a rise in the ground hid it from the house. Lady Somerton found this intensely annoying and had tried hard to persuade her husband to have the ground levelled so that what she called 'a vista' might be obtained. This the Earl steadfastly refused to do on the grounds that, whatever current fashion might dictate, he liked the element of surprise when one came upon the lake, and so it re-

mained a feature of the grounds. The Earl had also refused to allow the construction of a rustic bridge, but
had been happy to sanction a small belvedere in a grove
of expensively transplanted trees at one end of the lake.
The Countess was hoping to add a grotto beneath this
feature, but had not yet broached it to her husband.

It was towards this pleasant spot that Libby made her
way. The belvedere was in the classical style with a bench
on the marble floor beneath the small cupola that
afforded protection from the sun, and the view of the
lake afforded from here was one of her favourites. She
liked, in particular, to watch the birds: the resident pair
of swans with their brood of cygnets, and the Countess's
peafowl, who spent more time here than decorating the
terrace as their owner had originally intended.

As she sat enjoying the warmth and peace, she became
aware of the tall figure of Lord Charlbury approaching
from an angle which suggested he had come from the
stables rather than directly from the house. The Dowager,
had she been informed of his approach, would have
expected her companion to leave the belvedere immediately but without undue haste. Libby toyed with the idea
of doing what would have been expected of her, but only
briefly. She wanted Lord Charlbury's company, for
however short a time it might be made available, and,
in any case, they could not be observed from the house.

He paused at the top of the shallow flight of steps and
looked down at her, smiling. 'May I join you, Miss
Barton?'

'Of course, my lord,' she replied as she moved along
the seat to leave room for him to sit down, telling herself
that since there was only one seat, and that a long one,
it would be churlish to expect him to continue to stand.

'You've chosen a very pleasant spot, Miss Barton,' he
said.

'I like it here,' she replied. 'Unfortunately it's a
considerable distance from the house and I rarely come
this far in case old Lady Somerton wakes up and needs
me.'

'What made you come so far today?'

'She always sleeps much longer when the weather is really warm.'

'I see. What a practical female you are, Miss Barton.'

Libby considered this statement before responding. 'I think I must be. Lady Somerton is always remarking upon it, at all events. I think she regards being sensible—that's the other accolade she occasionally bestows upon me—and practical as being my two greatest virtues.'

'Indeed. May one enquire which characteristics she regards as your two greatest vices?'

Libby laughed unselfconsciously. 'A tendency to levity and an over-active imagination.'

'By the former I imagine she means a certain dry sense of humour, but I can't say I've observed in you this over-active imagination.'

Libby, conscious of the nature of some of her dreams, felt a faint blush as she replied. 'But imagination is an intensely private thing, don't you think?'

'I suppose in a paid companion it must be kept so, but in certain circumstances—as between husband and wife, for example—it could be happily shared.'

'As to that, Lord Charlbury, I'm hardly in a position to comment.'

'Not yet, no, but presumably you don't rule out the possibility?'

Libby was alarmed at the course the conversation was taking; the subject-matter was surely most unseemly even though the manner of it was distinctly matter-of-fact.

'No woman ever does, sir. The Dowager Countess feels I should set my cap at a country parson,' she added reflectively.

He laughed. 'You'd be wasted, my dear,' he said. 'Quite wasted.'

Electing to overlook the highly improper familiarity of this speech, and choosing to ignore the fact that she had no particular wish to wed a country parson, Libby's voice was indignant.

'I assure you, my lord, it would be considered quite a—quite a *catch* for a penniless companion to receive an offer from a country parson!'

'Which in no way alters the fact that you would be wasted should you ever be so foolish as to accept such an offer. And—forgive me for being indelicate—but I understood the Dowager Countess to imply that the salary she pays you is positively handsome.'

Libby laughed. 'It is, sir—for a companion, but since it would naturally cease upon my marriage I hardly think a prospective suitor would regard it as an inducement!'

'Do you want a suitor who needs an inducement?'

Libby thought for a moment. 'No, my lord,' she said, and then added, with a twinkle in her eye, 'But one must be practical.'

'Indeed one must. Some of us more than others, perhaps. In your case, however, your practicality is one of your charms. Incidentally—and I hope you won't mind my mentioning it—I do find this frequent "my lord" a shade trying. My name is Marcus.'

'And you cannot fail to be aware—my lord—that it would be most improper in me to use it!' Libby retorted.

'Not, however, if you were to marry me.'

Stunned, unable to believe her ears and quite sure he must be able to hear her beating heart, Libby stared at him, only looking away when a blush of pure anger suffused her cheeks. She stood up.

'Such a remark may be regarded as an amusing jest to someone in your position, Lord Charlbury, but to someone in mine it is both thoughtless and unkind.'

'Sit down!' he commanded, and such was Libby's surprise at his peremptory tone that she obeyed. 'Good God, woman, do you imagine I'm stupid enough to make such an offer in jest? If I did, it would serve me right if the recipient took me seriously and accepted the offer! I've committed follies enough in my time, madam, but proposing marriage for a joke isn't one of them, I assure you.'

Reassured by both the vehemence of his tone and the common sense of his words, Libby looked shyly up at him. 'Then why, sir?' she asked.

He looked down at her and seemed to hesitate. When he spoke, she was conscious that he picked his words with care.

'I'm thirty-five,' he said. 'It has been borne upon me recently that I should settle down. You're one of the few women I have ever met with whom I could be comfortable.' He paused. 'I'm sorry if you would prefer protestations of undying love.'

'I don't think I'd believe them,' she answered. 'You've not exactly behaved like an ardent swain, and frankly, sir, your reputation is one of frequently dying love.'

He laughed bitterly. 'That's not love, my dear, merely fancy. I can't offer you security and tranquillity as a country parson might. Indeed, at the moment I can offer you nothing but my name; but once we're married I fancy things will resolve themselves and, while I can't promise to reform my wicked ways, I can promise that they will not impinge upon you.'

Libby looked at him seriously. 'In all the conversations we've had, you've spoken like a sensible man and you've exhibited a discrimination of taste and feeling which one can but admire. It's difficult to equate that with your reputation.'

He took her hands in his, his thumbs unconsciously caressing them as he looked into her eyes.

'The reputation doesn't lie,' he said harshly, and then, his voice softening, 'Come, Libby, will you marry me?'

Libby gently removed her hands from his clasp, and moved a little away from him. She stood, her back to him, looking out over the sparkling waters of the lake. She knew the answer she wanted to give, but there were other considerations to be taken into account. He made no pretence of loving her. Well, that might be a disappointment, but it was hardly a surprise, and if love was important she was sure she had enough for both of them. It would be widely assumed she had married him for his title. Libby knew that was not so, and she suspected it hadn't crossed Charlbury's mind, either. The question was, did she mind others jumping to that conclusion? She thought not, but she was less sanguine about the interpretation those others might put on his having offered for her. Notorious for his liaisons with diamonds of the very first water, what would his friends make of his marriage to a provincial dowd, however well-born? Her common sense told her the Viscount must already have considered this and dismissed it as unimportant. Why, then, should she let it stand between them?

A voice from behind her broke into her thought. It was the first time she had heard uncertainty in his tone. 'Libby?' he said.

She smiled to herself. As if there could have been any real doubt, she thought. She turned towards him, her hands reaching out as she did so. 'Yes, my lord. I will.'

He took her hands and gently raised each to his lips in turn. Then he paused briefly, as if momentarily uncertain, and leaned over to kiss her gently on the lips. It was a tender kiss, quite different from any half-remembered peck from father or brothers. The Viscount's touch sent a shaft like fire through her veins. Her heart raced and her hands instinctively lifted towards his shoulders as if they sensed her need to be closer to him.

The Viscount understood his lady's actions with a clarity she did not, and was pleasantly surprised by a lack of reserve which he had not anticipated. Nevertheless, he was anxious not to endanger the innocence which he knew lay behind the greater familiarity of her approach, so that when he took her in his arms his kiss, though lingering, was still tender. He felt her heart flutter against his own, and found himself suddenly wondering about this sensible, practical woman who seemed to be unconsciously revealing depths he had not suspected.

Libby found herself longing for a more intense, more passionate embrace, but her practicality somehow managed to push its way through her more potent desires to remind her that, whatever her feelings for Lord Charlbury might be, he had offered his hand for purely practical considerations, and it would never do to exhibit a warmth he might well find distasteful. So she withdrew from his arms and tried to suppress the disappointment she felt that he made no attempt to restrain her, composing herself instead to discuss with him the practicalities of her new situation.

CHAPTER FOUR

LORD Charlbury having made it clear that he saw little reason to delay their marriage, Libby felt it incumbent upon her to tell the Dowager Lady Somerton as soon as possible of her planned change of status, especially since she felt that that lady might well wish to seek a replacement with the minimum of delay. She had expected her employer to express some surprise; she would not have been surprised to encounter strong displeasure at the shortness of the notice she was giving. She was not at all prepared for the furore which burst about her after the initial prolonged, stunned silence that greeted her somewhat diffidently expressed announcement.

'Viscount Charlbury,' the old lady repeated in an ominously quiet voice.

'Yes, ma'am.'

'Let me get this quite clear. You say Viscount Charlbury has asked you to marry him?'

'Yes, ma'am.'

'And you have accepted?'

'Yes, ma'am.'

'Are you mad?'

'I think not, ma'am.'

'Yet only the other day I warned you against setting your cap at him! I hadn't thought it of you—which just goes to show how mistaken one can be. You, miss, are a deceitful hussy!'

Libby flushed. 'That's unfair, my lady. As I recall it, you said you paid me the compliment of suspecting I didn't know how to set a cap.'

'Don't bandy words with me, my girl,' the Dowager said angrily. 'That merely underlines how seriously I misjudged you. So—you have a fancy to be Lady Charlbury, have you? Well, that's about all you will have,

36

for I tell you to your face, Charlbury has neither money nor estates. The latter have been mortgaged to the hilt for years, and rumour has it the creditors have fore-closed. And even if the noble Viscount manages to stay out of Newgate, how long do you think you can hold his interest?' She looked her companion scathingly up and down before ringing her bell and ordering her dresser to beg Lady Somerton's immediate attendance upon her mama-in-law.

Flushed and angry, Libby said nothing, realising that if a storm was about to burst then the sooner it did so, the sooner it would be over.

The Countess, recognising in the dresser's carefully worded message an unwontedly peremptory command, was with her mama-in-law within minutes. One look around her as she opened the door told her that here in the making was a scene of the first order.

'Amelia,' commanded the Dowager, 'close the door and sit down. Elizabeth, explain matters to Lady Somerton.'

Quietly, and with a great effort to stop the quiver in her voice, Libby did as instructed.

The Countess's reaction was much quieter than that of the Dowager. 'Well, well, well,' she said. 'Who would have guessed you were such a sly minx? Perhaps you thought we'd be grateful that you deflected his interest from Selina or Jane?'

'Lady Somerton, you know full well Lord Charlbury has never exhibited the slightest interest in them to be deflected.'

'That's quite beside the point. In any case, Selina is a beauty. What on earth do you imagine has made him offer for you?'

The Dowager interrupted. 'That is precisely the point, Amelia. She's only passable, and she has no portion. Yet Charlbury hasn't been here long enough to give her a slip on the shoulder—or at least, not long enough for it to be certain.'

Libby could contain herself no longer.

'You're insulting, my lady. Charlbury has been nothing but courtesy itself. I don't know why he should offer for me—I know I can't compare with the women with whom his name has been linked. He says he needs to settle down and that he will be comfortable with me,' she added, the words sounding lame even as she uttered them.

'Huh!' snorted the now irate Dowager. 'There must be a reason beyond that. With Charlbury there has to be. He's not a stupid man, for all his disreputable ways. There has to be a reason for his offering for a nobody, and I doubt it has anything to do with comfort.'

The Countess broke in upon these speculations. 'Rupert,' she said. 'Rupert will know. We shall ask him.'

Stung, Libby suggested they ask Lord Charlbury himself since, as she pointed out, he was the person best placed to account for his apparently inexplicable conduct.

'Don't be pert, miss,' snapped the Dowager. 'As if one could ask a guest so personal a question.'

'It being no such solecism to interrogate his best friend. What strange values you do have, ladies!' With that, Libby unceremoniously left the room.

Her own bedchamber was on the opposite side of the staircase to that of her employer, and she crossed the landing just as Lord Wilcote reached the top stair.

'Libby!' he said. 'I hear that I must offer you my felicitations.'

Her cheeks burning, she could bring herself to do no more than nod.

'I see,' he went on. 'You've already told Grandmama and my mother. I gather Grandmama was not congratulatory?'

Libby smiled weakly. 'I guessed she would be surprised. I had no idea she would be so angry.'

'She has taken you for granted, you see. It has probably never occurred to her that you might wish to leave—or would make that decision without asking her opinion.' He paused. 'I wish you well, Libby, but I confess I hope you know what you're taking upon yourself.'

She smiled up at him through incipient tears. 'To tell the truth, Lord Wilcote, I suspect that I don't, but I love Lord Charlbury—I've done so for a long time. I think that will help.'

He returned the smile. 'I'm sure it will—it can hardly be an obstacle, after all. Tell me, is Charlbury aware of your feelings?'

Libby shook her head. 'The subject didn't arise,' she said. 'Lord Charlbury said he needed to settle down, by which he means he needs to produce an heir, and that he felt he'd be comfortable with me. I didn't feel it appropriate to enlarge upon my own feelings, and I trust you'll not enlighten him.'

Lord Wilcote looked puzzled. He wondered why his friend had given that particular reason and not the truth. Did Charlbury believe the reason he had given would be more acceptable? He knew his friend well and was by no means sure that so cold-blooded an arrangement as this one seemed to be was what Charlbury really wanted from a marriage.

'If that's your wish,' he said doubtfully. 'I'm not sure that you're wise, however.'

'Possibly not, my lord, but I should prefer to make my own mistakes,' she assured him.

Lady Somerton was denied an opportunity to buttonhole her son until they met in the drawing-room before dinner. Had Lord Wilcote realised that only his mother and the Dowager were present, it was likely he would have delayed his entrance, but as soon as he realised the ladies were the sole occupants of the room he was not surprised to be accosted as soon as the doors closed behind him.

'Ah, Rupert,' declared his grandmama. 'Have you heard this ludicrous story?'

'I've heard no story that could be so described,' he replied, his heart sinking.

'You mean you haven't heard that Charlbury has offered for Libby Barton?'

'And been accepted, Grandmama. Yes, of course I've heard. I do not, however, regard it as ludicrous.'

'Well, of course not,' his mother broke in. 'Incongruous, perhaps—and almost certainly tragic. Libby must be mad; she's much better off with Mama. But what on earth possessed Charlbury to make the offer?'

Ignoring this question, her son confined himself to her previous comment. 'You're unfair to Libby, Mama. However generously she's treated as a paid companion, she is nevertheless at someone's beck and call, but, no matter how straitened Marcus's circumstances may be, as Viscountess Charlbury she will be at no one's. I mean no disrespect, Grandmama, when I say that most observers would regard that as an improvement in her lot.'

The Dowager snorted, but Lady Somerton was not to be side-tracked.

'Very pretty, Rupert, but you've avoided the real question. Why has Charlbury proposed? He's well-nigh under the hatches and Libby has no money at all, nor any expectations against which he can borrow. She's not one of his high-fliers. She's not even of his world. In short, she has nothing whatever to offer.'

'On the contrary, Mama, she has much to offer: she's well-bred, sensible, of strong character, and has most assuredly acquired habits of economy.'

Both ladies stared at him, dumb-founded. It was his grandmother who broke the silence.

'She has *what*?'

A sardonic voice from the door startled the two ladies into an awareness that one of the subjects of their conversation had entered the room. Lord Charlbury closed the door behind him.

'Rupert, I'm sorry you've been placed in so invidious a position. Miss Barton, ladies, possesses precisely those virtues that Rupert has so succinctly described. Do you disagree?'

The Countess looked somewhat abashed at the unexpected appearance at that precise moment of their guest, but her mother-in-law was made of sterner stuff.

'Since when have these virtues—or, indeed, any other virtues—appealed to you, my lord?'

'To be precise, since the reading of my uncle's Will.
Rupert has clearly been the soul of discretion. I assure
you, Lady Somerton, neither of your closely guarded
daughters would be remotely suitable. As Rupert can
tell you, unless my wife has those precise characteristics
I cannot inherit the unentailed portion of my uncle's
estate.'

'And does Libby know of this very flattering reason
for your offer?' the Dowager demanded sarcastically.

'I rather fancy that's a matter between Miss Barton
and myself,' he answered icily.

'So she doesn't,' the old lady declared triumphantly.
'Well, she will before the night's out.'

'I don't doubt it, ma'am.'

'Really, Grandmama,' Lord Wilcote expostulated.
'Marcus is right. It's none of your business. It's entirely
a matter between him and Libby, and it would be quite
inexcusable for you to tell tales out of school.'

'That's as may be,' the Dowager replied haughtily,
though a flush betrayed the fact that she knew herself
to be in the wrong. She might revise her intention in the
light of her grandson's criticism, but she was not about
to give him the satisfaction of telling him so. 'Libby is
my companion, and I feel I have a duty to protect her
from her own folly.'

'On the contrary, ma'am, your duty ends when you
pay my salary.' This time it was Libby's voice which
broke the engrossment of the party gathered by the empty
hearth. 'My folly, as you so charitably put it,' she went
on, 'is entirely my own affair. I am not, after all, a complete ninnyhammer.'

'You will be if you marry Charlbury,' retorted the
Dowager, stung. 'Lord, Libby, you know the man's
reputation. What sort of a marriage do you think you
will have, married to a man like that? And purely, I
suspect, for his own convenience.'

'No, ma'am,' Libby answered firmly. 'Not purely for
his lordship's convenience. I'm not being forced into this
marriage, you know. I'm fully aware that Lord
Charlbury has severely practical reasons for offering for

me. He needs an heir, and it will suit me very well to be married. I've therefore accepted his offer. Besides, ma'am, I seem to recall frequent occasions when you have expounded the virtues of marriages of convenience.'

'Pfui,' snapped the Dowager. 'Marriages of convenience arranged by parents are quite a different kettle of fish from this misbegotten affair. Think again, Libby. No announcement has yet been made. You can cry off now without anyone's being the wiser. Everyone makes mistakes. Admit this one now, for if the marriage goes forward you will live to regret it.'

'I've no wish to cry off and I doubt very much that I shall regret the marriage, but I can tell you this, ma'am: if I do, I shall make sure no one has the satisfaction of knowing it.'

'Bravo,' murmured her betrothed. 'Checkmate, I think, Lady Somerton!'

The Dowager cast him a fulminating glance, and he wondered whether she was angry enough to tell Libby he had other reasons for making his offer beyond a desire to 'settle down'. It appeared she was not, however, and the conversation became desultory and general. Lord Wilcote did what he could to ease the inevitable constraint that ensued, but it was not until the arrival of the Honourable Robert Wilcote and his sisters that the atmosphere more resembled that normally associated with such a gathering, and when the Earl finally appeared he gave no indication of sensing anything untoward.

Next morning, however, Libby received a note from him suggesting that she might be kind enough to wait upon him when she had a little time.

She wrinkled her nose. 'Is his lordship free to see me now, do you think?' she asked the footman who had delivered the note.

'It's not for me to say, miss,' he replied stiffly, and added, unbending a little, 'but he don't appear to be overly busy as it were, right now. His lordship's in the library,' he added informatively.

Deciding that procrastination only led to apprehension, Libby put aside her hemming and went down to the library, a handsome room on the first floor which was generally regarded in the family as Earl's exclusive domain, a matter about which that gentleman had mixed feelings: on the one hand it meant he could be left undisturbed, an aspect which had many advantages to one of such scholarly disposition; on the other, it suggested that none of his family shared his interest in academic pursuits, although he cherished a hope that Rupert might veer towards the academic as he grew older.

He rose when Libby entered, and indicated a chair for her. He came straight to the point—a characteristic of his which never failed to surprise Libby, for it seemed at variance with the customary abstracted air with which he went about his daily life.

'I gather Charlbury has offered for you and you've accepted?'

'Yes, my lord.'

'My mother appears to believe that this is—at least on Charlbury's side—entirely a matter of convenience. Are you aware of this?'

'Of Lady Somerton's opinion? Oh, yes, sir, she has made it quite clear.'

'Is she right?'

'I think she may well be.'

'And that doesn't disturb you?'

Libby looked up at him. 'Should it, sir? The Dowager had previously made it clear to me that I would do well if I married a country parson. A Viscount can surely only be considered an improvement.'

'Don't you think that might rather depend upon the Viscount? Unless, of course, you're solely concerned with social standing, and somehow, Libby, I don't think you are.'

'No, sir, I'm not, though the world will probably think otherwise.' She paused. 'I've taken all the possible objections into account and I am quite fixed in my determination to accept Lord Charlbury.'

Lord Somerton looked at her thoughtfully. 'My mother thinks you fancy yourself in love with him,' he said. 'Be that as it may, you'll have a hard road ahead but, if you're sure, then I wish you very well.'

'Thank you, my lord.'

'Which leaves me with a problem, Libby,' he went on as if she had not spoken. 'We think of you almost as a member of the family, so I shall be blunt. The Dowager insists that if you persist in going ahead with this betrothal she will not have you under her roof for one more night. I've pointed out to her that, at the moment, neither of you is living under her roof and so it isn't within her power to cast you into the streets forthwith. Nor would I allow it if it were. But you can see the position becomes a little awkward.' He paused. 'I've taken the liberty of speaking to Charlbury about this. It appears that a long betrothal isn't envisaged and since, in view of my mother's somewhat intransigent attitude, you can hardly be married from here, I think you'll find Charlbury is making other arrangements for you. At all events, he didn't think it an insuperable problem.'

There was little for Libby to say, save to thank him for his offices on her behalf and to undertake to be as small an embarrassment as possible in the ensuing days before taking her leave of him.

CHAPTER FIVE

THE HONOURABLE MAX ASTHALL was not pleased when he rode into the stable-yard at Chase to be greeted with the news that his brother had arrived and was awaiting him in the library.

He was still scowling when he entered the room. The Viscount had ordered a fire to be lit, for the house was distinctly chill, and this proprietorial act served only to deepen the scowl on his younger brother's face. The Viscount raised his quizzing-glass and scrutinised his brother for a few moments before speaking.

'How heart-warming it is,' he observed, 'to note the delight which suffuses one's brother's face when one visits.'

'You could have let me know you were coming,' Max grumbled.

'Possibly, but I chose not to. I particularly wished to get here without delay.'

'What do you mean?' Max demanded, colouring.

'Nothing beyond what I said,' the Viscount said blandly. 'Why? What should I have meant?'

'Nothing, I suppose. I mean, I don't know—I spoke without thinking.'

The Viscount shook his head. 'Always a mistake. You seem confused, Max. Now that's unlike you—or so I should have thought, but then we meet so infrequently that perhaps I no longer really know you. You look pale. Are you ill?'

'No, of course not, merely tired—and surprised by this unexpected arrival. What do you want?'

'So gracious!' his elder brother murmured to no one in particular. 'For myself, at the moment—nothing,' he continued. 'I shall ride on to Byfield and rusticate there for a while if the duns haven't moved in.'

45

'They haven't. Not yet, at all events. I thought you were rusticating with Wilcote?'

'I was, I was, but I seemed to have outstayed my welcome.'

Max laughed. 'Cast a lure to Lady Selina, did you? Might have known that wouldn't serve. Shouldn't think she'd fit the conditions anyway,' he added thoughtfully.

'I wouldn't be surprised if you were right,' his brother commented affably. 'However, I cast the lure, as you so elegantly phrased it, to Miss Elizabeth Barton. And she took it,' he added.

'Elizabeth Barton? I've never heard of her!'

'Possibly not, but then you do move in the most restricted circles, don't you? Really, you know, Max, you look most unwell—I'm almost concerned for you. But to more important matters. Miss Barton is more often called Libby. She is—or rather, she has been—companion to the Dowager Countess of Somerton. I assure you she fulfils all the conditions.'

'Does she know about them?'

'I made it quite clear it was a marriage of convenience. She is an extremely practical woman.'

'She sounds a dead bore.'

'Possibly. I don't find her so, however, and you'll do well to remember that.'

Max flushed. 'So you've come to take over Chase?'

'I can hardly do so before I'm married. No, you will continue here—as I hope you will feel able to do for as long after the wedding as you need to establish yourself elsewhere. I'm asking you to make the house available to Libby—as your guest—until the wedding. I've sent for Widford, our old nurse, to act as chaperon, and I shall stay at Byfield unless the duns take it over.'

'And if I don't choose to make Chase available?'

'Then Libby will go to Byfield and I shall stay here. You would be hard put to it to stop me, and I'm quite impervious to snubs.'

'Why can't you both go to Byfield? It's big enough!'

'And have all the old tabbies gossiping? That would never do.'

'All propriety all of a sudden, Marcus? Not like you.'

'If you expect me to treat my future wife as I do my mistresses, you much misjudge me, Max. You'd do well to bear that in mind.'

At this moment the housekeeper bustled in to assure his lordship that the green bedroom would soon be ready for Miss Barton, and was there anything else, please?

'I'm sure you've done all that is necessary. I expect her here before nightfall. Doubtless she will be hungry, but I know I may depend upon you, Mrs Chadlington, to provide a respectable meal. Lord Wilcote will also be here; he is accompanying Miss Barton and then will come on to Byfield.'

She curtsied and left the room, delighted that things were at last looking up. It was a long time since any entertaining had been done at Chase.

'You took a lot upon yourself, Marcus,' Max said angrily as the door closed behind the housekeeper. 'I've half a mind to refuse to have her here.'

'As you are perfectly entitled to do,' his brother said pleasantly. 'Only then you'd have me here, and I've an odd feeling you'd like that even less. I admit I've been high-handed in making these arrangements without first consulting your convenience, but it has been for Libby's sake. The Dowager made it difficult for her to continue at Copthorne, and Chase will, after all, be her home after the wedding. Libby's a good girl and she won't bother you.' He paused, and regarded Max with some sympathy in his eyes. 'Yes, I know how hard it was. You wanted Chase. Well, believe it or not, so did I. I always have. Did you really think I wouldn't comply with the old man's wishes? You'll lose Chase, Max, but I'll see you're not penniless. I'm not totally heartless, you know.'

Max flushed. 'I don't need your charity,' he said.

'It won't be charity. It will be some recompense for all you've done for the estate. You were treated shabbily in the Will; I intend to redress the balance.'

'When you're married.'

'Naturally, when I'm married.'

'But you're not married yet, Marcus.'

'Don't be childish, Max, and don't, I beg you, start nurturing dreams that I shan't get married. I have every intention of marrying Libby Barton, and it will take more than you to stop me.'

A sudden, unexpectedly boyish grin swept across Max's face. 'I might cut you out,' he said.

'You might try, young 'un,' his brother replied, an answering gleam in his own eye. 'But I'll lay odds you don't succeed.'

So it was that when the chaise with Libby and the Asthalls' old nurse, Mrs Widford arrived, accompanied by Lord Wilcote, the two Asthall brothers greeted them with every appearance of amity—to such an extent, indeed, that Rupert murmured, 'Well done, Marcus. How did you achieve such rapport?'

To which his friend replied, 'All things are possible, Rupert. It only requires a little effort.'

Libby pronounced herself delighted with the green bedchamber and with the adjacent turret room that was to be her sitting-room, an announcement which clearly came as a surprise to Max, giving Libby the odd notion that he was not altogether pleased. She complimented Mrs Chadlington on the obvious care that had been lavished on the house over the years, thus ensuring that good lady's high opinion of her understanding. Widford, having unpacked her new, if temporary mistress's bags, took herself off to the nether regions to chat to her old friend the housekeeper and in particular to regale her with the strange tale of Lord Charlbury's coming conversion to the married state.

After dinner, Lord Charlbury and Lord Wilcote rode on to Byfield Manor, the former's heavily mortgaged ancestral home whose lands marched with those of Chase. Libby had little compunction in making her excuses to Max and going to bed almost as soon as the door closed behind her betrothed and his friend. Max was her host, but the amiability of her initial reception had waned over the ensuing hours. It was nothing Libby could put her finger on; he was as polite as he had been at the beginning, there was nothing to be read into his utterances that hinted at something else, as was sometimes the case with Lord Charlbury; it was just an intangible change in the atmosphere which she rather thought had first been apparent when the housekeeper revealed that she had also set aside a sitting-room for Miss Barton. Libby was quite prepared to admit that the whole thing might well be her fancy. The last few days at Copthorne had not been pleasant, and doubtless her anxiety that Charlbury's family should not react as had the Dowager and her daughter-in-law was leading her to imagine a displeasure that wasn't really there.

In the morning Libby enjoyed the unwonted luxury of a cup of hot chocolate in bed, brought to her by Widford, who intercepted Mrs Chadlington at the door and insisted that Miss Libby should call her 'Nurse'. She was already exhibiting certain proprietorial tendencies which, Libby knew, would increase with the wedding and become positively restricting on that happy day when she would be told that the new Viscountess was increasing.

So Libby sat up against the pillows—thoughtfully plumped up by Nurse—and sipped her chocolate while Nurse ensured she was *au fait* with the situation in the Asthall family and particularly as it related to the two estates, Byfield and Chase.

It was clear that the Viscount's rakish reputation did him no harm in the eyes of his old nurse, though she regretted the almost certain loss of Byfield Manor, which had been acquired on his lordship's grandfather elevation to the peerage.

'It was always the old Viscount's wish—Lord Charlbury's father, that is—that his son should marry a daughter of Lord Denmead and join the two estates, and he did bring the boy up to expect Chase as part of a marriage settlement. The two families were on good terms with each other, and when the present Viscount was a boy he ran wild over both estates, so I suppose it's not to be wondered at that he was inclined to think of Chase as his rightful property eventually. Only Denmead didn't have a daughter—nor a son, neither, if

it comes to that—and nor did his brother, the present
Earl, and, since Chase was unentailed, the old Earl was
free to leave it to Lord Charlbury if he wanted and join
them that way. Still, he chose not to do so. I can't pretend
to know all the ins and outs, of course, but from the
gossip I've picked up, whether his lordship gets this place
depends on his finding a wife. Still, you'll know more
about that than me, and by rights I've no business to
be passing on gossip anyway.'

So that was why Lord Charlbury was so anxious to
'settle down'! Libby was dismayed. She had assumed
Charlbury had wanted an heir, an understandable if not
entirely flattering reason for a marriage of convenience.
Now it appeared his purpose was more venal—the ac-
quisition of more land. She could only assume he had
offered for the first female he met who was not in a
position lightly to refuse—a circumstance which was, if
anything, even less flattering. Nurse obviously assumed
she had known all this, and Libby was not about to dis-
abuse her. Nor was she inclined to stop her prattling,
despite knowing that she should. There were still too
many unanswered questions.

'What did you mean when you said it was too late?'
she asked.

'Lord, miss, we expect the creditors to move into
Byfield any day. Very uncertain it makes everyone, too.
Not like his lordship to leave us hanging on a cliff-face,
as you might say, and there's some as thinks that, once
the news gets out that his lordship's likely to get Chase,
the Byfield duns will hold off in the expectation of being
paid out of Chase. I certainly hope so.'

Libby knew she must now change the subject, fascinating as it might be. There were limits to what one could
discuss with a servant, even a privileged one, and one's
betrothed's financial position certainly came outside
those limits. 'Tell me about Max Asthall,' she suggested.

'Ah, Master Max—Mr Asthall, I should say, though
it's hard to remember he's a grown man. I reared him
myself, his mama having died when he was born, and
mostly a nurse gets overly fond of a child in that situ-

ation, but Master Max was never what you might call a taking child. He was a weak, fretful baby—as is not surprising, all things considered—and as he grew up he was jealous of his lordship. It didn't make for a happy household that his lordship blamed his younger brother for their mother's death, as if the poor lad could help it. Mind you, his lordship grew out of that idea.'

'But Max is still jealous, I think.'

'Well, he would be, wouldn't he? To see his elder brother inherit and squander all that money. It's no wonder he tried to make himself indispensable to Lord Denmead, but the Earl wouldn't let him try out his new-fangled ideas, and sometimes stopped him from maintaining what's there.'

'What do you mean?'

'Chase is a peculiar estate, Miss Libby, carved out between the sea and the forest. Little enough land round here is privately held, just Chase and Byfield and Beaulieu. The forest creeps forward year by year if it isn't kept back, and if ever it creeps back over Chase then the land reverts to the Crown. The old Earl, he would sometimes refuse Master Max permission to hack back undergrowth. Then, after a year or two, he'd change his mind. Whenever he came down here—which wasn't often, for he preferred Leicestershire—they had rows, Mrs Chadlington says. Not but what I didn't know, for that sort of thing gets talked about.'

'Poor Max. It must be galling to see it slip away to his brother. I'm surprised the Earl didn't leave it to the younger brother in return for all he'd done.'

'Ay, but Lord Charlbury was always the old Earl's favourite. Myself, I think he'd heard a thing or two about Master Max.'

Knowing she should put an end to this conversation which had stepped far beyond the bounds of what was proper, but becoming increasingly fascinated by it, Libby put her scruples firmly behind her and asked Nurse to explain.

This Mrs Widford was happy to do but, for someone who kept her finger firmly on the pulse of family affairs, her information was disappointingly vague.

It seemed that Master Max, as she persisted in calling him, had strange friends in strange places. He had been seen by unspecified observers in the less salubrious areas of Southampton, and when he returned to Chase or Byfield after a few days' absence he was, declared Nurse, a different person: vague, almost carefree for a while and then frequently depressed and ill. He usually developed a nasty chill a few days after his return, shivering as with an ague, and sometimes he complained of stomach cramps. Goodness only knew what he ate or where he went while he was away. Still, it had to be borne in mind that he was never what you might call a little ray of sunshine, and at least when he came back from this little change of scene he was always a lot better—and a lot more cheerful, too. It was just a pity it didn't last.

'Perhaps he has a sweetheart in Southhampton?' Libby suggested.

Nurse snorted. 'A lightskirt, more likely, in that town. Not but what there's no reason he shouldn't have, I suppose.'

'Oh, come, Nurse, there must be plenty of perfectly respectable girls in Southampton. Perhaps he's met one he fears will not be acceptable to his family because, though she may be respectable enough, her birth may not approach his.'

'Which, seeing as how his family is the Viscount, don't hold much water. If she was respectable, the Viscount'd not object.'

Regretfully, Libby decided this intriguing topic had gone far enough, especially since it was now entering the realms of pure speculation, so she brought it to an abrupt end by announcing that she had lain around chit-chattering long enough, and declaring her intention of getting up with no further delay.

CHAPTER SIX

As a result of Nurse's revelations, Libby felt extremely sorry for Max, who must surely see her own presence at Chase as salt rubbed into the wound. It was hardly surprising that he should resent her being here and, while there was nothing she could do to alter the underlying situation—nor, if she were honest, would she wish to do so even if it were in her power—she could at least do whatever she could to ease the feelings he must be enduring. She had never been a victim of jealousy, but she had observed that emotion in others and knew it to be corrosive and ultimately destructive. It would probably be a long time before Max Asthall would be able to regard her with equanimity, but perhaps she should help the process along by remaining amiable and ignoring any darts he might later choose to let fly.

She arose, therefore, determined to put her good intentions into practice forthwith, and was disappointed to be thwarted of the opportunity. Max had almost finished breakfast when she appeared and, after apologising for the fact that he made a point of rising early in order to set in train such work on the estate as was not a matter of routine, he then added that this was not the only reason for his being obliged to leave her to her own devices.

'I have to leave Chase for a few days on business,' he told her baldly.

'So soon?' she said involuntarily. Good manners, if nothing else, should surely have kept him there long enough to enable her to find her feet. 'What a pity. I'd been hoping you would show me around. Still, it can't be helped, I suppose.'

'No, it can't. This was arranged some time ago, and your own arrival was entirely unexpected, so I've had no chance to make alternative arrangements.'

Libby ignored his rudeness and smiled understandingly. 'There's really no need to apologise, Mr Asthall. I quite understand the position. Business must always take precedence, I think. You'll be going to Southampton, I collect.'

She was startled by the force of his reaction. He flushed angrily.

'Southampton? Why should I go to Southampton? No, my business lies elsewhere, though what it is to you I can't conceive,' he added rudely.

'It's nothing to me, of course,' she replied, refusing to be goaded into a rudeness comparable with his own. 'I merely thought your brother might wish to have converse with you, and if he knows where you've gone he would find it helpful in gauging whether your absence is likely to be prolonged.'

Max's anger seemed to subside, and he appeared genuinely contrite.

'I'm sorry, Miss Barton. I didn't mean to be rude. It's just that matters...that there are many things to be taken into account just now. Please accept my apologies.' He paused as she inclined her head to indicate that she regarded the matter as closed. 'I'll be well on my way before Marcus rides over,' he continued. 'I expect to be away for two or three days—no more than four, I feel sure.' He hesitated. 'Do, please, regard Chase as your own home. It will become so soon, after all,' he added, unable at the last to keep the bitterness out of his voice.

It was, however, not until dinner time that the Viscount learned of his brother's absence. He had spent a busy day with the vicar of Byfield, arranging the banns. He had sent an announcement of his betrothal to the London papers and instructed his man of business to see that all his creditors were acquainted with the broad terms of his late uncle's Will, at least in so far as they affected himself.

He was therefore entirely unperturbed by the visions of impending creditors that haunted his retainers, realising full well that those gentlemen would stay their writs once they were aware that his present financial situation was in a fair way to being reversed.

He rode across his encumbered estates with his friend, feeling able, for the first time in years, to plan repairs and even improvements. Lord Wilcote listened in some surprise. Never before had he heard Marcus Charlbury exhibit the slightest interest in his rents except as a source of gaming stakes, and he said as much.

The Viscount laughed. 'Very true, Rupert,' he said. 'But don't you see? I've been caught in a vicious downward spiral. Now, for the first time, I have the chance not only to halt that downward trend, but also to get back to the top half of that curve, if not to its zenith.'

'And will you hurtle downwards again with the same speed?' his friend enquired gently.

The Viscount was serious. 'No,' he said vehemently. 'I won't. When I came into my majority all I wanted to do was to snap my fingers at my trustees in order to show them I was my own man and not the product of their moulding. And I enjoyed it. You've never been an out-and-out gambler, Rupert. I don't think the tables have ever held the heady lure for you that they had for me. By the time I realised where it was leading I was so far on the way down that there was no way back except through a windfall—and a substantial one at that.' He paused. 'I thought of marrying into money, but I discovered that rich fathers are loath to see their daughters' money go down the drain that had already swallowed mine, and they were unimpressed by any protestation that this time it was going to be different. Not even a wealthy cit who fancied a title for his daughter was prepared to contemplate that sort of folly, and I knew I had only two chances of retrieving my position. One was to have a run of luck on the cards. The other, surer, path was to inherit Chase—and I knew I was the old man's favourite, despite his disapproval of the way I lived.'

'And Libby? Does she deserve to be simply the tool that hauls you out of the quagmire?'

'No, she doesn't. I must admit that as soon as I saw her at Copthorne it crossed my mind that here might be the solution to my problem, and I'll not deny I pursued the acquaintance with the intention of finding out to what extent she really did fit the old man's specifications. She does, of course, but I soon realised that there's more to Libby Barton than at first appears. She's no mousy doormat that can be alternately bullied and ignored. For the first time in my life I've found a woman I actually like and with whom I fancy it will be no great punishment to live. Nothing can alter my reason for offering for her, but I'll see she doesn't live to regret marrying me.'

'Very laudable, Marcus, if a trifle…sober. You know, my grandmother thinks she's in love with you.'

Charlbury laughed. 'If she is, she disguises it remarkably well. No cloying looks and little gasps of delight at the least attention paid her. No fluttering eyelashes over a cunningly deployed fan. But then,' he added thoughtfully, 'she's not in the usual run of females, anyway. I suspect she doesn't wear her heart on her sleeve.'

It was Rupert's turn to laugh. 'She's certainly not in the usual run of *your* females, Marcus. But she is a good girl. I wouldn't want to see her hurt.'

'She won't be, I promise you. Which reminds me, Rupert; she has no family at all, I gather?'

'Not so far as we've ever been able to find out.'

'Then will you give her away? I had hoped to ask your father, but the Dowager's attitude makes that difficult.'

'Of course I will, if Libby has no objection. What will you do for a groom's man?'

'Oh, Max, of course. He won't like it, but he'll do it.'

'Cruel, Marcus.'

'Yes, I suppose it is, but he's got to come to terms with it some time, and I am certainly not going to give the gossips any excuse for deducing there might be bad feeling between us. I don't want Libby to find herself the butt of impertinent hints and innuendoes.'

Lord Charlbury was more than a little annoyed to find that his brother had chosen to absent himself instead of playing host to Libby. It was a straightforward snub and, as such, quite intolerable. He said as much, and Lord Wilcote, who disliked being critical of anyone, felt bound to agree that Max had not behaved as he ought.

'Let it go,' Libby urged. 'He's plainly very put out, and he's oddly immature in his attitudes. To take him to task will merely set his back up the more.'

'I can't feel that immaturity is any excuse for bad manners,' Lord Charlbury answered, 'and as soon as he comes through that door I shall tell him so. I am very angry.'

'I expect your anger will have evaporated by the time he comes back,' Libby said calmly. 'It does if you try to keep it on the boil, you know.'

'He can't be long delayed,' Lord Wilcote pointed out gently. 'It's nearly dark already.'

'Oh, dear,' Libby remarked. 'I don't seem to have explained matters very well. Mr Asthall won't be back tonight. He expects to be away for two or three days—four at the most, he said.'

'Four days!' the Viscount exclaimed. 'What on earth will he be doing for four days? What business can he possibly have which will take four days?'

'As to that, sir, I couldn't say. All I can tell you is that he insists it is not in Southampton.'

Her betrothed looked at her suspiciously. 'I'm beginning to learn to be wary when you are being informative and imperturbable.'

She smiled at him. 'Then I must take care never to be imperturbable when I want something,' she said. 'I must practise fluttering my eyelashes over the top of a fan.'

'Don't you dare!'

'No, my lord,' she replied with a meekness that was belied by the twitch of her lips. Lord Wilcote laughed.

'Lord, Marcus, I think you've met your match!'

'That was my intention when I offered for Miss Barton, though not, perhaps, in quite the way you meant the expression,' the Viscount replied, the irony in his voice causing Libby to chuckle. 'Perhaps one might en-

quire what prompted my brother to insist that his
business did *not* lie in Southampton?'

'I asked him if it did.'

Her betrothed was clearly taken aback. 'That seems
rather extraordinary. May I enquire whether you propose
to ask me my destination every time I leave the house
after we're married?'

'Almost certainly, I should think,' Libby replied
cheerfully. 'It's called feminine curiosity, you know. I'm
surprised you've not encountered it before,' she added
thoughtfully.

Wisely choosing to ignore this sally, the Viscount asked
whether it was feminine curiosity that had prompted her
to enquire into his brother's destination.

'Oh, I didn't ask his destination, my lord. I merely
enquired whether it was Southampton. It is, after all,
the only town of any notable size in the area, so it was
a reasonable assumption. Besides, I gather he often goes
there,' she added.

'Servants' gossip, Miss Barton?' his lordship asked
sardonically.

'What else?' she answered cheerfully. 'Reprehensible,
I know, but so interesting. Of course,' she added, 'I do
realise that I shall have to mend my ways when I'm a
great lady.'

'You know what, Marcus?' his friend said. 'She's
going to be like my grandmother—never asks the servants more than two well-chosen questions and the next
you know she has a complete picture of the private lives
of everyone within a twenty-mile radius.'

'Good God!' uttered the Viscount, an image of the
Dowager Countess of Somerton springing before his
eyes.

Libby rose. 'Never mind, my lord,' she said, patting
him on the sleeve as she passed him on her way out of
the room. 'It will be years before I'm as good as she.'

In the event, Max Asthall was away for three days, every
one of which his elder brother spent at Chase awaiting
his return. The mood of the returned truant was so sunny
and so different from the one he had displayed when he
last saw his brother that Lord Charlbury did little more

than remonstrate with him for his lack of courtesy. Max was cheerfully contrite, and made Libby a very pretty apology, but he was very vague about where he had been and why. He smiled broadly when asked to be his brother's groomsman, and expressed himself delighted.

Lord Wilcote was glad that Max had accepted the inevitable so quickly and so well. Marcus was less happy. It was not like Max to put aside a grudge, real or imaginary, so easily. He felt there was some other reason for Max's change of mood, but for the life of him he couldn't think what it might be, and he took very good care not to communicate his unease to anyone else. Libby seemed not to have given the matter any further thought, but this might be because her time was taken up visiting cloth warehouses in Southampton and—together with Nurse, who, it transpired, wielded no mean needle—sewing her bride-clothes.

The weeks before the wedding passed quietly and uneventfully. Lord Charlbury drove Libby over to Byfield Manor on several occasions, and she noted with dismay the level of disrepair that had been allowed to develop. It was an old house, and one to which no alterations had been made for two generations, the present owner having spent the means, and his father having had a romantic notion of leaving it unaltered. Libby could think of many alterations that could only be improvements, but had to confess to herself that, while they would certainly make the Manor a more convenient place in which to live, it would remain a house in which she felt ill at ease. There was no accountable reason for this—the house was rambling but not particularly large, nor, despite its age, was it the sort of house that might lead the impressionable to Gothic imaginings. It was simply an old, inconvenient, poorly proportioned, outsized farmhouse.

More puzzling was the fact that the Viscount did not intend to remain in what was, after all, his ancestral home and, since her own ponderings on the subject brought no enlightenment, she eventually asked him.

He grimaced. 'My ancestral home? Yes, I suppose it is, in a way. That was certainly my grandfather's idea when he bought the Manor, but I've always felt that it has been in the family for far too short a time to qualify. I don't like the place. I never have, though I suppose I only really became aware of that after my mother died there. Maybe my feelings about it all stem from there— I don't know.'

'So you won't be unduly upset if your creditors take it?' she went on.

He laughed shortly. 'Listening to gossip again? Yes, I'd object, but not from reasons of affection. I'd object because property is not something one should rid oneself of lightly—and certainly not for any reason as foolish as gaming debts. Besides, when we have a son, he'll need somewhere to live eventually, and Byfield will probably suit him very well.'

'Then we must hope he doesn't share your aversion to the place,' Libby commented.

Marcus threw her a quick glance, unsure whether there was irony behind her words. 'And what is your preference?' he asked. 'Do you fancy the romantic inconveniences of Byfield? I own, I prefer Chase, and I must confess it hadn't occurred to me until now that you might not share that opinion. That was thoughtless of me. Will you forgive me? And tell me honestly which house you prefer?'

Libby smiled up at him, delighted to be able to give him the answer she knew he would prefer without having to disguise a different preference. 'To be honest, I don't much like Byfield,' she told him. 'There's an atmosphere here which is less than welcoming—and it has nothing whatever to do with the staff,' she added hastily, in case he took it up with them when she had returned to Chase. 'I just don't like it. Chase is a very different matter.'

He looked at her as if unsure whether she was simply saying what would please him and, having decided that her words reflected her true feelings, he raised her hand to his lips, his grey eyes seeing his own reflection in her brown ones. 'I'm glad we think alike,' he said. 'It bodes well for the future.'

Libby felt suddenly very shy. This was the first time since his proposal that he had exhibited any of the warmth she longed for. It might have been because he had no wish to embarrass her—after all, he was totally unaware of the strength of her feelings towards him— and it might have been because he had no particular desire to share any intensity of feeling with her. She preferred to believe the former was the correct explanation. Whatever the reason for his extreme propriety, the indication that he was capable of greater warmth, an indication that was more a matter of tone and expression than of gesture, took her unawares, and she was unsure how to respond. So she simply blushed and smiled and— with some difficulty—averted her glance. It was a reaction that did her no harm in the Viscount's eyes.

Chase was indeed a different matter. Libby fell almost as deeply in love with Chase as she had with its presumptive inheritor. She realised the spell it had cast over both brothers. Far older in origin than Byfield, it was said to stand on the precise site of a Roman villa and, indeed, the dairy had a mosaic floor of that period. It was a strange mixture. From the front it presented an entirely modern aspect in grey stone—taken, its records showed, from a nearby abbey ruin—with a pillared portico balanced by matching wings, but the back of the house was quite different, being constructed entirely of brick except where the corner of a medieval wall was incorporated. Indeed, it looked as if the height of the house had been determined by a wish to utilise the full height of this turret, but to do so in such a way that the turret itself was not apparent from the front. From the rear there was no denying the fact that it was a turret— a self-contained tower of rooms with massively thick walls, sufficiently modernised to provide pleasant, south-facing apartments that caught the sun through the enlarged windows on two sides through which the eye could take in views that went far out to sea. From the one that had been given to Libby as her sitting-room—and from nowhere else in the house, for elsewhere the view was screened by trees—she could make out the great white jagged stacks of the Needles to the east.

Libby enjoyed sewing in this room. Unfamiliar with the sea, she found endless fascination in watching its changing moods and changing colours. It was no penance to retire here to work and, although she still had the distinct impression that Max would have preferred her to be elsewhere, she told herself that this was probably because he was afraid she would feel cut off in this part of the house, for, although her bedroom was in fact adjacent to it, access to the stairs of the turret was through a heavy oaken door which effectively eliminated any sound from the rest of the house.

So it was here that she and Nurse worked on her modest bride-clothes. There was to be no wedding-journey, but the dresses suitable for an old lady's companion were scarcely eligible for the wife of one of Society's more dashing blades, and so the two women put their heads together and the result was several outfits in which Libby would not hesitate to appear beside her future husband. She had a good eye for fashion and an ability to sketch what she had in mind. Since she also wore her clothes with considerable style, she was confident of her appearance in any but the most exacting and exalted circles.

Certainly, when Lord Wilcote drove over to accompany her to Byfield church, that high stickler found nothing amiss with her modestly cut dress of ivory crêpe with long, close-fitting sleeves that puffed at the top, the high bosom and three finely pleated frills at the hem trimmed with a fine old lace Libby had found in a coffer at Chase and which both the Viscount and his brother assured her she could have.

This was not to be the wedding that the bride of a Viscount might have expected. Apart from the groom, the groomsman and the rector, the only people to witness the marriage from the body of the church were the Viscount's old nurse, his housekeeper and William Fratton, his groom. Libby, however, was not in the least dismayed by the quiet arrangements that both she and her future husband had agreed were appropriate. Rupert, glancing at her as they walked slowly up the aisle, thought he had never seen her look so radiant. Whether the groom really doubted Libby's love, Lord Wilcote could not decide, but one look at her face today would surely remove all doubt.

The rector observed Libby's arrival with some curiosity. He wondered how much the bride knew of her husband's past and of his reputation and, if so, whether she cherished illusions of reforming him. As she came closer and he noticed that determined chin, he decided that perhaps she might not be so naïve as he had at first supposed. He moved forward to the edge of the nave steps. 'Dearly beloved,' he began.

Libby looked up sideways under her lashes at the man standing beside her and thought how lucky she was. She knew not everyone would agree that she was the recipient of good fortune, but how many women had the chance to marry the man they loved so much that it was almost a physical pain to be separated from him, and hardly less so to be with him and obliged by both decorum and his expectations to disguise her feelings? True, there was the small grey cloud of his not feeling the same about her, but Libby reminded herself of the old saying about half a loaf being better than no bread. Libby was essentially a practical woman.

'Therefore if any man can show any just cause,' the rector's voice intoned, and Libby, with a sudden childish instinct, crossed her fingers and hoped no one noticed, 'why they may not lawfully be joined together, let him now speak, or else hereafter for ever hold his peace.'

There followed the customary nerve-racking pause, those few moments dreaded by every woman—and perhaps every man, too—as they waited and prayed that the total silence they expect will indeed be unbroken. Libby was no different from any other woman. Her already crossed fingers tightened, and she briefly closed her eyes, the better to concentrate on her brief prayer for silence.

As the rector himself broke that silence with, 'I require and judge you both,' Libby uncrossed her fingers, and a small sigh of relief escaped her. It was too soon. Before the rector could go on, a rough voice from the back of the church broke in.

''Ang on a minute, there, yer honour. I'm 'ere to show a just cause and whatever-it-was.'

Aghast, the small congregation turned to stare at the unsavoury-looking character with an unshaven chin and a rolling gait who had stepped into the aisle and was coming forward.

Libby's first thought was the inconsequential one that she should not have uncrossed her fingers so soon. Then she realised that she was breathing in quick, shallow breaths, and forced herself to breathe more slowly and deeply. She appeared outwardly calm despite the turmoil within, but she had involuntarily reached for the Viscount's arm as the man finished speaking, and only Lord Charlbury was aware of how tightly his arm was being grasped.

The rector was the first person to recover his composure sufficiently to speak. 'I suggest you go outside and sober up,' he said severely.

'Lor' love you, I ain't drunk,' replied the stranger. 'I'm simply a-doin' of my dooty, as it were.' His eye flickered fleetingly over the Viscount's shoulder to where Max Asthall stood, and then back to the rector.

It was Lord Wilcote who suggested they retire to the vestry to find out the precise nature of the stranger's objection to the marriage, but Lord Charlbury shook his head.

'The objection was not lodged within the time allotted,' he said. 'Surely therefore the marriage must go ahead?'

For a few brief seconds Libby's spirits rose, but were quickly dashed by the rector's next words.

'I'm afraid not,' he said, shaking his head. 'The objection must be listened to no matter how false or malicious it may prove to be. Lord Wilcote's suggestion is a good one. I think we should implement it.'

He led the way to the vestry, where Libby was persuaded to take a seat. She was relieved that Lord Charlbury stayed at her side, one hand reassuringly on her shoulder. The stranger seemed unconcerned by the stupefaction on the faces of his audience. He turned to the Viscount.

'I don't suppose you remembers me, my lord,' he began. 'And I must say 'ow you've changed a bit in nigh on twenty year: yer wisage looks a mite more lived in, like, but then it would if the 'alf of what I 'ear is true.'

'I don't recall having met you before,' Lord Charlbury replied stiffly, having subjected the man to a very intense scrutiny. 'I guess from your gait you're a sailor, though I can't say that takes me very far forward.'

'Right in one, me lord. Tom Bosham's the name, not but what that won't mean much to you, neither. I was a crewman on the Dover packet once, the time you came back from France in a bit if a 'urry. Only a lad you was, but a Viscount all the same, and you'd brought your Viscountess with you. Eye-talian, she were, or so they said, and newly wed, but seemingly she 'adn't no sealegs, and that were a rough passage.'

'It sounds as if you never actually set eyes on this Viscountess,' interrupted Lord Wilcote.

'I 'ates to contradict a gennelman, sir, but on this occasion I fears I must,' Bosham replied, grinning broadly. 'I seed 'er full clear when they boarded, and a lovely girl she were, too, though the sort what gets full-blown early, if you follows me. Then again I seed 'er carried off, the journey 'aving laid 'er low, so to speak.'

'So what precisely is the nature of your objection to this marriage?' asked the rector, hoping against hope that Tom Bosham would fail to be specific.

'The nature of my objection, yer honour, is quite simply that 'is lordship already 'as a wife and therefore can't 'ardly marry this one.'

'And why are you raising this objection?' Lord Wilcote asked. 'What interest have you in this matter?'

'None, sir, none,' answered the sailor, his ingenuous tone at odds with the mendacious glint in his eye. 'I don't like to see a young gal led astray and a man's got to do 'is Christian dooty, don't 'e? Pure altruism, that's me reason. Pure altruism.'

'Laying it on a bit thick, aren't you?' murmured the Viscount, resisting with difficulty a pronounced desire to lay the sailor out on the flagstones of the vestry floor.

Bosham made no answer but only grinned.

The rector intervened. 'I'm sorry, my lord. You'll realise, of course, that no matter how preposterous this objection I cannot continue with the ceremony until we have cleared the matter up.' He turned to Bosham. 'You've done your work,' he said. 'You're not needed here. Go back and report to your masters—for I make no doubt this day's work has been at someone else's instigation.'

Bosham laughed. 'I've no call to report to no one,' he retorted, 'but I'm glad enough to leave. Good day, yer honours.' He turned to the unmarried couple. 'And long life and 'appiness to the both of you,' he said, and laughed again as he left the vestry.

His departure was followed by a prolonged silence broken at last, and reluctantly, by the rector.

'Well, my lord?' he said.

Lord Charlbury picked his words with care and spoke in a strangely flat voice. As he spoke, Libby sought his hand and held it. She thought he gained a certain strength from it, and told herself that impression was not entirely a figment of her imagination.

'What Bosham said is true—as far as it goes—though it presents no impediment to this marriage,' he said. 'I had badgered my trustees into letting me do the Grand Tour. I was accompanied by our chaplain—now dead, alas—and William Fratton. In Naples I met and fell in love with Maria-Giulietta di Santeramo. I was determined to marry her, and her family was very happy to see her allied to a wealthy English milord, being themselves well-born but penniless, even though he was a Protestant. She was as closely chaperoned as Italian girls always are, and we rarely snatched even a few words without the presence of her duenna—a situation guaranteed to enhance any young couple's infatuation with each other, you'll agree. Joshua Barnwell, my chaplain and tutor, was adamant that I should return to England, seek my trustees' consent and woo her formally, but I was impatient and determined. I persuaded Maria-Giulietta—with great difficulty, I might add—to elope with me. Inevitably, her family caught up with us the next day and insisted upon an immediate wedding, my age being in any case no barrier under Italian law. As you may imagine, I was overjoyed, but Joshua was dismayed: not only did he disapprove anyway, but he would have to answer to the trustees when we returned. However, he did persuade her parents to allow him to perform an Anglican wedding, thus assuaging some of his misgivings. He told them—quite wrongly—that my trustees would have a Catholic one set aside once we were in England. To this day I don't know whether our marriage was legal in either or both countries. At the time I didn't doubt it and later events made it immaterial.'

He paused as if uncertain how to continue. Libby felt her world was turning upside-down. She seemed to be listening through a mist of incomprehension yet at the same time clinging to the one certainty that she must at least appear to be calm for the next little while. She glanced up at the Viscount. 'Go on,' she urged quietly. Lord Charlbury looked down at her and his hold on her hand tightened imperceptibly.

'We returned through France—a foolish route which I insisted upon despite Joshua's protestations that the country was too unsettled to be safe. We reached Paris—which still glittered, though the tarnish was becoming apparent—and there Maria-Giulietta became ill. She convinced me—perhaps I wanted to be convinced—that it was no more than a digestive upset. Joshua was becoming more and more insistent that we should leave France without delay, and since stolid, unimaginative Fratton was equally adamant, I decided to follow their advice for once, and leave. We didn't consult a doctor until we were on the packet. He happened to be travelling back to Dover where he had his practice, and to our horror he diagnosed typhoid. We put it out that she was sea-sick, and Dr Jordan arranged for us to go straight to his own house when the packet docked. Bosham may well have seen Maria-Giulietta carried ashore. She died two days later and is buried in Dover.'

'How many people knew of this?' asked Lord Wilcote, knowing that no whisper of it had ever circulated among Marcus's friends.

'Of the marriage? The di Santeramo family, of course; Joshua Barnwell, who died ten years ago; and William Fratton, my groom. Her family was naturally informed of her death, but apart from that the only people who knew for a fact that she died were Dr Jordan and the vicar who buried her. Fratton had ridden on to get Byfield ready for us, so he heard later. The trustees were naturally told the full story. They regarded it as an unfortunate interlude and were emphatic that it should remain a secret, largely, I think, because of her religion. I was at the time too stunned, too shattered even to think, much less to protest, and so far as I know it has remained a secret ever since. Where Bosham can have got the information, I've no idea. I can't believe Fratton will have talked. He guessed before he left Dover that she was dying, and had only told the household that I was returning early. That's what he assured me, at all events, and certainly no member of the household ever referred to it, not even obliquely. My late uncle—Denmead—was one of the trustees,' he added thoughtfully.

The rector turned to Lord Wilcote. 'Ask William Fratton to come in, my lord. We can then see what he can confirm.'

Lord Wilcote was gone some little while, and when he returned to the vestry it was alone and with the intelligence that Fratton had taken himself off after the departing Bosham. He added that he had sent the distraught nurse and housekeeper home, adjuring them to hold their own counsel until matters could be untangled.

The rector sat at the vestry table, his head in his hands. 'I fancy there may well be some doubt about the Italian marriage, particularly in view of the fact that you were still a minor,' he said. 'But such things are beyond my ability to determine. It seems to me that it would be a great deal more simple, and certainly speedier, just to ascertain the death. If proof of the lady's death can be procured, the legality or otherwise of the marriage becomes irrelevant.'

Lord Charlbury nodded. 'That makes good sense. I shall leave for Dover immediately.' He turned to Libby, and the harshness that had characterised his voice since Bosham's unwelcome disclosure softened. He took her hand and held it gently, conscious that it was trembling. 'My dear, I am truly sorry for this, as you may well imagine. I would have moved heaven and earth to spare you such humiliation. Go back to Chase with Max. The first thing I must do is get the proof I need. When I return, we will talk together. Believe me, I shall fully understand if you decide you would prefer to be released from our betrothal. Max, look after her. Rupert—a word with you.'

He paused only to raise Libby's still trembling hand to his lips before taking his friend by the elbow and hurrying him outside.

CHAPTER SEVEN

THE drive back to Chase seemed endless, and Libby
strove to maintain the outward appearance of calm
dignity. It was an effort. Under that cool exterior she
seethed with disappointment and jealousy. She had
known Charlbury had had mistresses—they were, after
all, the prerequisites of a rake—and that fact had dis-
turbed her not at all, for he had, by definition, not
married any of them. The shock lay in finding that he
had previously married. The possible illegality of the
marriage was no consolation. He had certainly believed
it to be legal at the time, and had loved Maria-Giulietta
enough to go to considerable lengths to marry her. He
had never pretended that his offer for Libby was
prompted by anything more than convenience, so she
could hardly claim to have been misled. It was her own
heart that misled her, a heart so overwhelmed by her
own love for the Viscount that it had convinced itself
that one day its object could not fail to return that love.
That had been when she had believed his heart to be
untouched. Now she knew he had once loved at least as
much as she did and, since it was inconceivable that she
should ever come to love another man, so she could no
longer delude herself that this man would ever come to
love her.

Then there was the inevitable disappointment at the
postponement of an event which had meant so much to
her. It was not only a disappointment, of course, but a
humiliation as well. She felt that humiliation less keenly
than others did on her behalf, knowing that Charlbury's
humiliation must be ten times worse. She had no doubt
at all that he would return from Dover successful in his
quest. She knew him to be an honourable man, and not
for one moment did she doubt the truth of his story. It

70

seemed entirely possible, however, that so dramatic a turn of events could only alter dramatically the relationship between Charlbury and herself. She had no idea in what way that change might manifest itself, and she was not at all sure it was something she wanted to give much thought to in case the outcome made her even more unhappy than she already was.

Her escort back to Chase was the man who had come to give her away. It should have been Charlbury who brought her back from the church, she thought bitterly, and she was grateful that Lord Wilcote at least made no attempt to engage her in conversation, in some fatuous attempt to take her mind off the events of the last half-hour.

Despite her determination to appear in control of herself, the drive was long enough to tax that determination to the full, and long before the gates of Chase were reached the need to break down and weep was well-nigh irresistible. When the carriage drew up at the portico, Libby accepted Lord Wilcote's assistance in dismounting from it and, with a barely audible word of thanks, she ran up the steps with unseeing eyes and made her way immediately to her room, where, at last, her composure cracked and she collapsed on to her bed, her tears coming thick and fast in great, racking sobs.

Nurse, who together with the housekeeper had cobbled together a story for the rest of the household which was not exactly untrue but which dispensed with the more sensational elements of the truth, was hovering on the landing when she heard the crunch of wheels on the gravel. Rightly guessing that this was not the moment for words of consolation, she remained unobtrusively in the shadows until Libby's door had closed behind her, and then she unashamedly put her ear to the keyhole. Her heart bled at the sound of tears from within, and she longed to take the heart-broken bride in her arms as if she had been a child and rock her into some semblance of comfort. She recognised, however, that Libby was not a child and that Libby's needs were different. Let her have a good cry, she thought, comfort can be

offered later, and she fetched her knitting from her room
and sat herself down on a chair outside the door to knit
and wait for the sobs to abate.

When the worst paroxysms had abated and Libby had
had a little further time for reflection, Nurse collected
a tray of hot chocolate from the kitchen, to which she
added a plate of ratafia biscuits and some marchpane
bon-bons, and went quietly in to her mistress.

Libby shook her head, protesting dumbly that she
wanted nothing, but Nurse was a past mistress at coaxing
unwilling appetites.

'I know you think you don't want it, my dear, and I
can't say I blame you, but it's a fact that nothing seems
quite so bad if you've got something inside you. Now
just you take a sip of this chocolate and see if I'm not
telling you the truth.'

Libby did as she was bid, as much because it was easier
than to resist as because she had much faith in Nurse's
theory, and she found that it did indeed make a very
small difference. At least she felt a little calmer, and she
supposed that could hardly be a bad thing. The biscuits
and the marchpane remained uneaten, however, and
Nurse was wise enough not to press them.

'Now, my dear,' she said when she judged Libby to
be a little more composed. 'Why don't you tell me what
transpired in the vestry—if you want to, that is—and
then we'll put our heads together and see what we can
make of this whole faradiddle.'

Libby couldn't see what there was to be made of it
beyond the bald facts, but nevertheless, in between sips
and choking sobs, she recounted what had been said and
decided. Nurse nodded thoughtfully.

'I guessed as much,' she said. 'When his lordship came
back from the Tour he was in a very bad way—moody
and sullen-like, as if the world owed him something. We
all guessed there was a lady in the case, of course, but
no one thought there was more to it than that, except I
had a suspicion.' She paused, and Libby urged her to
continue. 'Like this it was: Master Max came down with
the measles, and naturally they brought him back to the

nursery for me to look after. He had it bad, poor little soul—Master Max always did take sickness hard—and Mr Barnwell came into the nursery to see how he was. His lordship had been very unfeeling about his poor brother: "Why should he live when others die?" he'd said the day before, and I thought he was meaning their mother, and said as much to Mr Barnwell. "Oh, no," replies the chaplain. "I don't think he was referring to *that* Viscountess,"—with the emphasis on the "that", if you know what I mean, Miss Libby—so naturally I asked what he meant, and he coloured up and said he didn't mean anything in particular, and left the room. Now, when the door was closed, Milly—she was kitchen-maid but I'd been given her to help with the work in the sick-room and she never did learn to keep a still tongue in her head—she says to me, "I reckon I knows what he meant. I reckon his lordship went and married some foreigner and she died." Well, naturally I told her she had an imagination as big as her mouth and his lordship wasn't of an age to get married without permission and she was to hush up and not be so silly, but I did wonder. So a day or two later I had a quiet word with William Fratton and he didn't say yes and he didn't say no, but he did say as how some people should know their place and keep mum—meaning Milly, of course—so I decided that maybe Milly had hit the nail fairly on the head.'

'Does Milly still work at Byfield?' Libby asked.

'Lord, no, miss, not this many a year. She married a seaman from Lymington soon after. Last I'd heard—and it wasn't recently by any means—she'd set up in some kind of business near the docks in Southampton. By all accounts nothing very respectable, but more than that I couldn't say.'

She watched while Libby finished the cup of choc-olate and then whisked the tray away. 'Now,' she said, 'what you need is a few hours' sleep. Let me help you out of that dress—which I'm sure we'll have you wearing again before long—and into your night-shift. I'm going to draw the curtains and then I'll get Cook to make you

up a nice little something for dinner, and you'll be feeling
better in no time.'

Libby let her undo the small buttons that fastened the
back of her dress, but she protested that she wouldn't
want anything to eat.

'Nonsense,' Nurse declared stoutly. 'Of course you
will. Besides, it will never do for his lordship to come
back and find you've wasted away to nothing. Now you
lie down like a good girl and get some sleep.'

Libby slid thankfully between the sheets in the now
darkened room, but sleep eluded her. The secret of
Marcus's marriage was not as well-kept as everyone had
supposed, and it was probably inevitable that Milly,
sooner or later, had talked. It sounded as if she was
hardly the most discreet of women. Where Tom Bosham
came into it Libby had no idea, and she had even less
notion why he should have felt impelled to interrupt the
wedding. He obviously didn't know the former Lady
Charlbury had died, but what had been his true motive?
The least probable motive was the one he had himself
given. If Libby could be sure of one thing, it was that
altruism had never figured prominently behind any of
Tom Bosham's actions.

No matter how she turned considerations such as these
over in her mind, she was no nearer discovering their
true explanation, so she turned her thoughts instead to
the more profitable area of how she now felt about
Marcus. She had already decided she believed his story,
and she saw no reason to change her opinion. The
jealousy still hurt and she knew it would go on hurting
whenever she thought of the beautiful Italian who had
captured his heart. He had told her they would talk when
he returned and he would not hold her to their contract
if she wished to be released from it. There had been a
brief moment when she had felt she never wanted to set
eyes on him again, but that had faded now. If she decided to go ahead and marry him after all, she must first
resign herself to the knowledge that, no matter how good
a wife she became, no matter how efficient a provider
of heirs, she could never replace Maria-Giulietta in his

heart. That was a bitter fact to face, a painful one to accept. It brought her back to that half a loaf. When she had previously decided the proverb was right, at the back of her mind had been the thought—no, the conviction—that in time she would have the whole loaf. Now she knew that could never be so. The question she had to ask herself was whether she could accept that and live with a daily reminder that it was so. She was unsure until she turned the question around and asked herself whether she wanted to spend the rest of her life never seeing Marcus again. The very thought brought an involuntary smile to her lips, and her question was answered. She would marry Lord Charlbury on any terms he chose to lay down. Her only remaining fear was that it might be he who changed his mind, either out of a misguided wish to save her further embarrassment or because the day's disastrous events meant that he would never be able to look at her again without remembering the love he had lost. In the former instance he would undoubtedly raise the matter himself, and it would be up to Libby to convince him that he was mistaken. The latter posed greater problems.

Lord Charlbury was a gentleman. If he thought Libby wanted to go through with the wedding and he did not, for reasons he would be loath to share, then he would go through with it for her sake. Half a loaf was all very well, but what sort of marriage would it be if every time he looked at her he was reminded of what might have been? No, that was a situation in which no bread would be preferable in order to save him a lifetime of pain. If Charlbury expressed a willingness to resume their plans, it was up to Libby to make quite sure that that was what he really wanted.

Only one other query niggled at the back of her mind. She had no doubt at all that things had happened exactly as Marcus had said, but it had been a long time ago. No one had thought to mention his age at that time, but she supposed he must have been about eighteen. A lot could have happened in the ensuing seventeen years. Already one witness, the chaplain, had died. Might not Dr

Jordan also have died, to say nothing of the vicar who had officiated at the funeral? What if the church register had been burnt or that volume mislaid? Marcus was going to have to bring back proof before any marriage to him could go ahead, and it was an uncomfortable thought that such proof might be very difficult indeed to obtain after such a length of time.

There was a limit to the amount of churning any brain could indulge in before becoming exhausted, and it was perhaps as well for Libby's sanity that hers decided enough was enough and she fell into a deep if uneasy sleep that lasted until Nurse crept back into her room with the news that Cook had made her a nice little dinner to be served in her room, but that if Miss Libby preferred she could always join Master Max and Lord Wilcote in the dining-room.

No one was surprised that she decided to eat in her room, if eat she must, so the tray was sent up, its contents carefully selected by Nurse as being likely to tempt a depressed appetite: a small piece of turbot in a white wine sauce; a poached and stuffed chicken breast; button mushrooms and sweet young carrots; and a syllabub, the whole being so beautifully presented that Libby found herself tempted into tasting, despite her inclination to the contrary and, having tasted, found no difficulty in demolishing the meal, greatly to the satisfaction of Nurse and the cook, the latter having initially been reluctant to make a special effort which she felt sure would be untouched and therefore unappreciated.

When Libby awoke next day she felt a great deal calmer, and though it would have been foolish to expect her nerves to be completely mended they were considerably less frayed than they had been when Nurse had left her the previous evening, a fact which Nurse observed and remarked upon when she brought in a cup of chocolate.

.   'Now you'll not want to face the world yet awhile, I dare say, so if you let me know what you fancy for breakfast I'll get one of the girls to bring it up.'

Libby sipped her drink and considered the suggestion. 'I don't think so,' she said at last. 'I've got to face everyone sooner or later, so I may as well get it over with. No, I'll go down to breakfast.'

She saw no reason to hurry herself, however, and when she eventually entered the breakfast-room it was to find that Lord Wilcote had already ridden over from Byfield to see how she did, and was refreshing himself with some coffee. His concern for her was obviously heartfelt and genuine, in odd contrast to Max, who had been keeping him company and whose enquiry into how she did seemed to be made as a matter of form rather than interest and who did not appear to be paying much attention to the answer. He seemed irritable and jumpy, though neither Libby nor Lord Wilcote had much difficulty ascribing that to the upsets of the day before. He added his mite to the conversation, but only when he was directly addressed and, although he repaired with them to the morning-room when the meal was concluded, he was still on edge and seemed ill-at-ease in their company. Midway through the morning he made his first unprompted contribution to the conversation by announcing his intention of going away, adding that he would be back on the morrow.

Lord Wilcote suggested quietly that politeness—and Marcus's parting words—required Max's remaining at Chase until his brother returned.

'Oh, rubbish!' Max said impatiently. 'There's business to attend to. You're perfectly capable of looking after Libby.'

'Undoubtedly,' replied Lord Wilcote, casting an embarrassed glance in her direction. 'That's hardly the point, however. You are host here, not I, and you can very easily send an agent to attend to business in your name if it's so urgent.'

'Well, I can't,' was the petulant answer. 'I have to go myself, and I *am* going. So far as I'm concerned, you may make yourself free of this house. I shan't mind, and I'm quite sure neither Marcus nor Libby will.' And with that, he slammed out of the room.

Lord Wilcote turned to Libby. 'I'm sorry,' he said. 'That was an inexcusable display of bad manners—and not least by discussing you as if you weren't present.'

Libby smiled. It was a rather uncertain smile because she, too, had been taken aback by Max's rudeness. 'There's no reason why you should feel obliged to apologise. It's not as if Max is your brother. I know I shouldn't criticise my future brother-in-law, but he does seem to be a very strange young man. I think he labours under a strong sense of grievance, not all of it unjustified.'

Before her companion could answer, they heard the sound of hoofs on gravel. Lord Wilcote crossed over to the window and saw their host riding down the drive on a serviceable cob that was built for endurance rather than speed. He turned back to Libby. 'It seems we must amuse ourselves as best we can,' he said. 'We shall get no help from our host.'

Max was away for the remainder of that day and most of the next, returning early the following evening, his mood completely changed: he was affable and friendly, evincing every sign of sympathetic concern for Libby in her present unenviable position. Libby could not entirely disguise her surprise at so complete a volte-face. She was becoming accustomed to his changes of mood, resembling, as they did, those sudden changes from the depths to the heights that often characterised children when they were at that difficult age between childhood and adulthood, but Max was far too old to come into that category, and his present concern was so totally at variance with his previous complete lack of it that she was not at all sure how best to respond.

Lord Wilcote made no comment on the change, but his concern was greater than Libby's. He knew Max had always been an unaccountable creature and not an easy person either to know or like, but he was now seeing rather more of the young man that he had ever done before, and he was puzzled. Had he not known the Asthall family so well, he would have been inclined to suspect Max of bouts of insanity and, while that could not be entirely discounted, he felt there might be another cause. These were not suspicions to pass on to Libby, but it was perhaps something he should at least mention to Marcus when he returned. In the meantime, he would keep his own counsel, and spend as much of his time as possible at Chase.

Both Libby and Max breakfasted early next morning, and Libby was happy to see that her host's sunny good mood was undiminished. She decided it could only be beneficial to try to build on his improved humour and so she raised with him an old wives' tale Nurse had related when they were sewing in the turret room.

'It's such a lovely day that I thought I'd go to Tipper's Wood and see if I can find the magic spring,' she said. 'Is it far?'

He laughed—indulgently, she thought. 'I gather Nurse has been filling your head with all the local stories,' he remarked. 'No, it's not far. A good, brisk walk across two fields, that's all, and the track through the woods is well marked. What are you going to wish for?'

She shook her head. 'Oh, no, Max, you'll not catch me out that way. Nurse told me to be very sure never to reveal to *anyone* the nature of my wish because, if I do, not only will it not be granted—which is quite usual in that sort of situation, I believe—but it will guarantee the very reverse happens. That's a risk I'm not prepared to take.'

'You'd better get Rupert to stand out of earshot, then, or whisper it very quietly indeed,' he told her.

'Lord Wilcote will be over much later today. He feels he has been neglecting his family, and intends to devote the better part of the morning to writing to his mother. I thought it would make a pleasant walk, and give me a chance to get to know a part of the estate I haven't yet seen.'

'That sounds as if you intend to stay. Wouldn't it be wiser to wait until you know whether the objection to the wedding was valid?'

His tone was perfectly affable, but the subject-matter brought back the cloud that Libby had only just succeeded in putting to one side. She must not let the comment get her down. 'I still have a morning to fill,' she said briskly. 'As to whether I intend to stay, that's really a matter for discussion between your brother and me, don't you think?' She paused. 'I don't suppose you'd like to come with me?' she asked.

'What a pity you didn't mention it last night,' he said with apparently genuine regret. 'I'm afraid there are matters on the estate to be attended to, and unfortunately they're not in that direction. Do you mind terribly?'

'Of course not,' she told him truthfully. Libby liked her own company and had made her suggestion entirely in the interest of trying to find some sort of common ground with Max.

By the time she had put on her pelisse and a country-woman's bonnet to keep the sun from her complexion, he had left the house, and she was quite content to set out on her own.

Lord Wilcote was engaged in the difficult task of keeping his mother *au fait* with events in Hampshire without giving her gossip-fodder. He knew all too well the speed with which a nice piece of scandal could circulate, and he had no desire to be the source of one which would embarrass both Libby and Marcus, whether or not they eventually married. At the same time, he had no intention of lying to his mother. The wedding had been called off. That must be stated, but he decided that a tactical vagueness as to the cause might be best, and so the indisposition that had struck Libby as a direct consequence of Bosham's interruption became instead the cause of the postponement—or rather, he succeeded in so wording his account that that was the impression it gave.

This tricky task finally completed to his satisfaction, he was waiting for his horse to be brought around when a discreet cough drew his attention to his valet, who stood at the door of the morning-room and, apologising for the intrusion, asked whether Lord Charlbury's groom might have speech with him.

'He's back, then? Yes, of course, Minden. Ask him to step in.'

Clearly William Fratton had been waiting immediately outside for he entered the room before the valet had had the time to beckon him in.

'Seeing as how Lord Charlbury's away, me lord, I thought I'd best report to you.'

'Quite right. When we looked for you after the brouhaha, we gathered you had gone after that seaman—Bosham, I believe he said his name was.'

'Ay, that's it, me lord. He were heading towards Lymington, and the road don't hardly go anywhere else, so I took the risk of losing sight of him while I went back to Chase for a horse and, sure enough, he were still heading Lymington-way, jaunty as you like. He tried to find a boat going to Southampton—which worried me, I can tell you, for how was I to follow? Still, I needn't have fretted, for there wasn't one, seemingly, and in the end he cadges a ride on a carrier's cart instead.

'It were a bit difficult when he got to Southampton, for he made straight for the docks and a good horse sticks out like a sore thumb down there. But as luck would have it the head ostler at the Dolphin were standing on the flagway outside, and he knows Lord Charlbury's horses, so I flings him the reins and says to look after the 'oss till I gets back, so I didn't lose sight of our Bosham.'

He paused, and Lord Wilcote resisted the urge to tell him to hurry up, knowing it would be quicker in the long run to let the groom take his own time.

'I followed our Mr Bosham right down into the stews—and a right place that is, down there by the docks, me lord—and where should he go but into an alehouse—the Spliced Mainbrace, it were called—so of course in I goes, too. Not a nice house, me lord. Not a nice house at all. Anyway, I gets inside just in time to see Bosham go behind the bar, and who should be a-standing there but Milly Radlett. You wouldn't know Milly Radlett, me lord, but she were kitchen-maid here around the time Lord Charlbury went on the Tour. I did hear as how she married a sailor and set up a business in Southampton. The Mainbrace was crowded, so she didn't see me, and I slipped out—if she knew Bosham, I didn't want him knowing I'd followed him. I asked around, and she's called Milly Bosham now, so seemingly they're wed, though it doesn't always follow, not in that neck of the woods.

'It were a strange alehouse, though, me lord. I couldn't rightly put my finger on it until I left, and as I were riding home it struck me, like. It were the smell. Not just beer and baccy—nor gin and baccy, for that matter—but something else, sweet and sickly. Not strong. Just a hint as if it had drifted in from the back.'

'So,' said Lord Wilcote, 'we know where to find Tom Bosham, and I suppose he must have had his information from his wife. But why should he lay information against Lord Charlbury? Did his wife have a grudge against him or the family?'

'Not so far as I know, me lord,' the groom answered, shaking his head. 'I'll ask Mrs Widford—she knew her quite well—but as I recall, she left for love of a sailor—Tom Bosham, as like as not. No question of her being dismissed, of that I'm certain sure.'

'Pity. I fancy the answer to that question may tell us a great deal. What I'd like you to do, Fratton, is to take yourself to Chase and install yourself there—say it's Lord Charlbury's orders—and keep an eye on what goes on. Especially on Miss Barton. Lord Charlbury seems to think she should be carefully watched. I go over each day, but you, I fancy, would be in a better position to watch unobtrusively.'

'Consider it done, me lord. I'll be off almost immediately,' Fratton bowed and walked to the door. When he reached it, he stopped suddenly as if a thought had just struck him. He turned back to Lord Wilcote.

'There was another thing, me lord. Funny really, though I hope you won't think it's none of my business. Well, it isn't, except it involves Mr Max.'

Lord Wilcote looked at him sharply. 'Mr Max?' he asked.

'Yes, me lord. As I were going back to the Dolphin I saw him—funny part of the town to be in, I thought—with a young lady.'

'I think you're right and it may well be none of your business, Fratton,' Lord Wilcote said repressively. 'Gentlemen do expect to be free to pursue...other interests.'

'Yes, me lord, but I think you mistake my meaning. This were a young *lady*, no doubt about it, and not an English lady, neither. Frenchie, she seemed, from the way she waved her hands about. Very excited she were, and Mr Max seemed right put out. Course, I didn't get close enough for them to see me, so I didn't hear what they was saying.'

'Thank you, Fratton. I don't think we need refine too much upon this particular encounter. Pray don't let me keep you from your work.' Thus dismissed, Fratton bowed again and made his way back to the stables, prior to setting out for Chase.

Although Lord Wilcote had been ready to leave Byfield Manor for Chase before talking to Fratton, his urgency seemed to leave him after this conversation, and an observer would have noticed how very thoughtful he had become. Eventually, however, he threw off his apparently sombre thoughts with a quick shake of his head as if clearing his mind, and rode over to Chase.

As he rode into the stable-yard he was met by William Fratton, who took his horse from him as if they were in his own yard and not someone else's.

'Good morning, me lord,' he said, and then, more quietly, 'Miss Barton isn't here, seemingly. They tell me she set off for a walk some time ago and she's not back yet.'

'On her own?'

'So they say.'

'Did she happen to mention where she was going?'

'Apparently not, me lord.'

Lord Wilcote frowned. 'Then there's nothing to be done but to await her return.'

Leaving his horse with the groom, Lord Wilcote made
his way out of the yard and across the grass towards the
house. As he turned the corner a sturdy smock-clad
figure hurtled across the grass and collided with him.
Lord Wilcote opened his mouth to administer a severe
set-down to the impetuous youth, when he realised from
his ashen face that he was distraught. He was also too
breathless to be coherent. Fratton and two stable-lads,
hearing the commotion and his lordship's initial exple-
tives, rushed out to see what had happened. The
breathless youth, bent double and gasping for air, kept
pointing behind him in the general direction of the home
farm.

'That lady,' he gasped at last. 'I think she be called
Miss Barton—I dunno for sure but it's her as is to be
Lady Charlbury...' He stopped to catch a bit more
breath.

'What about her, man?' rasped Lord Wilcote. 'What
about Miss Barton?'

'Over there, my lord,' the youth went on between
gasps. 'She's dead, my lord. I reckon as how she's died
o' fright. Must have, for there's no blood—leastways,
none as I could see. Still as a rock, she is. Dead as a
stone.'

CHAPTER EIGHT

'FOR God's sake, man, where is she? What has happened?' Lord Wilcote exclaimed.

'Twenty Acre Ley, this side of Tipper's Wood,' the youth told him. 'I dragged her through the fence by the stile, but I think she's dead. Owld Sidney be there and he don't have no right to be in that field. I think he's done for her.'

Rupert looked from Fratton to the stable-lads. 'Who's "Owld Sidney", for goodness' sake?' he asked.

The two lads glanced at each other and shrugged. 'He's Mr Max's bull—one of they improved Longhorns.'

Not listening to anything beyond 'Owld Sidney''s basic identity, Fratton ordered the lads to get a hurdle and hasten to the stile, telling Ned Newbury, the still-gasping farm-hand, to lead the way. Lord Wilcote remounted his horse, and Fratton slung a bridle on the cob and followed him bareback across the fields to where Libby lay motionless just beyond the reach of 'Owld Sidney', who stamped and pawed the ground and threw his massive head with its extraordinary overstated horns from side to side so that the clods of earth caught up on them were scattered far and wide.

Both men flung themselves from their horses simultaneously and knelt down beside Libby's still body. Lord Wilcote took her wrist while the other stood round with bated breath. He felt a faint pulse, and when he looked up and nodded a sigh of relief escaped all of them in unison.

Whipping off his carefully arranged cravat, Rupert instructed the groom to wring it out in the nearby water-trough and, as he bathed Libby's head with its damp coolness, her eyelids fluttered and she looked up at him, temporarily bewildered as to her whereabouts.

'Lord Wilcote?' she whispered faintly.

'Hush, Libby,' he replied. 'Lie still and don't worry. We'll have you back at Chase very soon.' He turned to the groom. 'Fratton, do you ride off for Dr Kennet and urge him to make haste. I see more lads coming. I'll oversee Miss Barton's return. Put my saddle on the cob and make all speed.'

It was the work of moments before the cob was saddled and Fratton on his way. The stable-hands, with poor Ned Newbury puffing and panting as much as ever, came across the field with their hurdle. Libby was laid on this as gently as possible, but not without a tell-tale wince that indicated she was hurt, even if there was no sign of blood. It would have been more surprising, given the circumstances, if she had not been hurt, Lord Wilcote thought, and he prayed that her injuries would prove to be considerably less than fatal. He bade the lads have a care and jostle the hurdle as little as possible. There might well be none of the blood by which Ned Newbury set so much store, but he feared what internal injuries might have occurred, and dreaded that a careless step might aggravate them.

By the mysterious workings of the rural grapevine, word of Libby's accident had reached Chase ahead of the party of rescuers, and Mrs Chadlington and Nurse were already hovering at the front steps in anticipation of the arrival of Libby's corpse. Both were delighted that the event was not yet as severe as the portents had predicted, and both relished the opportunity to be of service to the probable future mistress of Chase. Indeed, to such an extent did the two ladies vie with one another that Lord Wilcote thought it expedient to direct their activities into different, though equally necessary channels. Thus, the old nurse saw to Libby's comfortable disposal in her bedroom to await the doctor's arrival, while the housekeeper consulted with the cook as to a suitable diet and boiled kettles in anticipation of the doctor's calling for them. She had no very precise notion why they should be needed, but had a firmly entrenched idea that they would not come amiss.

Of Max Asthall there was no sign.

Fortunately William Fratton had found Dr Kennet at home, so the physician was able to arrive at Chase before anyone had had time to become any more anxious than they already were. He found Libby hovering between the conscious and unconscious state and was not sorry when, after giving him a weak smile, she drifted away. He privately hoped she would sink back into unconsciousness after his examination, which was unlikely to be painless.

Nothing appeared to be broken. That, at least, was a cause of congratulation. Even better was the doctor's inability to detect the slightest sign of internal bleeding. It seemed extraordinary that anyone should emerge from an encounter with Old Sidney with nothing more than severe bruising and shock, but so it appeared. Dr Kennet was not entirely satisfied, simply because the improbability was too great. He would return next morning, and exhorted Nurse to send for him immediately should there be any adverse change in Miss Barton's condition. The patient was to be kept warm at all costs, and fed a light, nourishing diet. Neat's-foot jelly, perhaps, and a coddled egg if she could be persuaded to eat. No, he didn't anticipate fever, and insisted upon being called should any such signs develop, or should Miss Barton complain of any pain not accounted for by bruising, or of a sharp nature. Indeed, anything untoward would, he felt, justify sending for him at once.

To Lord Wilcote he expressed himself bluntly.

'Miss Barton seems to have been remarkably fortunate,' he said.

'I doubt if Miss Barton sees it in quite that light,' Lord Wilcote commented drily.

The doctor laughed. 'I take your point, my lord, but I fancy you take mine. That bull is notorious in these parts. He may be new and improved, but his temper is vile and is well-known to be so. What was he doing in Twenty Acre Ley? The footpath is a frequently used one to Tipper's Wood, and the old Earl was always adamant that people should be free to use it without hindrance, however stupid the reason.'

'What was their reason?' Lord Wilcote asked, intrigued. 'What's the attraction of Tipper's Wood?'

'A spring generally credited with powers both curative and magical. It's reputed to make wishes come true. Pure superstition, of course, though I have noticed the waters can be beneficial in certain conditions. But this, with all due respect, my lord, is not the point. That animal should not have been there at all, and certainly not without his cows, as seems to have been the case today. What is Lord Charlbury thinking of?'

'Lord Charlbury isn't here,' his friend answered. 'Nor has he been for some days. I assure you the matter will be brought to his attention.'

When Max Asthall returned for a very belated luncheon after what he described as a good long gallop, his concern for Libby and his insistence on knowing all the details surprised Lord Wilcote. It struck him as somewhat excessive coming, as it did, from one who had been a host casual to the point of rudeness.

'You have charge of this estate,' Rupert reminded him. 'That bull appears to be a byword for bad temper in this locality. You can hardly have been unaware of this, so what was he doing in that field?'

Max's expression was one of wide-eyed surprise. 'Old Sidney? Of course he shouldn't have been in Twenty Acre Ley, but I've no idea how he got there. I can only assume the gate from his normal field had been left open. I don't suppose you'll find anyone who'll admit to having done so, however.'

'I'm sure you're right,' was Lord Wilcote's only comment. He noticed that Max made no enquiry as to whether the gate had been found to be open—and it seemed improbable that Old Sidney should have closed it behind him—and nor did he wonder why, if it had been so left, the cows hadn't followed their bull into the fresh pasture. Lord Wilcote volunteered no information on either count, but he made a mental note of his host's singularly one-sided curiosity. Perhaps it was right and proper that Max should be more concerned with Libby's well-being, but without establishing how the accident could have occurred it would be difficult to prevent its happening again. If, indeed, it had been an accident.

Libby remained in bed, bruised and shaken, under Nurse's watchful eye, and when Viscount Charlbury returned late next day he was greeted with the news of her misadventure almost before his foot had left the stirrup. He had no desire to hear a garbled version from the under-groom's lips, so, learning that Fratton had gone off earlier, he made straight for the dining-room where his friend was finishing a sustaining meal. Of Max there was no sign. Marcus saw no reason to stand on ceremony.

'Libby—how is she?' he demanded. 'What's all this about the bull, and why was that damned vicious animal in Twenty Acre Ley in the first place?'

'Sit down, Marcus, and have something to calm your nerves,' his friend answered, pouring him a glass of wine. 'Libby is shaken and badly bruised, but happily seems to have sustained no other hurt. I gather from Dr Kennet—who says she goes on extremely well, by the way—that, given the known temperament of that animal, she's been remarkably fortunate. She has remained in bed on his advice and, truth to tell, I very much doubt if she is in any condition to do otherwise, for Nurse says she's very badly bruised. As to the whys and wherefores of the bull's being in that field, I think you'd do well to enquire. As a guest, it was hardly my province, though my natural curiosity produced some relevant facts.'

Lord Charlbury laughed harshly. 'And what relevant facts did this entirely natural curiosity produce?'

'That the gate was securely closed, thus precluding its having been left open accidentally and at the same time preventing "Owld Sidney's" zenana from following him through—and possibly mitigating the worst excesses of his bad temper.'

'What has Max to say about it all?'

Rupert appeared to be studying his well-manicured nails. 'He was off on "a good long gallop" at the time.

He assumed the gate had been left open. I didn't enlighten him, and I fancy he hasn't pursued the matter.'

'Where is he now?'

'I'm afraid I've no idea. He went out this afternoon and, so far as I know, hasn't yet returned.'

'I see. Do you know when he left on this "good long gallop", or where it took him?'

'Ah, now that's where being a guest puts me at such a disadvantage. One can hardly enquire of the servants into the actions of one's host, now can one?'

'Too nice by half, Rupert! But I take your point. And now I must see Libby.'

Nurse tut-tutted at the impropriety of his lordship's entering the bedroom of an unmarried lady.

His lordship grinned. 'Would there be more propriety if she were married?' he asked.

'Only if it were to you, my lord, and then I couldn't possibly have an objection,' his old nurse conceded.

'I'm relieved to hear it,' he laughed. 'Now, since Miss Barton will, I hope, shortly be my wife, and since the circumstances are exceptional, and since I shall naturally expect you to stay in the room, do you think that perhaps on this one occasion propriety might be stretched?'

Mrs Widford was no more impervious to his lordship's considerable charm than any other woman upon whom he exerted it and, after animadverting on his cozening ways, agreed that he might indeed visit his betrothed.

'And to tell you the truth,' she went on confidentially, 'since Miss Barton's only able to move with great pain and is certainly in no position to be led astray, I don't really think I need be there at all, so if you'll not mind, my lord, I'll go down to the kitchen for a change of scene.'

'Now that's what I call tact,' he told her. 'You may rest assured your charge will come to no harm with me.'

Nurse snorted. 'If I thought anything else, I'd not be leaving her, my lord,' she retorted.

Libby lay among the deep feather pillows, her head to one side and one hand resting on the pillow, level with her head, but otherwise completely enveloped in the warm bedclothes. She smiled drowsily at Lord Charlbury as he sat on the edge of the bed and gently took her hand.

'You came back, Marcus,' she murmured.

He noted her unprompted use of his Christian name, but made no comment upon it. 'Of course I came back, my dear. Did you doubt that I would?' A glance at the bottle on the small cupboard beside the bed told him that laudanum was a more probable cause of her drowsiness than either exhaustion or injury.

'I don't know. I thought . . . I wondered . . .' Her voice trailed off.

'What on earth prompted you to go to Twenty Acre Ley in the first place?' he asked.

'Tipper's Wood,' she answered. 'The magic spring,' she added, and she smiled a little sheepishly.

'So you've heard about that.' Lord Charlbury laughed. 'And what took you there—surely not rheumatism? I don't think I could marry one so young and already afflicted.'

'Don't be silly,' she replied with something of her old spirit. 'It was to wish for your return—and that your errand should prove successful.' She looked up at him, an expression which combined both hope and doubt in her eyes. 'I can see the first wish was granted,' she continued. 'But what about the second?'

'Greedy girl,' he said. 'Didn't anyone tell you the well is said only to grant one wish to any individual, so you have to be sure the one you make is the most important one in your life?' He saw the look of utter dismay that crossed her features, and hastened to reassure her. He took her hand in both of his. 'Don't let your imagination run ahead of you,' he told her. 'The gods must smile on you, for not only am I here but yes, my errand was successful. Not only were Dr Jordan and the vicar still in Dover, but the church records were intact, and a local magistrate has verified the statements and the

documents. I am proved to be a widower. Does that make
you happier?'

So great was Libby's relief that she tried to sit up with
the understandable, if unladylike, intention of throwing
her arms round the neck of her betrothed, but, with a
cry of pain, she fell back upon the pillows.

Marcus winced in sympathy and tightened his clasp.
'Lie still,' he told her. 'You need rest and sleep. When
you're rather more recovered we'll discuss whether you
wish to release me from our contract.'

'I don't have to think about it, Marcus,' she whispered. 'I'm content that it should go ahead.'

He shook his head. 'I'm very flattered, my dear, but
I don't think you're in any condition just yet to make a
rational judgement. We'll leave it a day or two.'

Libby hoped she disguised the disappointment she felt
at so clear an indication that the Viscount no longer
wished the wedding to take place. Had his wish been
otherwise, he would surely have welcomed her words with
some show of enthusiasm.

'Did you love her very much?' she asked wistfully.

She had the disconcerting impression that a shutter
had come down across his features, cutting her off from
any display of feeling.

'Very much indeed,' he said shortly.

'I see,' she said, and thought she did.

Nurse came bustling back in at this moment and tut-
tutted as she came over to the bed. 'Now just you lie
still,' she admonished her charge. 'You've been moving,
I can tell. And as for you, my lord, don't you be en-
couraging the poor thing to move, for she's a mass of
bruises which you'll have to take my word for, and needs
to lie as still as she can if she's not to be in agony.'

'I'll leave Miss Barton shortly to enable her to sleep,'
he promised. 'But before I go there are one or two things
I must know.'

Nurse sniffed her disapproval. 'Then make it brief,
my lord, for I'll have to send you packing shortly.' And
to demonstrate that though she was in the room she was
not a participant in any conversation, she set herself the

task of tidying—or rather, of rearranging, for the maids at Chase did their work well—Libby's modest dressing-set.

'Were you on your way to Tipper's Wood or were you returning from it?' he asked.

'I was on my way back,' Libby replied.

'And was Old Sidney—the bull, I mean—in that field when you crossed it the first time?'

Libby wrinkled her brows in the effort to recollect. 'I think not. I certainly didn't see any stock in the field, but I suppose he might have been out of sight.'

The Viscount forbore to inform her that the topography of Twenty Acre Ley was such that the whole field could be seen from each of the stiles.

'One more question, Libby. Did anyone know you were going?'

'Oh, yes. I mentioned it at breakfast, so the servants would have heard—and Max, of course, since it was to him that I mentioned it.'

He kissed her hand gently then and tucked it under the coverlet. 'Go to sleep now, Libby. If Nurse can bear the impropriety, I'll visit you again tomorrow.'

She smiled hazily and obediently closed her eyes. It was a great comfort to her that he had returned safely. The more worrying aspects that would follow were best left until she felt able to grapple with them. For the present, her mind was too hazy to hold any thought for very long.

Lord Charlbury's face was grim when he left the bedroom and returned to Lord Wilcote, who had made himself comfortable in the old Earl's rarely used study. He looked up enquiringly as his host came in.

The Viscount threw himself into a chair and stared at the logs blazing in the hearth. It was summer, but the evenings were chill.

'She was on her way back from Tipper's Wood,' he said shortly. 'The bull had not been in the field when she first crossed it. She had told Max at breakfast that she was going.'

'I see. And the rest of your business?'

'The rest of my business?' Lord Charlbury seemed almost to have forgotten what had taken him away from Chase in the first place. 'Oh, that. All's well. Both the doctor and the vicar are still there, though the latter only just. The record, too, is clear enough. I have a deposition from the local magistrate, and that will be proof enough. What did Fratton find out?'

Briefly, Lord Wilcote gave him the essence of the groom's discoveries. The Viscount was thoughtful.

'I've been loath to think too ill of Max,' he said. 'He is my brother, after all, but I confess I've had suspicions, as I'm sure you've already guessed. Now I'm forced to the conclusion that there have been too many coincidences to be entirely coincidental. If you hadn't appeared on the scene, I doubt whether I should have survived the attack on the way to Copthorne. It wasn't a road which attracts enough traffic to make it worth highwaymen lying in wait on the off-chance; Max knew I was going to Copthorne, and when. What he didn't know was that you had been delayed and that we had, in fact, left together and decided to make a race of it. He knew Libby had gone to Tipper's Wood. It would be an easy matter for a mounted man to let the bull—and only the bull—out of his field. It was his bad luck that Old Sidney for some reason didn't notice Libby until she was very nearly across the field. Then there was the wedding,' he paused.

'Max must have known Milly Bosham when he was a child,' Rupert said. 'But would he have heard about the earlier marriage? And we musn't forget that we've no evidence he knows her now.'

'No, that's true. It's the stumbling-block in my case and, believe me, there's nothing I'd like better than to be able to absolve my brother of any complicity in this. There are, however, some coincidental circumstances and a close proximity. Then there's the undeniable fact that Max is the only person who can benefit either by having me killed or by stopping my marriage, and if he felt I could overset the obstacle he put up to the wedding then if Libby is disposed of it rather increases the odds against my being able to fulfil the terms of the Will within the required six months. There are none too many Libbys about—and most wouldn't have me at any price,' he added ruefully.

'The answer would seem to be for you to get the knot tied without further delay,' his friend suggested.

'So it would seem,' Lord Charlbury agreed. 'I'm by no means so sure, though. If Max is desperate enough to go to those lengths to which he seems already to have gone, then I must ensure not only my marriage, but an heir and, having ensured an heir, may I not also need to keep him safe? No, I think this whole matter needs to be settled first.'

'How?'

'How, indeed! I need proof that Max knows the Boshams. Then he has to be persuaded to act as groomsman again—for scandal I will avoid if I possibly can—and to leave the country afterwards. He could follow the example of other members of the family and go to India. No doubt the new Earl will provide him with letters of introduction once the situation has been explained to him.'

'And if he's not prepared to oblige?'

'Then I shall have to think again. But I shall have Chase, Rupert, and I don't intend to lose Libby if I can help it. Of those two facts you may be certain.'

'Do I conclude you think there may be some doubt about Libby?' Rupert asked.

Marcus frowned and shrugged. 'I don't know. I hope not, but there's no denying her opinion of me may have taken quite a drubbing. It's one thing to know you've been offered for as a matter of convenience. Most women of the right sort understand that. To find that the man you've accepted had previously been married to a woman he loved very much must be daunting—the more so if, as your grandmother suspects, Libby has a fondness for me.'

'Is that your opinion as well?'

'I don't know. Sometimes I have thought... But then she shows her entirely practical face and I suspect that I've been deluding myself.'

'Would it make any difference if you were sure, one way or another?'

'Not as to whether I wanted to marry her. It might make quite a difference as to how I went about wooing her.'

'That sounds cold-bloodedly cynical,' Rupert said drily.

'I suppose it does. Maybe it is. It's certainly practical.'

Rupert looked at him gravely. 'I've no doubt you could seduce her if you'd a mind to,' he said. 'But what are your true feelings towards her, Marcus?'

He was conscious of the same shutter that Libby had noticed earlier.

'That's hardly a matter which need concern you, Rupert,' the Viscount said stiffly. 'All that is relevant for the time being is that I need to fulfil the terms of my uncle's Will, and the inescapable fact is that, if Libby cries off, it won't be easy to find the right woman.'

Lord Charlbury resisted the temptation to wait up for his brother. He knew he would lose his temper with Max if he did so, and he was anxious that his temper should not inadvertently let slip anything that might put the younger man on his guard. It was therefore at a belated breakfast that he first had an opportunity to tackle him.

Max's reaction to enquiry about the bull was off-hand and accompanied by a sigh of exasperation at being obliged to go over the ground yet again.

'Of course Old Sidney should not have been in Twenty Acre Ley,' he snapped. 'I can only conclude someone had accidentally left the gate open.'

'And who do you think that might have been?'

'How should I know? Plenty of people use the footpath across that field.'

'True, but the path takes them well away from that particular gate. Who had any business opening Old Sidney's gate?'

'I don't know. Plenty of people may have done—someone must have taken them all back after milking. Perhaps the gate opened accidentally.'

'Perhaps it did. That would imply a faulty catch. Have you checked the catch?'

Max shifted uncomfortably. 'No, I saw no need. If it hadn't been properly fastened, all this business will have ensured the men take better care next time, and if one of them had subsequently found it faulty he'd have reported it. I can't see why you're making all this fuss, Marcus. After all, Libby escaped with nothing much worse than a few bruises.'

Lord Charlbury controlled his anger with an effort, and resisted the temptation to slap his brother's unconcerned face into some exhibition of feeling.

'Tell me, Max,' he said, an edge to his voice. 'What do you really want in all this? I should have thought, if you want to continue running Chase, that you would be showing greater concern for the occurrence of such . . . carelessness . . . on the estate.'

Max turned on him, his normally pale face ablaze. 'I would—if it were my estate. What's the point of doing anything now if Chase is to be yours? You've ruined Byfield and you'll do the same to Chase.'

'Would you believe me if I said that's not my intention.'

'Oh, I'm willing to believe it isn't your *intention*,' Max said scornfully. 'What I doubt is your ability to change the habits of a lifetime. You've never made the least push to change them in the past, so what on earth is going to make you succeed now?'

'The love of a good woman, perhaps,' Lord Charlbury replied sardonically. His eyes were fixed on his brother, a cold light in them that underlined the significance of his words, had Max been in a humour to observe such details.

Max snorted. 'You wouldn't recognise a good woman if she cut you dead,' he sneered.

He gasped as the back of his brother's hand whipped hard across his face.

'Let that be the last time you say anything derogatory
of Miss Barton,' he snapped. 'And be sure of one thing,
Max. I intend to have Chase, and nothing you can do
will stop me.'

CHAPTER NINE

WHEN Nurse brought Libby her morning chocolate the day after Lord Charlbury's confrontation with his brother, she let slip the fact that his lordship intended to ride over early that morning and breakfast at Chase.

'In that case I shall get up and join him,' Libby declared.

'Now don't be foolish,' Mrs Widford chided her. 'You're in no fit state to go gallivanting about downstairs.'

Libby smiled wryly. 'I don't think there will be much "gallivanting",' she said. 'More of a cautious step-by-step amble.'

'All the more reason for you to stay where you are,' Nurse declared, but the obstinate set of Libby's chin told her her protestations were wasted.

Libby had had plenty of time to go over and over her present situation. Sooner or later she and Marcus would have to discuss whether the marriage was to go ahead, and she needed to be absolutely sure what her own wishes were.

She supposed there had never really been any doubt that she wanted to marry Marcus, no matter what problems there might be and despite the more recent discovery that the love he had borne his first wife meant that Libby would be well advised to forget any hope she might have had that he in time would come to love her. She was more concerned to discover whether he was himself still of the same mind, now that he had been inescapably reminded of his Italian Viscountess and must inevitably have drawn comparisons between her and Libby. She was also afraid that sheer gallantry might preclude his being absolutely truthful about his feelings and thus lead him to condemn himself to a lifetime of unhappiness. 'Misery' was the word that first sprang to her mind, but she discounted it. If ever she found out that Marcus had married her from a misguided sense of honour, she could at least ensure that he wasn't miserable. In that situation she supposed she would have to face up to the fact that sooner or later he would set up a mistress. That was a possibility—no, a probability—she viewed with dismay. All the same, she wanted with all her heart and soul to be Marcus's wife, and only if he admitted—or she seriously suspected—that he was no longer of the same mind would she willingly stand aside.

All the more reason to get up and join him at the breakfast-table. Nurse might protest, and Libby herself might have preferred to stay where she was, but she had absolutely no intention of presenting herself for too long as a languorous invalid. She fancied it was an image of which he might quickly tire, so she hastened her own dressing so that she could time her descent to the breakfast-room in order to arrive slightly after he had taken his seat.

He sprang to his feet as she entered, an expression of mingled concern and astonishment on his face as he came round the table to pull out a chair for her.

'My dear Libby, are you sure you should be up and about so soon?' he asked solicitously.

'Probably not,' she answered with a cheerfulness which she hoped disguised the entirely physical pain she was enduring. 'Not in Dr Kennet's opinion, at least, and Nurse has done her best to prevent me, but I prefer to be up and doing. Mind you, since I'm forced to admit that I do still ache somewhat, I fancy I shan't actually be "doing" very much.' She looked around the room. 'Has Max breakfasted, do you know?'

'It would appear so,' Lord Charlbury answered, indicating the remains of a breakfast. 'I'm informed he has dashed off somewhere. He seems to do quite a lot of "dashing off" these days. Rupert will be over later. Now, since I can't have you putting yourself to the discomfort of jumping up and down to get your breakfast,

you must allow me to serve you. What will you have?'
He went over to the chafing dishes on the sideboard.
'Nurse tells me you're particularly partial to the devilled
kidneys. She says it's a most unladylike fancy. Is that
what you'd like today?'

Libby chuckled. 'Yes, she does disapprove. Apparently, ladies should eat blander dishes. I do enjoy the
kidneys—and the kedgeree as well—but today I'll do as
Nurse would prefer. Some scrambled egg, if you please,
and a couple of slices of ham will suit me very well.'

She watched him thoughtfully, trying to assess his
mood and wondering how best to broach some of the
things that were in her mind. She decided on a straightforward approach.

'Marcus, while I've been in bed I've had time to think;
even the laudanum didn't dull my senses all the time,
you know, and there was plenty of time left over. Only
I'm afraid you'll consider it grossly impertinent because
it concerns your brother, and I shouldn't discuss him
with you behind his back. The trouble is, I can't very
well say what's in my mind to his face.'

He put her plate before her and poured her some
coffee. 'If I undertake not to be offended and promise
not to tell tales out of school, perhaps I can encourage
you to speak freely.'

He smiled reassuringly as he spoke, but Libby still felt
diffident about raising the first part of her concern.

'It seems to me that there have been three incidents
which may fairly be described as "unfortunate",' she
began. 'They're all apparently unconnected. First there
was the attack upon you on your way to Copthorne.
You played it down at the time, but I'm not so stupid
as to realise that highwaymen don't customarily lie in
wait on little-used rural lanes on the off-chance of rich
pickings. Then there was the objection to our marriage
from a man no one seemed to know and for an unclear
purpose. Lastly there was the previously unheard-of
straying of Old Sidney into Twenty Acre Ley. I have to
admit that I don't fully understand why there should be
one particular link between these events, but there is,

and it seems to be Max. At least, it is if he knew you were going to Copthorne.'

'He knew it, but he thought Rupert had gone on ahead to advise his family that I should be joining them. Had Rupert not changed his plans, I rather fancy I should have been left dead at the roadside. His connection with the bull is obvious and, since he has taken no steps to check whether there was a faulty catch, and since the cows didn't follow their lord and master, I can only conclude he was deliberately let out and the gate fastened behind him. The connection with Max only falls down over the matter of my earlier marriage. Max cannot have known about it. He was very young indeed, and the whole business was kept very quiet. I doubt there was any gossip.'

'But there was,' Libby told him, and recounted what she had learned from Nurse. 'Of course,' she went on, 'Max was very young at the time. I suppose it is stretching probability to assume he understood what was being said, and it's not even certain if he remembers it. What significance he would have attached to the remarks at so young an age is also debatable.'

Lord Charlbury was thoughtful. 'Max was never a stupid child,' he said. 'He might well have remembered enough to seek out Milly Radlett after the set-to on the road to Copthorne had failed and our betrothal was announced. Tom Bosham, by the way, is no longer a stranger. That's to say, we know his connection: Milly Radlett is now Milly Bosham.'

'So now we have a very strong connection between the three incidents and Max,' Libby said thoughtfully. 'I can understand why he might want you out of the way, because I gather he would then inherit Chase. But why should he want to stop the marriage or put *me* in danger?'

The Viscount studied his fingernails for a long time before answering, and then Libby learned for the first time the precise terms of his uncle's Will and Lord Charlbury's reason for proposing to her. In finally telling her the whole story, Marcus was prepared for outrage, for an expression of deep hurt, perhaps even for tears. The last thing he expected was that she would giggle. He looked up, startled, an expression on his face which did nothing to abate his humour.

'When I entered the drawing-room at Copthorne partway through a conversation I wasn't intended to hear, I realised the marriage you proposed was purely one of convenience. I don't think I ever deluded myself it was anything else, since nothing in your behaviour could fairly be described as amorous. I'm sure you recall that I acknowledged at the time that I had few illusions on the subject. I don't suppose it would have surprised me to learn that the inheritance was subject to your marrying. Such things are not unusual, I believe. But I should never have imagined how specific were the Earl's instructions!' She chuckled again. 'Oh, my lord, did you know of no one else to fit the bill?'

He looked into those brown eyes, alight now with mischief, and smiled ruefully. 'No one, Miss Barton—and certainly no one else with whom I could bear the thought of a life-long shackle.'

Libby blushed with pleasure at this comment. 'Is that really how you felt?' she asked eagerly.

Lord Charlbury was disconcerted that so very mild a compliment should give so disproportionate an amount of pleasure, and perceived that he should tread cautiously. 'I felt it would be no penance,' he said. 'Why did you accept?'

Libby toyed briefly with the idea of a bantering reply, and discarded it; she similarly discarded giving the matter-of-fact explanation that marriage to a viscount— even one who was a penniless rake—was preferable either to marrying a country parson or remaining an old lady's companion. The latter explanation would undoubtedly be believed, and Libby suspected there might even be more than a grain of truth in it, but it was not the real reason, and she had the feeling that this was no time to beat around the bush.

She smiled apologetically. 'I'm afraid you may decide to withdraw your offer because, you see, I'm not really

as sensible as you thought. The very first time you visited
Copthorne when I was there, and without the slightest
encouragement from you, I fell in love with you, and
I've never fallen out again. The most I ever looked for
from you was the chance to exchange a few words from
time to time. Your proposal was the realisation of a
dream. Of course I accepted.'

'Even though I made no pretense of loving you and
you must have guessed it was pure convenience on my
side?'

'That was where common sense reasserted itself, my
lord. I recalled those old saws about "half a loaf" and
"a bird in the hand".'

'I've been accused—behind my back, of course—of
being too high in the instep by far, and arrogant,' Lord
Charlbury commented. 'To be compared—and to my
face—with half a loaf of bread is distinctly lowering.'

'You don't *look* distinctly lowered,' Libby answered
in a matter-of-fact voice after studying him
dispassionately.

'But I hide my feelings well, you see,' he replied,
getting out of his seat and coming round to her side of
the table. He held his hand out to her and she put her
own in it, rising from her seat with a wince which did
not escape the Viscount's eye. He led her to the window
that looked over the park to the darkness of the forest
beyond, and stood there, one hand holding hers, the
other gently round her waist.

'One rarely has a second chance at life,' he said
seriously. 'I've been given one. I love Chase. I always
have. If I win Chase I can save Byfield as well. Libby,
a rake and a libertine *can* reform, though they seldom
do. I must, or lose all. I asked you to marry me in part
because you fitted the specifications and in part in a fit
of selfish pique at my uncle's Will.'

'Selfish?' Libby queried.

'Yes, selfish, because, to be quite truthful, I gave no
thought at all to how you felt or what you wanted. Part
of my arrogance, I suppose, that I assumed the acqui-
sition of a title would be all the inducement necessary.

However, in mitigation of the selfishness, there was a
third reason. It wasn't a major part of my calculations,
but it was there. There was a certain something that, as
I became better acquainted with you, I found I liked. I
can't pretend it was love. Believe me when I say I wish
for your sake I could. Love was what I felt, overwhelm-
ingly, for Maria-Giulietta, and it was a love of such an
intensity that I don't believe one can feel it twice. Rupert
told me his mother thought you had a *tendre* for me. I
know now that was true, but you hid it well. I don't
know—I can't gauge—how intensely you feel, but if you
harbour a hope that I shall one day feel as strongly as
you do I can only say that I can make no promises. I
can, however, tell you with perfect truth that in the weeks
since you accepted me I've become increasingly content
with our arrangement. Libby, this, as honestly as I know
how to express it, is how I feel. I realise that it must be
a disappointment to you, and if you feel in the circumstances that you would rather cry off I shall understand
and release you, but if you're prepared to let the betrothal stand I shall be both happy and grateful. What
do you say?'

Libby gazed out at the view before her with unseeing
eyes. She could no longer deceive herself as to the nature
of Marcus's feelings towards her, nor would she ever
again be able to persuade herself that his feelings would
ever change. If she married him she would, for the rest
of her life, have to be content with that half a loaf, and
deep inside her something cried that that simply wasn't
enough. Well, the voice of common sense insisted, it will
have to be. It's that or nothing. Do you really want to
spend the rest of your life never seeing him again?

She turned her face towards him and smiled, hoping
the smile would keep the tears at bay. 'Why should I cry
off?' she asked. 'After all, I may never get another
chance to be a viscountess.'

The comment, implying something which both of them
knew to be quite untrue, eased the tension that lay between them. Marcus laughed and, tightening his grip on
her waist in a way that was, in the circumstances, very

painful, kissed her full and long on the mouth. Libby responded as eagerly as her bruised body allowed, but there was a desolation in her heart. She knew he was demonstrating that she would encounter no outward signs of his lack of any deep feeling for her and, in a way, that was almost worse than if he had contented himself with a peck on the cheek or a handshake.

Lord Charlbury felt her tense as her bruises protested, and assumed the tears welling in her eyes were in response to the pain. He kissed her again, gently, and released her.

'Forgive me, my dear,' he said. 'I should have remembered your injuries. I had no wish to cause you pain.'

Libby had recovered her equilibrium by this time, and smiled up at him. 'Think nothing of it, sir. If it weren't for the fact that I'm anxious to retain your good opinion, I'd be inclined to tell you it was a pleasure. Well,' she amended in the interests of veracity, '*almost* a pleasure.'

He laughed. 'Minx!' was his only comment as he led her back to her seat and they continued their interrupted breakfast.

The meal was nearly over when Libby bethought herself of a seemingly loose end.

'Marcus,' she said. 'Why should the Boshams be willing to help Max?'

'I presume he made it worth their while.'

'I thought he had very little money of his own?'

Lord Charlbury looked amused. 'True, my dear, but these things are relative, you know. I dare say the Boshams regard him as wealthy, and the odd guinea's not to be sneezed at.'

'Do they really need "the odd guinea"? Their tavern was sufficiently crowded for Fratton not to be noticed. That suggests they're doing rather well; and for Tom Bosham to leave a prosperous business for two or three days—as he must have done—implies either that Max paid them rather generously or perhaps owes them money which can only be paid if he wins Chase. And he needed their help for that.'

Lord Charlbury considered the suggestion. 'Ingenious,' he said, 'but preposterous. He couldn't be that much in debt.'

Libby looked at him steadily. 'Couldn't he?' she said.

The implication was not lost upon the Viscount, and he was none too pleased at having it drawn to his attention. He flung his napkin on the table and pushed back his chair.

'Our cases are quite different,' he said sharply, before bowing briefly and leaving the room, irrationally annoyed that she had hit the nail so unerringly on the head. It was, he supposed, one of the snags of finding a woman of common sense.

Libby watched him go with a renewal of her dismay. The last thing she wanted to do was to diminish in the least degree such regard as he had for her. Clearly there were aspects to which he was extremely sensitive. She would have to tread warily.

When Marcus opened the door of his late uncle's study, he was surprised to see his groom standing there. He raised one eyebrow in silent question.

'Sorry to come in here uninvited, as it were, me lord,' Fratton said. 'But I couldn't be sure as you'd be back at the stables yet awhile, and there's something I thought as how you'd like to see.' He held out a small brown bottle which the Viscount had a vague recollection of having seen before. 'Mrs Widford brought it down to the kitchen,' the groom went on, and was interrupted by his master.

'I thought I'd seen it before. I rather fancy it's Miss Barton's laudanum.'

'Yes, sir, it is. She told Mrs Widford she'd not be needing it, so Nurse took it out but put it to one side, being not as convinced as Miss Barton that she'd not be needing it again, seeing as how she's still badly bruised, by all accounts.'

'What of it?'

'Well, me lord, seeing it on the side, like, and being a mortal curious man, I takes the stopper out and has a sniff——' He held the bottle out to Lord Charlbury, who duly sniffed.

'It smells exactly like laudanum to me, Fratton. What's your point?'

'This, me lord: that smell's remarkably similar to the smell in Tom Bosham's alehouse—the smell that weren't beer or baccy that I couldn't quite put me finger on.'

'And, as I recall, you said it seemed to come from a back room,' continued the Viscount.

'That's right, me lord.'

Lord Charlbury handed him back the bottle. 'What exactly are you trying to tell me, Fratton?'

'I don't quite like to spell it out, me lord. I'd liefer you worked it out for yourself.'

'Come, William. We've known each other a long time. I suspect we're already thinking along the same lines. Don't concern yourself with subtleties and inferences. Tell me straight what you think.'

'Opium, me lord.'

The Viscount sighed, as if he had been hoping against hope for a different answer. 'As I said, we think along the same lines. You're sure about the smell?'

'Certain sure, me lord.' He hesitated. 'And I wish I wasn't.'

'Then take the bottle back and put it where you found it. Nurse is probably right to keep it awhile. I don't think there's any need for you to mention this conversation to anyone else for the time being.'

'Quite so, me lord.'

Seeing that the groom still made no attempt to go, and seemed to be hesitating, the Viscount asked if there was anything else.

'Yes, me lord. I did a bit of digging yesterday, seeing as how I didn't seem to be needed here or at Byfield.'

Lord Charlbury tried to appear interested. 'I didn't know you were a gardener, Fratton.'

'No, sir, nor am I. I dug in a manner of speaking, as it were. That young lady Mr Max met in Southampton. Lord Wilcote don't think she's more than a fancy-piece and none of my business, and happen he's right, but

Lord Wilcote didn't see them, and I did. Not easy to track down, me lord, given the sort of place Southampton is, but I had a bit of luck, and it seems she's fixed at Lymington. Very distinctive lady, me lord. Once seen, always remembered. A French mam'zelle, name of Héloïse d'Angers, I hear.'

Lord Charlbury was amused. 'So Max has a French lightskirt, has he? Good for him. I didn't think he had it in him!'

'No, sir, that's just it, as I tried to explain to Lord Wilcote. A lightskirt she isn't, by all accounts, nor she don't look like one. She's fixed at Lymington now, like I said, but seemingly she was at Southampton—which we know about—and before that at Portsmouth. Word is she's been seen in Plymouth.'

'Whose word?'

'Ah, well, now, there's things I'm swore not to tell, if you'll forgive me, sir. But I wouldn't doubt the truth of anything from that source.'

'I presume the lady to be an emigrée?'

'It would seem so, me lord.'

'Who is possibly searching for relatives at various ports?'

'Quite possibly, me lord.'

'But you—or your sources—don't think so.'

'As to that, me lord, I'm not at liberty to say.'

'Why should she be connected to my brother?'

'That would seem to be the crunch of the matter, me lord.'

'Watch him.'

'I am, me lord. I formed the opinion some time ago that it might be a good idea.'

He left his employer deep in thought. What was the precise nature of the connection between the Honourable Max Asthall and the disreputable Boshams on the one hand, and this striking Frenchwoman on the other? And was there also a connection between Mademoiselle d'Angers and the Boshams? These were questions which caused Lord Charlbury to ponder long after his groom had left him.

* * *

Max returned after luncheon in a singularly benign frame
of mind. Meeting Libby for the first time since her accident, he enquired most solicitously after her health and
professed himself delighted that she had had so fortunate an escape and was now making so rapid a
recovery.

'I've ordered that gate to be padlocked,' he went on.
'A nuisance, of course, but it will make it impossible
for it to be opened accidentally.'

'Please don't put yourself to any inconvenience on my
account,' Libby replied blandly. 'You may rest assured
I shall go nowhere near Twenty Acre Ley again.'

'You may do so, however, with perfect peace of mind,'
Max assured her, oblivious to the sarcasm in Libby's
voice.

Apparently determined to make good his previous de-
ficiencies as a host, Max offered to take her on a tour
of the estate. Since Libby had already been staying at
Chase for some weeks, and since she was hardly in a
physical condition to enjoy riding at the moment, she
found this offer a little odd, and perhaps the oddest thing
about it was that Max himself seemed to see nothing
untoward in it. He seemed genuinely surprised when she
declined on the grounds that Lord Charlbury had shown
her round some time ago, but that revelation did nothing
to make him any more conscious of the tardiness of his
own offer.

'I suppose he had. Sort of thing Marcus would do,'
he commented. 'How do you find him?'

Libby stared at his pale, unconcerned face. '"How
do I find him?"' she echoed. 'You talk as if your brother
were a...a *horse* I'd just acquired!'

'Well, isn't he? You've only got to look at that long
nose and those long legs to realise how like a hunter he
is. Well turned out, too, though that's mostly on tick.
Of course, you haven't actually acquired him yet, have
you?'

Libby continued to stare at him, her amazement
deepening. He appeared totally unaware of the improper nature of his remarks which, despite being ut-

tered in a pleasant enough tone, were clearly intended to be malicious. Had he still been a schoolboy she would have known how to deal with him, but he was not, and there was now some evidence to suggest that he might in fact be an extremely dangerous young man, in which case, his remarks might be better ignored.

On the other hand, it might be wiser to behave as he must surely expect her to, and she would not normally have let such comments go unremarked.

'That's hardly a proper way to speak of your brother, Mr Asthall,' she said.

'My brother is hardly a proper person, Miss Barton,' he replied mockingly. 'Or are you following the old adage about not looking gift-horses in the mouth? I assure you, Marcus will prove to be no gift. On the contrary, I suspect you'll find you'll pay dearly for the title, though not necessarily with money.'

Flushing with anger at the implication of this remark, Libby rose from her chair and stuffed the flounce she had been repairing into her sewing-box. 'Quite frankly, Mr Asthall, I find this conversation intolerable. You must excuse me.' She made her way to the door. A laugh followed her.

'Not one half as intolerable as Charlbury's behaviour will be once he has secured both you and Chase!' he called after her.

Libby slammed the door behind her with the most satisfying and unladylike force.

In the hall she encountered Lord Wilcote, who had spent most of the morning with the Viscount. He cast one look at her face.

'Angry about something, Libby?' he asked in his usual mild tone.

'Furious,' she replied. 'I've just had to endure the comments of that . . . that odious little toad in there.' She nodded in the direction of the room she had just left.

'I imagine we can absolve Marcus of that description, since I fancy you don't see him in quite that light—and in any case I know he isn't in there because I've just left him. In a very brief process of elimination that seems to leave Max. What has he been saying?'

'Nothing. Everything. It would be most improper to repeat it.'

'Tell Marcus,' he advised.

'How can I? To do so would only cause bad blood between them, and that would make me as objectionable as Max.'

'Shouldn't think it would make much difference to the feeling between them, myself,' Lord Wilcote commented. 'But of course you're right. You can't repeat something that will only aggravate the situation. Why not tell me?'

'I'm tempted to,' Libby confessed. 'But I'm calming down now and, really, the remarks were what you might expect from a spoiled child who has had his favourite toy taken away. Such comments don't really warrant repetition.'

'Except that Max is no longer a child.'

'True, but haven't you observed that he often reacts like one? Be that as it may, I gave the door a most satisfactory slam.'

'I heard. Most reprehensible, I thought.'

Libby laughed. 'But entirely satisfying, I assure you!' With that, she removed herself and her needlework to her own room in the turret. It was here that the Viscount found her shortly afterwards.

'Rupert thought you had come here,' he said. 'I gather Max has been offensive.'

She looked up at him. 'So Lord Wilcote told you? I wondered if he might. I was very angry at the time, but I've calmed down now, and in truth his comments were much the sort of thing one might expect from a spoiled child.'

'Max isn't a child.'

'That's precisely what Lord Wilcote said. All the same, I really don't think any more importance should be placed upon them than would be accorded to those of a child.'

'Will you tell me what he said?'

'I'd rather not, Marcus. I think his intention was perhaps to make me wonder whether I should change my mind about marrying you.'

'I gather it hasn't succeeded.'

'It has not.' She looked up at him under her lashes. 'Not yet, at all events. Who knows what results he might achieve by continuing to harp upon it?'

The Viscount observed her dispassionately. 'Miss Barton,' he said with mock severity. 'I do believe you're acquiring the tricks of a flirt. They are not becoming on one selected for her common sense—and I'm not at all sure I like them.'

The look Libby bestowed on him was one of wide-eyed innocence. 'Indeed, my lord? You surprise me. I had rather thought—on past performance, you know—that you frequently found them irresistible.'

'I'll have you know, Miss Barton, that there's a shrewish turn to your tongue which bodes ill for the future.'

Libby threw up her hands in a gesture of despair. 'Alas, sir, I understand that a shrewish tongue frequently accompanies women brought up in habits of economy. It comes of continually economising.'

'I suppose that that is also the cause of their continually expecting to have the last word.'

Libby appeared to give the suggestion some thought. 'I suppose it might be so, my lord. I own I hadn't thought of it in that light before, but no doubt you're right. I bow to your superior understanding.'

'Coming it a bit too strong, Libby,' he laughed, and flicked her chin in a careless gesture that made her heart skip a beat. Libby dropped her gaze self-consciously and found that her sewing required very concentrated examination. Lord Charlbury watched her, the hint of a smile on his lips, a smile that Libby's absorption in her sewing prevented her noticing. Then he walked over to the window and stood looking out for some time. When he spoke again, his tone was matter-of-fact.

'I'm not surprised you like this room. I'd forgotten how far one could see from here. Do you often come here at night?'

'At night?' Libby said, surprised. 'No, indeed. Never. Why should I? The view is superb but it's not precisely visible after dark, you know.'

'Exactly. So why do you have this rather ugly lamp? It would be more at home in the stables. I should have thought the estate could run to candles up here, or is that one of Max's little idiosyncrasies?'

'The lamp has always been here. I thought it incongruous, too, but it has never been in the way, so it doesn't bother me.'

He picked the lamp up. 'I'll take it with me and have candles sent in instead. Now, to my purpose in seeking you out.'

Libby looked up, surprised. 'I thought you came to find out precisely what your brother had said.'

'Strangely enough, I did not. From what Rupert had told me, I formed a shrewd idea that you'd prefer to keep your own counsel. My purpose was quite different, but first of all, how are your bruises progressing?'

'A great deal more colourful but a great deal less painful. Unless I actually bump into something I'm scarcely aware of them most of the time.'

'Good. Do you feel they are sufficiently ameliorated to allow you to accompany me to Southampton tomorrow in the curricle?'

'Why?'

'The correct answer, Miss Barton, is either, "Thank you for the honour you do me, my lord, and I shall be delighted to accompany you", or "Thank you for the honour you do me, my lord but, alas, I fear I am not yet sufficiently recovered to accompany you." The correct answer is certainly not a bald "Why?"'

Libby did her best to look demurely abashed. 'I stand corrected, my lord, but all the same—why?'

'Because I have to go there; because your company will be more enjoyable than William Fratton's alone; and because I feel you would benefit from a change of scene, however brief. Besides,' he added, 'Rupert is keeping Max occupied tomorrow. He's very nobly expressing a hitherto undisclosed but none the less passionate interest in new farming methods.'

Libby laughed. 'Poor man,' she remarked. 'What can I say in the face of such a sacrifice?'

'The sacrifice is all Rupert's, and you may thank him at dinner. Will you come?'

Libby fluttered her eyelashes in what she hoped was a suitably flirtatious manner. 'Thank you, my lord, for the honour you do me. I shall be delighted to accept.'

They left the next morning after an early breakfast. Fratton stood at the horses' heads with pursed lips as the Viscount handed Libby up into the curricle and then, when his lordship had safe hold of the reins, climbed up behind and sat with his arms folded and his lips, had anyone turned round to see, still pursed. Fratton had nothing against Miss Barton. She was quite a taking little thing, given that she wasn't one of your high-fliers, and he had a shrewd suspicion she might prove to be the making of his lordship in the long run, not that Fratton would have dreamed of hinting as much to his employer, not being one to want to put people on their guard. No, the identity of the passenger was not the source of his disapproval. Fratton firmly believed that females, no matter who they might be, had no business dashing around the countryside in sporting vehicles. He felt, besides, that it displayed a sad lack of dignity on the part of the Viscount to drive his betrothed in such an unsuitable conveyance when a chaise could have been used instead. His disapproval was not lessened one whit by the knowledge, engendered through long years of service, that his lordship had never been known to stand upon his dignity except when it specifically suited his purpose.

Libby knew when she accepted Marcus's invitation that her bruises might have subsided to a bearable level while all she had to do was walk from one room to another and to get up or sit down, but that a long journey in a curricle would put a nearly intolerable strain upon them, for they were by no means as well-healed as she had implied. But a whole day in Marcus's company was not something she was prepared to forgo for no better reason than a few aches and pains. She told herself that the curricle was well-sprung, and if she disposed herself carefully against its squabs she would be able to cut the discomfort to a minimum.

In fact, she was distinctly uncomfortable, and silently grateful to Lord Charlbury for not pushing the pace. He held his horses to a steady trot—very different, the groom reflected, from his normal break-neck speed—and seemed to select as far as possible the smoothest stretches of road, sometimes leaving the road altogether when a stretch of open forest bade fair to being smoother than the rutted track that basked in the unwarranted glory of the title 'road'. Libby kept very quiet about her discomfort, however, for the happiness of the prospect of a whole day in Marcus's company was something for which she would cheerfully have endured much more, and, besides, she very much feared he would insist on turning back if she hinted at her aches.

Had she but known it, Lord Charlbury had a shrewd idea how she felt. He noticed the rigidity with which she had eased herself on to the seat and the grip she exerted initially upon the side of the curricle to keep herself erect. He noted, too, the gradual easing of her body as she realised that he was driving with exceptional care and that the combination of the springing and the well-padded squabs did make it possible for her to relax a little without increasing her discomfort too much. Had Libby expressed a desire to return, he would have acceded to it without demur; had she openly referred to her discomfort, he would have suggested a return; but she did neither and, since Lord Charlbury did not for one moment delude himself into thinking she might be diffident about mentioning it, he took it as a tacit indication that she preferred to continue. She really was a most unusual woman, with depths both of feeling and of resolve that he was only now beginning to appreciate. He should perhaps be congratulating himself on the fact that the first woman he had met who fitted his uncle's conditions was proving to be one to whom it would be no penance to be tied for the rest of his life. He glanced down at the resolute chin and firm mouth beside him and decided that, congratulate himself though he might, marriage to Libby was unlikely to be invariably calm and unruffled. In the meantime he must ensure that this journey was accomplished as smoothly as his skill and the carriage-maker's craft could ensure.

It was Lord Charlbury's custom to bait his horse at the Dolphin and on this occasion he also proposed a light luncheon for himself and Libby. He felt it highly probable that she would appreciate some refreshment after what must have been a trying journey, and that notion was fully endorsed when she agreed with some alacrity that it would be just the thing. Negotiating the traffic took all his concentration then, and he was not pleased when his groom attracted his attention by unceremoniously tapping him on the back.

He reined his horses in, cursing Fratton with a fluency that caused Libby to giggle, so clearly did it indicate that he had momentarily forgotten her presence. Fratton was unmoved and unrepentant.

'Over there, me lord. That tall lady turning into the Dolphin. That's Mr Max's French mam'zelle.'

'Are you sure?'

'Certain sure, me lord.'

'How fortunate, then, that we too shall be going to the Dolphin.' He drove his horses carefully into the yard of the hotel, handed them over to his groom, and assisted Libby's descent. He took her by the arm as they entered the inn.

'I don't know how it can be arranged,' he said, 'but I want converse with that lady if we can somehow bring it about.'

'I could claim acquaintance from some years back, perhaps,' Libby suggested.

'Have you ever been in France?'

'No, but I have a vivid imagination.'

He laughed. 'I don't doubt it. However, with nothing more than imagination to rely on, you wouldn't be able to sustain the role for long enough. No, we must play our cards as they're dealt.'

'Then let us hope for six or seven aces in the pack.'

Lord Charlbury grinned. 'Miss Barton, you shock me. How could a lady of breeding contemplate playing with a stacked deck?'

'You must put it down to a conflict between my breeding on the one hand and my common sense on the other,' she retorted.

Once over the threshold, they paused. Mademoiselle d'Angers was engaged in conversation with a waiter. If the vehemence of her gesticulations and the expression of rigid politeness on his face were anything to go by, there was some disagreement. Libby suddenly began to chatter with unwonted loquacity and banality which, had he suspected it to be her normal conversational style, would have caused her betrothed to cry off forthwith. As it was, he hid his surprise and smiled at her inane comments with an urbanity which surprised himself and would have amazed his friends.

Having loudly and rapidly disposed of the weather—far too hot for comfort; the roads—appalling, really quite unbelievably dreadful; his lordship's horses—slugs by comparison with what she was used to; and the Southampton traffic—indescribable; Libby proceeded to that subject of eternal fascination to the male listener, female apparel.

'Indeed, sir, I vow I've seldom seen anything so pretty as the new Mameluke sleeves. I am determined to have them on all my street dresses this season. No——'and here she put up a hand to prevent the objection her escort had no intention of making '—I will hear nothing against them,' she went on, apparently oblivious to the fact that his lordship had done nothing beyond stare at her in awed fascination. 'They're admittedly unusual—avant-garde, one might say with truth—but I declare they will be all the rage, and you would hardly wish me to appear *démodée*, now would you?' And, since she was looking earnestly up into his bemused face as she spoke, it was probably inevitable that she should accidentally cannon into the tall woman talking to the waiter.

His lordship, never slow on the uptake, instantly dropped his companion's arm in order to support her victim, who had been sent staggering back against the newel post.

Libby clapped her gloved hand to her mouth. 'Oh, la, ma'am,' she exclaimed vulgarly. 'My deepest apologies. I vow I can't imagine how it should have happened, except that I do get *so* carried away by my little enthusiasms. You must permit me to make amends. We were about to partake of some light refreshment. You will, of course, be our guest.' She turned to the waiter. 'You will show us to a private parlour. Come, ma'am, I insist.'

Lord Charlbury observed with amusement that his betrothed could, when it suited her purpose, move with the awful inexorability of lava from a volcano, bearing all before her and smothering resistance. He ignored the surprise on the waiter's face, and exhorted him to follow the instructions he had been given.

Thus Mademoiselle d'Angers found herself seated in the Dolphin's best private parlour, a glass of Madeira pressed into her hand.

'For I'm sure,' Libby insisted, 'that a shock such as you have just received—for which I am most truly sorry—requires more than a mere cordial to offset. Besides, a Frenchwoman such as you—for such I can see you are by your fashion; the braid on your dress is quite exquisite, ma'am, it has me positively green with envy, for you must know I am quite passionately interested in such things—you will be quite accustomed to wine at odd times, I dare say. I don't think I quite caught your name?'

'Héloïse d'Angers,' replied that lady faintly, overcome by her hostess's vulgarity and the incompatibility of her appearance and protestations.

Libby turned to her escort. 'There you are, you see, sir. Didn't I say she was French? We shall have some wafers of ham and perhaps some cheese—for, vulgar it may be, but I do *like* cheese, and I quite see why farm workers enjoy it so much—and then perhaps maca-

roons, and we can have a cosy prose about fashion. Do
you live in Southampton now?'

Lord Charlbury was uncertain whether to be appalled
at this unsuspected talent for acting which the Dowager's
demure erstwhile companion was exhibiting, or whether
to admire the skill with which she had confirmed
Mademoiselle d'Angers' identity without revealing their
own—a social solecism he really should correct even
though he knew that if he did he would surely put the
Frenchwoman on her guard, for she could hardly fail to
be aware of the name of Max's brother. He decided to
let ill alone.

Mademoiselle d'Angers, at first bemused by Libby's
continued prattle, decided that her hostess was vulgar
but kind-hearted. She was more perplexed by her hostess's escort. Everything about him proclaimed the
gentleman, yet he did nothing to curb her painful gar-
rulity. On the contrary, he seemed almost amused by it.
Héloïse could not quite establish to her own satisfaction
the precise relationship between the two, though they
constituted one of the most oddly assorted couples she
had ever come across. The woman seemed to have an
insatiable curiosity and no inhibitions about asking the
most searching questions, but there seemed little harm
in her, and Héloïse decided it was easier to succumb with
the appearance of good grace and answer them than to
try to put her down. As for the gentleman, he was
someone with whom Héloïse would be very happy to
become acquainted if he could but be separated from
his dreadful companion.

Yes, she was an emigrée; it *was* truly quite shocking,
some of the things that had been done in France in the
name of freedom and equality; how tragic the fate of
the poor queen; yes, life had been very difficult for those
of noble birth; well, yes, she must confess she came into
the latter category; sadly, no, she had been unable to
bring with her more than the clothes she had stood up
in—she was entirely dependent upon the kindnesses
shown her in England. No, she did not live in
Southampton; she couldn't truthfully claim to live any-

where in a permanent way, but she was at present re-
siding in Lymington. Yes, indeed, a pretty place but a
shade—she was sure Libby would agree—a shade provincial. Fortunately it was also cheap; dreadful to have
to mention anything so vulgar as money, of course, but
such were her straitened circumstances that it coloured
everything these days.

Lord Charlbury listened to the relentless stream of
largely inconsequential prattle, most of it from Libby,
with an air of detached resignation that belied the interest
he took in certain of their guest's answers. He reflected
grimly that Mademoiselle d'Angers' straitened circumstances did not seem to have exercised much practical
effect on her apparel, which had every appearance of
being inordinately expensive. The Viscount looked at
such things with the eye of a connoisseur who had paid
many a dressmaker's bill, and he wondered whether the
Frenchwoman took him for a flat.

And still Libby's unrelenting, impertinent questions
went on. God help her husband if she suspected him of
transferring his affections! the Viscount thought—and
remembered suddenly that there was every likelihood he
would be that husband. He sighed and consoled himself
with the thought that forewarned was forearmed, and
returned to the task of disentangling the possible truth
from the probable falsehood.

Mademoiselle d'Angers' parents had, it appeared, died
in time to escape the Revolution; her elder brother had
misguidedly spoken out against the new régime and his
head had paid the price; Héloise and the younger brother
had escaped to relatives; she had subsequently made her
way to England because the aunt and uncle who had so
gladly offered shelter could ill afford two extra mouths
to feed once their property had been confiscated, and
so Héloise had thought that perhaps she might find employment as a governess in England.

Not dressed like that, I fancy, Lord Charlbury found
himself thinking, while Libby, the picture of credulous
gullibility, her eyes like saucers, gave every appearance

of drinking in the Frenchwoman's tragic, yet romantic story.

It was a story to which Mademoiselle d'Angers found herself insensibly warming. She was encouraged by her uncritical audience—for the gentleman said nothing and his interest seemed to be merely that demanded by common politeness—and felt able to expand a little, prompted by the fascinated Libby.

No, alas, she had not yet been successful in her quest for a post—there were so many other Frenchwomen similarly placed, but she hadn't been entirely luckless, either: she had every expectation of marrying well and becoming mistress of a large estate. No, nothing formal had been declared, but the understanding was firm. But there were, how did one say?—obstacles.

Libby nodded sympathetically. 'Let me guess,' she said. 'His parents are against it. They've already settled on someone else, the daughter of a neighbour, no doubt.'

If Mademoiselle d'Angers spotted in this ingenious theory the plot of a popular novel, she gave no indication. 'Nothing like that,' she told her audience. 'As a matter of fact he is an orphan—an orphan but, unfortunately in the circumstances, not alone. He has a brother who is determined to prevent him from claiming what is rightfully his.'

Libby gasped and shook her head. 'The selfishness of my fellow men never ceases to amaze me,' she declared. She put out a hand impulsively towards her new-found friend. 'Let me guess—you've come to Southampton to keep an assignation with your intended.' She clasped her hands together and raised her eyes towards the ceiling. 'Oh, how romantic!' she breathed.

Mademoiselle d'Angers made a small, deprecating gesture. 'No, not on this occasion. It is my young brother, you see. I am in daily expectation of his arrival. We are both so anxious that he should get to England, but it is so very difficult in the present circumstances, you understand. First he has to get out of France—and that is not easy, I assure you.'

Libby nodded her understanding. 'I can imagine it must be fraught with difficulty,' she said, wondering if her eyes would ever revert to their normal size again.

'And then, of course, when any Frenchman reaches England... I may be frank?' Libby assured her she might. 'The English—not the people who are so charming, like yourself, but the officials—they are so suspicious. In every Frenchman they see a spy. I suppose there must be one or two from time to time, but who can imagine anyone of breeding spying for that Corsican upstart?'

Libby agreed that it was unthinkable but, sadly, her new acquaintance seemed to have come to the end of her unhappy tale, and Lord Charlbury thought it politic to bring the luncheon to an end. He rather thought they had learned all they were likely to learn, and he didn't think he could bear very much more of his betrothed's inane prattle and artless questions.

'My dear,' he said mildly, 'loath as I am to bring this conversation to an end, we do have business in Southampton. I'm sure Mademoiselle d'Angers will forgive us if we take our leave.'

Héloïse instantly rose to her feet, begging their pardon for keeping them so long and saying that she, too, must be attending to matters, the nature of which remained unspecified.

Lord Charlbury held open the door and both ladies passed through into the foyer of the inn, Libby still chatting of this and that, but saying nothing of importance. A large, rubicund man was divesting himself of his driving coat as the Viscount asked Mademoiselle d'Angers whether they might drive her to her destination, since they had already taken so much of her time. An observer would have noticed that the new arrival seemed on the brink of addressing Lord Charlbury but, after a glance at his companions, thought better of it.

Héloïse declined the offer with a shake of the head. 'You are very kind, sir, but my destination is but a step or two from the Dolphin, and I have need of neither a carriage nor an escort. You are most courteous, but truly it is unnecessary.'

Lord Charlbury bowed his acquiescence and, taking Libby's arm, guided her from the inn.

'Which,' Libby said severely, once they were safely out of earshot, 'is just as well since there's room for only one passenger. Or was I expected to sit up on the box, arms folded, like William Fratton?'

He laughed. 'I don't think there was much danger of that,' he said. 'I suspect Mademoiselle d'Angers had had quite enough of your mindless prattle. And to tell you the truth, I shan't be entirely sorry for myself when you revert to normal.'

'How charmingly you use the art of flattery,' Libby retorted. 'And when I think how much my "mindless prattle", as you call it, was instrumental in discovering! Even if, as I suspect, a good deal of it was lies,' she added thoughtfully. She flashed him a sideways glance, and then lowered her eyes demurely. 'You must know, my lord, I'm quite at a loss to understand how you ever became a rake if you sought to attract your victims with derogatory remarks about their conversational style.'

'A lady of delicacy would not refer to such matters,' he said repressively, a gleam in his eye.

'Very true,' Libby replied. 'But a lady of delicacy doesn't behave as I've been doing this past hour, so that excuses me.'

'You have a point,' he conceded. 'But you see, my "victims"—who, I assure you, never saw themselves in that light—were always ladies of delicacy and never needed a set-down.'

Libby laughed. 'Touché, I suppose,' she said cheerfully. 'I hope you're resigned to the head-shaking and tut-tutting that will take place in the neighbourhood when they realise what a vulgar piece you've had to marry. My heart almost bleeds for you.'

'Oh, I think I can survive the horrors I've seen today,' he said. 'If the worst comes to the worst, I can always incarcerate you in the turret at Chase.'

'So you can,' Libby agreed, as if struck for the first time by the felicity of this suggestion. 'Dare I extend my vulgarity to asking the nature of the business that brought us here, and enquiring whether we haven't wasted enough time already?'

Lord Charlbury looked uncharacteristically sheepish. 'My business was really just a pretext,' he admitted. 'I thought it was about time you got away from Chase for a few hours and, in addition, it seemed a useful way of our becoming better acquainted.'

Libby giggled. 'Then it's a wonder you haven't decided to cry off, after my behaviour in there.'

'I keep telling myself that that was an assumed persona and doesn't reflect the true Elizabeth Barton.'

'And if you discover you're mistaken—that you've just seen me as I really am and that for all those years with the Dowager I was just play-acting?'

'I shall be forced to implore you to play-act for the rest of your life.'

'You have, of course, already considered that that would give me a very potent weapon to use against you in the future: either I get my way or I behave in public as I've been doing today.'

'You're forgetting the turret room.'

Libby chuckled. 'The ultimate weapon. And now, sir, since we are here to provide me with a change of scene, do you think you could be prevailed upon to take me to one or two warehouses?'

'Didn't the preparation of your bride-clothes give you a surfeit of silk warehouses?'

'No woman can *ever* have a surfeit of such places,' she said adamantly.

'I have an uncomfortable feeling you may be right,' he told her, and resigned himself to his fate.

CHAPTER TEN

LORD CHARLBURY was lingering over his breakfast the next day at Byfield Manor, mulling over the previous day's encounter, when his housekeeper announced Sir John Bere. The Viscount looked up in some surprise. Sir John was a magistrate with whom he was superficially acquainted, but whose blunt, didactic manner and lack of interest in anything more profound than the condition of his coverts left him with no wish to know the older man better. Sir John had never called on him before, and this was an extraordinarily early hour to be making a social visit. The housekeeper was equally surprised.

'Will you see him in the study or the morning-room at this hour, my lord?' she asked. 'Or would you prefer me to deny you altogether?'

'No, don't do that,' the Viscount replied, frowning. 'He must have some reason. Show him in here—and bring another cup. Perhaps he'll join me in some coffee.'

'Very good of you, my lord,' the gentleman in question said, coming into the breakfast-room as he spoke, and divesting himself of his hat and gloves and handing them to the startled housekeeper.

'Still at breakfast, I see. Good. I hoped I'd catch you before you left. Never take a man away from his breakfast, I always say. Most important meal of the day. Had mine, of course, but I'll not say no to some coffee.'

Lord Charlbury dismissed the housekeeper with a nod, and a mask of careful politeness replaced the momentary astonishment which he hoped his visitor hadn't seen. 'I imagine you breakfasted some time ago,' he said courteously, though with no warmth in his voice.

'Hours,' Sir John agreed bluffly. 'Came early because it seems you ride over to Chase most days as soon as you've eaten. Not that I blame you. After the little brouhaha in the church it won't do to be backward in any attention, what?'

Lord Charlbury's mask of politeness froze on his face. Having for so many years pursued a way of life that seldom brought him into contact with the bluff squire, it had never crossed his mind that Sir John was anything other than a gentleman. It was inevitable that there had been gossip locally, of course, but there were limits which he would have expected to be observed. Everything about this visit was surprising—the time, the manner, and the extraordinary way in which his visitor seemed to have familiarised himself with his present host's affairs.

Choosing to ignore the familiarity of his visitor's final remark, Lord Charlbury asked him to what he owned the honour of this visit. His words were polite enough, but the tone in which they were spoken was sufficiently arctic to freeze a polar bear, a fact which did not escape Sir John's notice.

People who did not know the squire well were inclined to think him rather stupid. He was a large man, ruddy-cheeked, permanently cheerful, a good judge of a horse, and a bruising rider to hounds, but there seemed little more to him than that. People who did business with him found him to be surprisingly shrewd, while the very small circle of his acquaintance who knew him really well realised that his bluff and hearty manner disguised—opinions varied as to whether it was deliberate—a brain which moved when necessary with a rapier-like speed and incisiveness totally at variance with his appearance and his general manner. He had been the local magistrate for many years, a large and imposing figure on the bench who dispensed justice roughly but a great deal more fairly than many of his fellows. People were frequently surprised at the number of pies in which he appeared to have a finger. Those who gave more consideration to the matter—and fortunately they were few—realised that perhaps some of the pies were being baked in extremely deep dishes.

He was not one whit abashed by Lord Charlbury's icy tone.

'Aye, I know it's none of my business—or might seem not to be. We've not had a lot in common, and I doubt we ever shall have, but you're a byword in these parts, Charlbury—a rake-hell and a spend-thrift, they say, and I doubt if many would argue with that. But no one has ever suggested you were other than a gentleman.' He paused to take snuff—and to watch the Viscount's reaction to this blunt speech.

Lord Charlbury was plainly furious at the savage and unprovoked assessment of his character. That it was accurate merely served to annoy him the more. That it was stated quite baldly by an uninvited guest who had so far revealed no reason for this unprecedented visit was fuel to the fire. With considerable self-control, and mindful of the fact that this man was, for whatever reasons, a guest in his house, Lord Charlbury chose to ignore all but the last sentence.

'I'm obliged to them,' he said sarcastically.

Sir John laughed. 'No, you're not,' he said. 'You don't give a damn what they say about you. If you did you'd have mended your ways years ago. The thing that's annoying you just now is that this insensitive boor has turned up uninvited on your doorstep for no given reason and is insulting you to such a degree that the toe of your boot is itching to kick him back out again. Only the laws of hospitality preclude it.'

Lord Charlbury's surprised laugh now had some warmth in it. 'Thus proving that you're neither so insensitive nor so boorish as might have been thought,' he said. 'Sit down, man, and join me in that coffee that was mentioned.'

His guest did so. 'I begin to think we may yet come to an understanding, my lord.'

'Indeed? You perceive me agog to learn more.'

'No, you're not. You're being extremely careful not to be at all agog. But nevertheless you are curious.' He paused. 'Shall I go on?'

'The—er—floor appears to be yours,' his host replied.

'I believe that yesterday you and the estimable Miss Barton were in Southampton.'

'We were.'

'Precisely. You drove there, after an early breakfast, in your curricle with William Fratton up behind. You lunched at the Dolphin and later visited a silk warehouse—hardly your milieu, I should have thought, but let that pass.'

'Pray, do.'

Ignoring his host's sarcasm, Sir John continued. 'While you were gone, your other guest, Lord Wilcote, engaged your brother in a tour of Chase, expressing an interest in modern agriculture which is surprising in one who has previously been regarded as exclusively a connoisseur of oriental art. But doubtless he looks forward to putting young Max's theories into practice at Copthorne when Lord Somerton is no longer with us.'

'Doubtless.'

'On the other hand, the Earl is not, I understand, in expectation of an early demise, so perhaps the expressed interest in agriculture shouldn't be taken at its face value.'

'You take a devilish long time to make your point, sir.'

'I do, don't I? But then, I'm not at all sure that making a point is what I'm trying to do. Let us return to the Dolphin. I believe you and Miss Barton didn't lunch alone. A friend joined you. A female friend.'

Lord Charlbury's interest sharpened. 'An acquaintance, rather.'

'Indeed? An acquaintance of long standing?'

'No. Quite the contrary, in fact. Miss Barton bumped into her—quite literally, I'm afraid—only yesterday. To offer her hospitality seemed the least we could do.'

'Ah, yes, Miss Barton. Such a quiet, sensible young female, so I've been told—you know how local gossip is, and it's so rarely wrong.'

'Of course!' Lord Charlbury exclaimed. 'You were in the Dolphin when we left. My deepest apologies for having cut you dead but, to tell the truth, my attention was so taken up at the time that I didn't recognise you.'

'There's no need to apologise. I can quite see that Miss Barton might take up one's attention. I was in no position to judge how sensible she may be,' he added, 'but I shouldn't have described her as quiet. Strange, that, you know—domestic gossip is so rarely inaccurate.'

He took another pinch of snuff and looked at the Viscount's once more rigid face before continuing, impervious to his host's disapproval.

'But to return to your—er—acquaintance. I don't suppose she furnished you with her name?'

'At Miss Barton's insistence, yes. She said she was Héloise d'Angers.'

Sir John looked pleased. 'So she is, so she is. May I ask whether she told you anything else? She's generally held to be rather reticent, I believe.'

'I fancy she may be so, but Miss Barton has a perseverance which is quite amazing, and I think Mademoiselle d'Angers found it easier to satisfy her very vulgar curiosity than to maintain a ladylike reserve.'

Sir John's mouth twitched. 'Perhaps you'd be kind enough to tell me what she said?'

'Perhaps you'd be kind enough to tell me why I should?'

'A fair enough request. I'm being impertinent and inquisitive and you're finding it well-nigh intolerable—and I can't say I blame you—and, in any case, you want to be off to Chase. I've a reason for wanting to know, and it's a very good reason, but I'm not yet sure how much I can tell you. Trust me, Lord Charlbury, and I'll try to repay the compliment.'

For the first time in all the years Lord Charlbury had been acquainted, however slightly, with Sir John, the bluff, hearty voice had been dropped. Suddenly it seemed he was no longer talking to the hard-riding, back-slapping squire, but to a man of intellect and serious purpose. The difference was apparent. The reason was not. Briefly, Lord Charlbury told him Héloise's story.

Sir John listened intently and nodded from time to time. When Lord Charlbury had finished, he asked him

if the story sounded plausible to him. Lord Charlbury
thought for a few minutes.

'Plausible, yes, on the whole. It is, after all, the story
of many emigrées. It did occur to me, however, that,
for someone in straitened circumstances, she dresses remarkably well. It's an area in which I'm not without
experience,' he added apologetically.

'I don't doubt it,' Sir John said. 'Tell me, did this
disparity strike Miss Barton?'

'She didn't mention it, but it can hardly have failed
to do so. Miss Barton is far from stupid. There was
another thing.'

'Yes?'

'I've no personal experience of such matters, but I
would have thought that any governess who presented
herself in such a high degree of fashionable elegance
would be unlikely to be offered a position.'

'Never met one who wasn't an out-and-out dowd,
myself,' Sir John commented with a temporary return
to his more usual manner. 'Did she give you any idea
whom she might be marrying?'

'None,' Lord Charlbury replied shortly.

'And you feel disinclined to hazard a guess?'

'Quite.'

'Odd that you should have bumped into her like that,
really.'

'These things do happen.'

'True, very true. Never discount coincidence. Tell me,
how did she react when she learned your name?'

'She didn't do so.'

'Didn't react?'

'Didn't learn our identity. Somehow or other Miss
Barton omitted to mention it. She was somewhat carried
away,' he added by way of explanation.

'And you didn't rectify this omission?'

'The opportunity to do so didn't immediately present
itself, and it would have seemed a trifle odd later on to
have said, *à propos de* nothing in particular, "By the
way, this is Miss Barton and I'm Viscount Charlbury",
don't you think?'

'I'm sure you're right. Nevertheless, I find it interesting that you allowed that little solecism to go unrectified. So Mademoiselle d'Angers doesn't know who you are?'

'Not unless she asked at the Dolphin after we left.'

'Which is not impossible. However, she left almost immediately and seemed to speak to no one, so let us assume she remains unaware.'

'Sir John, I think the time has come for me to be as blunt as you.'

'Please do. What is it they say? That exchange is no robbery?'

'You didn't come here at this unearthly hour to make small talk, or to insult me. Nor did you come out of idle curiosity about Mademoiselle d'Angers. In fact, I fancy your curiosity about that lady is very far from idle. I want to know what this is all about.'

'And I, my lord, do not believe in coincidences. That they sometimes occur, I will accept intellectually as a possibility, but in my experience things that appear co-incidental very rarely prove to be so. I wish you would trust me enough to be quite frank with me.'

'I'd like to but, to tell the truth, I can't do so without involving someone else.'

'Your brother?'

'I see.' He paused for a long time. 'I think I must rely upon your discretion.'

'Then in fairness I must warn you that I can't guarantee total discretion, but I think you'd be agreeably surprised just how discreet I can be. I listen to gossip. Avidly. I seldom repeat it.'

Lord Charlbury nodded. 'I understand. There's not a great deal to tell. I had heard—from my groom—that Max was meeting a Frenchwoman in Southampton. Max hasn't mentioned her, and I knew nothing about her. It was Fratton who recognised her, yesterday and, on an impulse, we followed her into the Dolphin. It occurred to me that it might be useful to know more about one of Max's acquaintances.'

'Now that has a ring of truth about it,' Sir John said thoughtfully, 'as far as it goes, though I rather fancy it could go further. Do you think your brother is intending to marry her, or is that wishful thinking on Mademoiselle d'Angers' part?'

'I've no idea. I don't know Max all that well; he's a good many years my junior, and we've never had very much in common. He'd be better advised to hang out for a rich wife.'

'Which he wouldn't need if he inherited Chase. Oh, yes, Lord Charlbury, the conditions of your uncle's Will are well-known locally, and the outcome is awaited with interest. The publication of your banns disappointed many mothers who saw their plain—and, by inference, sensible—daughters elevated to the peerage and mistress of Chase while at the same time relieving their fathers who had no wish to see substantial marriage settlements go down the drain.'

Lord Charlbury laughed, genuinely amused at something by which he might reasonably have been expected to be offended. 'Thank God I was totally unaware of all these machinations,' he said. 'But I think you digress. What is the nature of your interest in Mademoiselle d'Angers?'

'She is indeed an emigrée and an orphan. Whether or not she has a younger brother living, I've no idea, but it's extremely unlikely she has any expectations of his imminent arrival on these shores—unless in the uniform of an invading force.'

'You think an invasion is imminent?'

'Imminent, no. Planned, certainly. Mademoiselle d'Angers has been a Bonapartist ever since she decided that her bread was buttered more thickly on that side. She's been waiting for her brother all along the Kent and Sussex coasts, but of course they're well fortified. There's a chance things may be more lax further west.'

'She's a spy?'

'We believe so. She listens and looks and learns, but most often, I'm delighted to say, she only learns what we choose her to. An invasion force is being prepared. We know that. The two questions are, when will it sail and where will it land?'

'Then why Southampton? Only Portsmouth could be a worse target—no enemy fleet could sail up the Solent undetected.'

'A reasonable assumption. But Portsmouth is important. It has that vital dockyard. Are you aware that the city is undefended on the landward side?'

'Frankly, I've never given the matter a thought, but, if that's so, how could an enemy make use of this information—which can hardly be a secret? How could an enemy assemble to the north without first landing—and being repulsed?'

'You've never been a military man, Lord Charlbury?'

'Never. I'm far too much of a hedonist.'

'Quite. I, on the other hand, found military strategy quite fascinating. In the Americas,' he added by way of explanation.

'Go on.'

'The eastern seaboard of America is very heavily forested. A most useful feature of the landscape if one wishes to disperse a band of troops.'

'I think I follow you: an invasion force that landed on the coast immediately south of the forest could disperse and move north to Southampton without being seen, provided the landing hadn't been spotted.'

'More than that. Forest—under one name or another—extends eastward well past Portsmouth. Assemble in the woods to the north of that city, be on the crest of the hill overlooking it at night, and in the morning your position is well-nigh impregnable, the more so because all the city's fortifications are designed to defend the city on the seaward side.'

'It sounds easy.'

'The manoeuvre is easy enough. The problems are twofold: it would require a very large force of men, and they would somehow have to be landed without being noticed. No easy task, I think you'll agree.' He paused before adding, 'Chase land runs along the Channel coast for several miles.'

Lord Charlbury stared at him, aghast. 'My God! Is that why the Frenchwoman is cultivating Max?'

'Possibly.'

'But it won't wash. Surely they wouldn't risk being seen from Hurst Castle?'

'Permit me the liberty of suggesting you go for an observant ride, my lord. You will see that Hurst looks out over Southampton Water and across the Solent to the Isle of Wight, but not back along the coast in this direction.'

The Viscount shook his head in disbelief, though not of his visitor's words. 'I can't believe my brother knows of these plans.'

'Perhaps not, but, if the plan is to land at Chase, then either he has to co-operate willingly or else Mademoiselle d'Angers is in a position to bring pressure to bear on him.'

'And whichever theory is correct, he must know what's in the wind,' Lord Charlbury summed up bitterly.

'So it would appear. Tell me, has your visit—and that of Miss Barton—been welcomed by him?'

'Hardly, though he has occasionally tried to put a good face on it. I feel bound to point out that the terms of my uncle's Will were enough to provoke that response from him in any case.'

'I take your point, but it does suggest that there may be more than one reason for his wanting you elsewhere.'

Lord Charlbury rose from his seat and paced the room, watched silently by the squire.

'I hope you're wrong,' he said at last. 'I hope you're wrong from start to finish, but especially about Max's possible involvement. It could be that he hasn't yet been brought into it.'

'It could be.'

'But you don't think so. Whatever the outcome, it must be arranged as far as possible for the Asthall family name to be kept out.'

'That would certainly be desirable, but it can't be guaranteed, my lord.'

'Will you leave this with me, Sir John? If your suspicions are correct, I'd like the chance to get Max away before any moves are made.'

'If you're asking me to drop the matter until Max is clear one way or another, you're asking too much. But if I have your co-operation in thwarting any specific plan that may be uncovered, then I shall be happy to give what help I can to keep your family name out of it.'

Sir John rose to his feet and shook his host's hand. 'It was good of you to see me, my lord,' he said, returning to his more familiar bluff manner. 'Give my respects to Miss Barton—and to Lord Wilcote who, I believe is staying with you. I knew his father well in the old days. Glad he's still fighting fit. Good day to you, Lord Charlbury.'

Libby was tired after her long day in Southampton and, more pertinently, perhaps, the long drive in Lord Charlbury's curricle. The sun was well up when she awoke, but she rejected Nurse's suggestion that she should breakfast in her room.

'No, I'll go down. Lord Charlbury will be driving over, and I've no wish for him to discover he's betrothed to an invalid. He's probably tapping his foot on the hearthstone already, wondering why he's being kept waiting.'

'Now that's where you're wrong,' Nurse informed her. 'If his lordship was here, you'd have been the first to be told—once you'd woken up, that is. If you want to eat in the comfort of your own bed, you've only to say the word.'

'Thank you, but I think not.'

Nurse knew better than to argue with that particular tone. Miss Barton might have been only the companion to a dowager, but she had clearly been brought up in a less subservient position and, in Nurse's opinion, bode fair to becoming a very competent mistress for Chase.

When Libby entered the breakfast-room, she was surprised to find Max still there. He was an invariably early riser, and she would have expected him to have been long gone about his business on the estate. She wondered what had delayed him on this occasion, but it never crossed her mind that he might have been waiting for her.

'Good morning,' she said affably. 'It's not like you to linger over breakfast.'

'I wanted to be sure you'd recovered from yesterday's drive,' he declared.

Libby's surprise was unfeigned. 'How very kind of you! Thank you, I seem to be entirely recovered.'

'You must have found it quite a strain.'

'It took a little time to get used to the carriage, but it's well sprung, and Marcus drove with punctilious care.'

Max snorted. 'Well, he would, wouldn't he? After all, the last thing he wants is to have you crying off.'

Libby bit her tongue, refusing to rise to the spite with which he was clearly baiting some as yet unperceived hook. She ignored his comment and instead helped herself to some kedgeree from the chafing dishes at the side.

'Are you still going to marry him?' Max persisted, his tone less barbed this time.

'I don't see why not. After all, it has now been established that there is absolutely no reason why not.'

'No legal barrier, I grant you, but you've always struck me as being a woman with a considerable degree of self-respect.'

'I hardly think your brother would have offered for me had it been otherwise,' Libby said coldly.

'Don't delude yourself. You fitted the bill, that's all. You do realise that marrying you—or someone very like you—is the only way Marcus can get his profligate hands on this estate, which, in turn, will enable him to hang on to Byfield as well—at least until he's run through this inheritance, too? Or did he profess eternal love? He's quite good at that, too, I believe.'

'This is no way to discuss your brother behind his back,' Libby replied in what she hoped were depressing tones.

Max caught the tone and knew perfectly well that the reprimand was well deserved, but he had his own reason for continuing in the same vein. 'No, you'd rather I didn't make you uncomfortable, wouldn't you?' he said. 'The fact remains that by accepting Marcus you've made

yourself a local laughing-stock. If you could only hear
the sniggers behind your back! Everyone who knows
Marcus knows perfectly well that in three years—maybe
five at the outside—he'll be as destitute as he is now.
And everyone who knows Marcus knows that within six
months of securing the estate by marrying you he'll have
set up a mistress to make up for his disappointments in
that area. In fact,' he went on, dropping his voice to a
more confidential level, 'someone was telling me only
the other day that he's already found a prime article with
whom to console himself for the tedium of staying here.
I haven't seen her for myself, of course, so I can't vouch
for the accuracy of the rumour.'

Libby was seething inside, but she managed with great
difficulty to control both her voice and her expression.
She smiled deliberately sweetly. 'Then it ill becomes you
to repeat it,' she said. 'Or don't you concern yourself
with the light in which you present yourself to others?'

Max shifted uneasily. He had hoped to see her needled.
In his experience, if you needled women, sooner or later
they burst into tears, and who would be more likely to
do just that than the dowdy former companion of a
singularly crotchety dowager? Perhaps Libby Barton was
quite simply insensitive. He hadn't thought so, but if she
were then it might prove very difficult to get her to cry
off. Perhaps nothing short of a public humiliation would
make her do so, though he felt bound to admit that the
last one hadn't worked too well. Still, there were more
ways than one of skinning a cat, and he did have the
beginnings of a very good idea. Meanwhile there was
another tack to be tried. He would change the subject.

'Actually, I'm glad to have caught you,' he began. 'I
know why Marcus wanted you here and not at Byfield,
but it seems to me you'd be more comfortable there for
the next few weeks. Before you came here so unexpectedly, I'd arranged for quite a lot of refurbishment
to be carried out at Chase, and it would be easiest for
everyone if you could persuade Marcus to let you move
to his own house. Besides,' he added maliciously, 'you'd

be in a better position to keep an eye on him if you were there.'

Libby, who had just finished her kedgeree, put her knife and fork very neatly together on her plate. Then she wiped her lips delicately with her napkin. Then she looked Max directly in the eye and smiled.

'No, Max, I don't think so,' she said. 'Let us be under no misapprehensions. I have no intention whatsoever of crying off from this marriage. I have a fancy to be a viscountess. It's a chance I never expected to have, and it's a chance that will never be offered again. If you think I've the slightest intention of letting that title slip through my fingers, then you're very much mistaken. That being the case, you may rest assured that before very long I shall be mistress of Chase. As for the refurbishment you talk of, in the circumstances I advise you to save the estate's money. Once the coronet is, so to speak, on my head, all your work will be undone, because I shall immediately replace it with refurbishments to suit my own taste—and I doubt whether that will concur with yours.'

With these words, Libby rose from her seat and left the room, leaving Max as white and angry as she herself felt inside. As the door closed behind her—it wasn't easy to refrain from slamming it—Max glowered at her now empty chair.

'You're not married yet,' he spat. 'I think I have one or two other aces to play before I'm out of the game.'

Libby went straight to the turret room, where she could be reasonably sure of being alone, at least for a little while. She was white and shaking with an anger that was all the worse because she was impotent to do anything about it. She had always known Marcus's proposal had been made as a matter of convenience. That was something between themselves. She didn't like it, but Marcus was not an insensitive man, and no one observing his behaviour towards her would have guessed how things lay. For that she must always be grateful. Of course, his family knew the situation. They could hardly fail to be aware of the conditions under which he might inherit Chase, but it was intolerable that Max should make so blatant an attempt to turn her from his brother. It was almost as if he had hoped his information would come as a surprise to her. Libby could guess how stunned she would have been had Marcus not already been entirely open with her. Even so, she wasn't happy to be subjected to such crass insensitivity, and regretted deeply that only by descending to Max's own level could she deal with him in kind.

What really hurt was Max's suggestion that it wouldn't be long before his brother set up a mistress. Libby knew that Marcus was reputed to have had several in the past. Those she could forget simply because they *were* in the past and therefore no longer relevant. Her common sense told her that a great many married men had mistresses and, if she was honest with herself, there was no reason to assume Marcus would not be one of them. She knew instinctively, however, that if he did it would be handled with the utmost discretion so that his wife would never be discomfited by the knowledge. It was something to which she had given no thought, and she was not the least bit grateful to Max for drawing her attention to the possibility. A possibility which he clearly regarded as an inevitability.

She glanced out of the window and saw, through a film of tears, Max gallop off somewhere on his horse. I hope a tree falls on him! she thought savagely, but she knew that would be little consolation. The damage was done, the seeds of distress had been sown. From now on, for the whole of her life with Marcus, there would always be that little maggot gnawing away at her happiness: the question, Has he taken a mistress yet? and then, after a few years, perhaps it might change to, I wonder who she is?

A falling tree was too good for Max, and she suspected that the most effective way to punish him for his unkindness was to behave as if she were entirely unconcerned. She knew she had disconcerted him by claiming to have accepted Marcus for the title she would acquire. It was precisely the sort of motive Max could understand and believe. It was also the one motive which would guarantee she wouldn't cry off. It would never occur to Max that her real reason for not crying off was simply that she loved his brother to distraction—and she had no intention of giving him any hint that that was so because, if she did, he would have no difficulty in forging from the information other weapons with which to hurt her.

Libby dabbed her eyes and sniffed, and then told herself that moping about would achieve nothing. She pulled her tambour-frame towards her and set about matching her silks, an activity which took at least part of her mind off Max's cruel words.

Despite the fact that Sir John's visit meant Lord Charlbury set out for Chase at a much later hour than he had originally intended, he made no effort to make up for lost time. On the contrary, he took his time over the ride, not because he was any less wishful of getting there with expedition, but because his visitor had given him so much food for thought.

The more he saw and heard of his younger brother the less he liked him and the more he wished that that young man were someone else's responsibility, that it was someone else's family name that would be besmirched by Max's behaviour. Such considerations were futile, of course: Max was his brother, and it was the name of Asthall that bade fair to being sullied. True, Marcus reflected sardonically, he had himself brought it rather less than fame and glory, but his misdeeds, while they might be frowned on by the strait-laced, were at least the misdeeds of a gentleman. Betraying one's country, for whatever reason, was acceptable to no one.

No one who knew Max could doubt that he wanted Chase for himself, and few would disagree that he had been shabbily treated by the late Earl. If Max had indeed been behind some of the recent incidents, it was reprehensible, but such actions were easily and understandably attributable to a desire to keep his elder brother from inheriting. That they might also be directed quite simply to keeping him off the property for a period was a possibility which Marcus now considered for the first time.

He had no doubt at all that the attack on the road to Copthorne had been intended quite simply to kill him before he had any opportunity to implement the terms of his uncle's Will. Had the attempt succeeded, it would have ended forever his claims to the estate, and in a manner which was unlikely to provoke awkward questions, highwaymen being all too prevalent these days.

However, that straightforward attempt having failed, subsequent incidents had been directed at Libby. Most women, if they hadn't cried off altogether, would have begged to be taken elsewhere, and Marcus had to admit that if Libby had asked him to do that he would have complied with her wishes and accompanied her. This would not have prevented the marriage—indeed, for propriety's sake it might well have precipitated it—so to that extent it wouldn't have served Max's interest, but it would have left the younger man with the free run of Chase at this crucial time and, if Marcus had married Libby, Max only had to act before they had a son to be sure of inheriting the estate on which he had set his heart.

Of course, the easiest way to achieve both goals was for Max to prevent Marcus's marrying within six months. If Libby could be persuaded to cry off on one pretext or another, Marcus would be hard put to it to find at such short notice another bride who conformed to Lord Denmead's criteria. He would certainly have to leave the estate while he hunted for one.

Max had always been subject to distempered freaks when he didn't get what he wanted, and Lord Charlbury had suspected Libby might be in danger from his moodiness and his acid tongue, while at the same time not entirely ruling out the possibility that a more concrete danger might present itself. Max would have taken a malicious pleasure in, for example, giving her a mount that was quite unsuitable for a lady and then pretending surprise and regret at the inevitable accident. With this sort of thing in mind, he had asked Lord Wilcote to keep a discreet eye on Libby while he tracked down proof

of his wife's death. Sir John Bere's visit had cast a far
more sinister light on Max's activities. The magistrate
clearly took him very seriously indeed and, as Marcus
went over both his conversation with Sir John and the
events that had taken place since the reading of the Will,
any remaining doubts that Libby's life was endangered
by her remaining at Chase faded away and he began to
grapple with the more difficult one of what to do for
the best.

He handed his horse over to a groom and noted that
Max's favourite mount was gone. Good. That meant he
had Libby to himself. Rupert was still recovering from
the previous day's mind-numbing exposition of modern
farming methods, and had already told his friend he deserved a day in bed.

'Do you realise,' he had said, 'that when you take up
your inheritance you are going to have to grapple with
turnips? I had a whole day of turnips. Turnips and clover
and drains and drills. Marcus, it isn't even interesting,
and it plays havoc with one's boots. You'll never stand
it.'

The Viscount had laughed. 'Hunting plays havoc with
one's boots, but I've not noticed you staying behind.'

'That's quite different and you know it. Hunting is
expected of one.'

'I think you found Max's enthusiasm exhausting—and
exhaustive. You have a day of inactivity and, if it's any
consolation to you, I'll undertake to hire a bailiff who
knows about turnips, and thereby do away with the need
to find out myself and bore my visitors into the ground.'

Glancing at the empty loose-box, Marcus wondered
wryly which of the esoteric activities of modern farming
his brother was pursuing today. Then he went in search
of Libby.

Since he had made no mention of a time at which he
might be expected at Chase, he was not surprised to learn
that Miss Barton had taken herself off to her turret. She
was seated at her tambour-frame close to the window,
where the light fell full on her stitches and coincidentally
on her face as well. She glanced up as the door opened,

and the delight that suddenly bathed her face when she recognised her visitor was unmistakable and unfeigned. She was always pleased to see him, but she had never exhibited quite such spontaneous pleasure before, and the Viscount was surprised at the degree of gratification her evident pleasure afforded him. He took her offered hand and kissed it with a warmth that brought a small blush to her cheeks, but not a strong enough blush, he noticed, to disguise the fact that she looked drawn and fatigued. Her smile almost, but not quite, disguised the underlying strain, though she was able to keep all trace of it out of her voice.

'Oh, Marcus, I *am* glad to see you. I thought that after a day spent pandering to my whims you might prefer to spend today attending to such matters at Byfield as must have been neglected yesterday.'

'There's nothing at Byfield so urgent as to justify neglecting you. Are you well? Tell me the truth, now. When I came in I formed the distinct impression that perhaps yesterday's drive had been too much for you.'

'Nothing of the sort,' she protested stoutly. 'A few aches and pains were beginning to set in by the time we arrived home, but a hot, scented bath soon saw to that, and this morning I'm as right as a trivet.'

'Really? I tell you bluntly you look a little fatigued still.' He glanced at her embroidery. 'Are you busy?'

'Not at all. Quite idle in fact. I spend most of my time looking out of the window—the embroidery is just a deception, an excuse I can use if I don't want to be interrupted.'

Lord Charlbury smiled wryly. 'Then I must hope I don't come into that category.'

'Of course you don't! That would be ingratitude of the highest order!'

'Would you think me churlish if I say I hope your willingness to receive me is due to a little more than gratitude?'

Libby, who was fast recovering her spirits, and had no intention of presenting herself as a cloying female hanging on his every word, looked at him speculatively.

'I wouldn't consider you churlish,' she conceded. 'Smug might be a more apt word, I think.'

She was quite pleased to observe that she had succeeded in disconcerting him, and chuckled. 'That was unkind, sir, but you'll allow it to have been irresistible. Your company is most welcome, and I hope I never have to have recourse to an excuse in order to avoid it.'

He bowed ironically. 'Thank you. We share our hopes. However, when I see you bent earnestly over your sewing in future, I'll be very careful how I approach you for fear of getting my *congé*.' He turned to the window and regarded the view before him in silence.

'It is beautiful, isn't it?' Libby commented.

He nodded. 'I'd forgotten just how lovely it was,' he said. He rested his hands on the deep sill and, leaning forward with his weight on his arms, took his first really intelligent look at a view which he had previously only considered in terms of its aesthetics.

Chase itself stood a good way back from the coast, although the sea formed the southern boundary of the whole estate. This little room was the only one in the house sufficiently elevated to provide a view right across to the sea. When it had first been built, in medieval times, there had been dense forest obscuring the view but at the same time protecting the house and the demesne lands from the sea-gales of winter. The late Earl of Denmead's father had cleared the forest to provide a broad vista from all the south-facing rooms, and it was certain that the house itself would be clearly visible from the sea, given reasonable visibility. However, from all the other rooms in the house, the view, while splendid and far-reaching, was simply of a tree-edged expanse of lawn stretching to the horizon, but from this room the grass could be seen to stop at the edge of the low cliffs so that they formed a natural ha-ha separating the lawns from the sea beyond. To the left he could make out the most westerly of the three great chalk stacks of the Needles. On a clear day, after rain, that last stack stood out sharp-edged and distinct; in summer's hazier days its edges were softer, more blurred; and in driving rain, Lord

Charlbury suspected, it would be totally invisible. A pity, but then few people attempted to admire views in driving rain.

Although it was well to the left of the picture framed by the casement, this final stack was none the less the focal point of the view, the very shape of the tree-lined lawn leading the eye to this particular feature of the seascape beyond the ha-ha. Never before had Lord Charlbury realised how skilfully the gardens at Chase had been designed to provide this superb view from one room and one room alone. Someone before Libby had appreciated what the turret could offer.

He turned back to Libby. 'I don't think I've ever looked at it properly before. I knew it was a superb vista, but I hadn't realised just how cunningly the gardens were laid out. Have you been down there yet? To the coast, I mean?'

She shook her head.

He hesitated. 'It's a beautiful day—a perfect day for a ride, in normal circumstances—but after yesterday's ordeal I imagine you'd rather not do anything strenuous today.'

'If this is a convoluted way of asking if I'll go riding with you, my lord, then the answer is yes, provided you find me a nice, quiet mount. I don't think I'm up to one of Max's beloved "good gallops" yet, and I am, besides, a no more than competent horsewoman.'

'Then put on your habit, and we'll have a quiet ride. It isn't very far, and I'm depending upon you to tell me the instant you feel you've had enough and want to return. There's one small snag, though: Fratton's away at the moment, so unless you insist on the company of one of the stable-lads it will have to be an unchaperoned ride. Do you mind?'

'To tell the truth, my lord—and at the risk of sounding fast—I don't mind at all. By all means let us manage without one of the stable-lads. I'm quite sure they've plenty to occupy themselves with in the yard.'

He laughed. 'I'm not sure whether that reveals you to be a shameless hussy or an immensely practical woman,' he said. 'I think we have something suitable for you in the stables. It will be ready by the time you've changed.'

Libby surprised him by being ready almost as soon as her mount, a superannuated bay mare quite accustomed to carrying a lady's saddle. She had hardly been thrown into the saddle when Lord Wilcote rode into the yard.

'Up at last, Rupert?' his friend mocked. 'I thought you were going to spend a day doing nothing?'

'I was, but I decided that would be even more soporific than listening to an enthusiast talking about agriculture. Morning, Libby.'

'Good morning, Lord Wilcote. I hope Max didn't suspect your lack of enthusiasm.'

'Lord, no. He took it for scepticism, but I must admit it was an effort to keep it up.'

'We're off for a ride, Rupert,' the Viscount said, stating the obvious. 'I've no wish to be inhospitable and, if you insist, you'll be welcome to join us, but frankly you'll be *de trop.*'

'I'll tell you something,' his friend offered, unperturbed by the warmth of the invitation. 'If you ever need to work for a living, don't try the diplomatic service.'

Lord Charlbury laughed. 'I won't,' he promised. 'Make yourself at home, Rupert. Shall we see you at luncheon?'

'Probably not. I think I may ride over to Southampton. Dinner perhaps?'

'At Chase. We shall look to see you.'

Libby enjoyed the ride. It was a long time since she had been on horseback, but Miranda was a kind beast, surprised but not upset at being brought out of retirement, and quick to sense that her present rider was less sure of herself than the very late Countess had been. As a result, Libby soon began to feel at home on her and able to concentrate at least as much on the landscape through which they rode as on her mount. Lord Charlbury's sense of propriety saw to it that she was rarely alone with him. This was as it should be, of course, but she would have appreciated far more of his company

without the restrictions inevitably imposed by the
presence of a third party, however discreet. It was
strange, she thought, how pronounced a sense of propriety he had. It was the last attribute one would have
expected a rake to exhibit. But then, perhaps there was
none so proper as a reformed rake. She smiled. The
expression conjured up a very satisfactory picture. But
then she recalled Max's spiteful remarks, and the smile
faded. Perhaps he was just determined that no hint of
scandal should attach to his wife's name. That didn't
mean he would no longer be the rake he had always been.

Few words passed between them. Lord Charlbury was
still weighing up the implications of Sir John Bere's visit,
and Libby, besides being wrapped up in her own not
entirely happy thoughts, was content simply to be with
him. She felt no impulse to break into his meditations,
though she would have welcomed the opportunity to be
brought into them. Lord Charlbury kept a careful eye
on his betrothed, correctly guessing that it would be up
to him to spot any signs that this little expedition was
proving too much for her, because she would not admit
to any fatigue. As always, he found her company surprisingly restful—surprisingly, because he had met no
other woman whom he would so describe. It was an extremely pleasant change to be in the company of a female
who didn't gabble the whole time and he supposed, recalling her performance of the preceding day, that he
was fortunate indeed that Libby's temperament made
her a more comfortable companion than most of her
sex. He never failed to be surprised—and most agreeably
so—at the way in which she seemed to sense his mood,
when he wanted to talk and when he preferred to be
silent. He was beginning to realise that in many ways he
had happened upon quite a remarkable woman.

They had taken a circuitous route north from the house
and then in a wide arc west and south, a route which
obliged them to ride through the woodlands of the forest,
a pleasantly shady ride on a hot summer's day. Eventually the trees thinned out and they were on the short,

springy grass that led to the cliff-edge, grass that cried out to be cantered over.

Libby glanced at her companion and sensed that it wasn't only his horse that was champing at the bit.

'Don't you think they'd enjoy the chance to stretch their legs?' she suggested.

He looked at her, surprised. 'Are you up to it?' he asked.

'I don't think Miranda has a headlong gallop in mind,' Libby told him. 'A sedate canter will suit her very well, and it won't do me any harm. We'll catch you up at the trees over there.'

'Too far for both of you,' the Viscount said, shaking his head. 'Half that distance will be ample.'

It was a short, sharp, exhilarating burst—at least, it was for Libby and Miranda. She rather suspected that the Viscount and his mount found it tantalisingly brief and much too slow, for he refused to pull ahead and wait for her, preferring to keep beside her in case anything untoward occurred. They reined in at the cliff-edge, and Libby looked with interested surprise at this hitherto unvisited part of the estate.

'What strange cliffs!' she exclaimed. 'I had been expecting them to be high and white—like Dover.'

'Instead of which, they're barely worthy of the name,' Lord Charlbury commented. 'Children scramble up them quite happily, but I fancy an adult would prefer to find an easier route. They're little more than compacted sand, you know, and as you scramble up them they give way under your feet. When the tide is out the beach is very sheltered under their lee. You can see the Needles quite clearly now.' He pointed them out with his crop.

They rode along, Libby enjoying the view and the fresh sea air, while the Viscount took particular note of the lie of the land, seeing terrain with which he was quite familiar from a completely different perspective. It was Libby who broke the companionable silence.

'I should have thought the Needles were extremely hazardous to shipping,' she remarked.

'They are, particularly to ships whose masters wish to tack round them and into the Solent. It's an exercise best not attempted save by expert seamen who are familiar with these waters. The fishermen of Lymington do it safely enough. When I was a boy I went out with them from time to time and it was a hair-raising experience, I assure you.'

'I'm surprised there's no warning-beacon.'

'There will be one day, I'm sure. In the meantime wise sailors give them a very wide berth.'

Libby's attention had been so taken with the novelties of the sea, with its shifting, changing colours and the endlessly varying patterns of the waves that she had given no thought at all to the landward view, and she now glanced inland for the first time. 'Oh, Marcus, look!' she exclaimed. 'How well one can see Chase!'

How well indeed, he thought grimly, and manoeuvred his horse to line up the turret, clearly visible from here, with the last great stack—the one which could be seen from that room and that room alone. He knew enough of seamanship to be able to put himself in a master's shoes at least for a brief spell. If a ship at sea steered to the left of a light in the topmost turret window it would avoid the Needles.

It remained to determine whether Sir John had been correct when he had said that the garrison at Hurst Castle would not be able to see along this part of the coast. The general shape of the castle itself could be seen from here, but it lay low and grey on the skyline. This was no medieval ruin built to spot invaders from afar, but one of Great Harry's fortresses designed to blast out of the sea any foe venturing eastwards up the Solent or, more probably, trapped in the Solent and seeking an escape to the west.

Lord Charlbury glanced anxiously at his betrothed. 'Do you think you can ride along here?' he asked, indicating the shingle spit that led to the Castle.

'I don't see why not,' Libby replied, not realising what heavy work the horses would make of the spit. The pace was necessarily slow because the horses' hoofs either sank into the shingle and had to pull themselves out, or else they slid on the displaced stones and were continually recovering themselves, neither eventuality being conducive to a comfortable ride. Libby gritted her teeth and stayed in the saddle, determined not to complain, but Lord Charlbury kept an eye on her, and about halfway along the mile of shingle that lay between the land and the Castle he drew rein and looked about him. No, he thought, Sir John is right. Any ship could land west of the Needles unseen except by a passer-by, and there were few enough of those even in daylight. There would be none at all at night save the occasional poacher.

'This shingle is heavy going for the horses. We'll go back,' he said, guiltily aware that for Libby's sake they should have turned round some time before. They turned their horses and returned, Libby telling herself it was easier to ride along the shingle than it would be to walk it, and sending up a silent prayer of gratitude that Lord Charlbury's concern for his horses had made him turn back at all.

As soon as they were once more on grass, he dismounted and lifted Libby from the saddle so that both horses' hoofs could be checked for stones. That done, he turned to Libby. 'How do you feel?' he asked. 'The horses need a rest and so, I suspect, do you. Do you prefer to stop here for a little while, or shall we walk gently towards the house until they're rested?'

'I think I can manage a gentle walk,' Libby told him, aware that a change of activity would benefit her more than simply a change of where she sat. He took her arm, and together they strolled towards the shade of the woodland lying over to their right.

'Do you recognise these trees?' he asked.

Libby frowned, puzzled. 'I recognise oak and ash and chestnut,' she said, 'but not individual trees. Why? Should I?'

'This is Tipper's Wood.' he told her. 'The shortest way back lies through it.'

'Does it, indeed? Speeded up by the presence of Old Sidney, no doubt,' she added with asperity.

He laughed. 'I promise you we'll remount if there's the slightest sign of him or of his harem. Tell me, Libby, did you find the magic spring?'

'Oh, yes. Nurse's directions were quite specific.'

'And have its magical powers exerted themselves? Have your wishes come true?'

Libby looked worried. 'I do hope I didn't tell anyone what I had wished for,' she said. 'I don't think I was in any fit state to control either my tongue or my brain when they first brought me back, but I will have you know, my lord, that if one reveals one's wishes to anyone the magic evaporates.'

'Then perhaps I should remind you that you told me you had wished for my safe return and to a successful conclusion to my visit to Dover. Both these eventualities came about—and have not so far evaporated. I wondered whether there were any more you hadn't revealed to me.'

'If there were, I'm certainly not taking a chance on their ultimate success by telling you what they were!' she retorted. 'Why, it could be disastrous!'

'Dear me, you make it sound just like a fairy-tale. And to think I offered for you because of your common sense!'

'Of course it sounds like a fairy-tale—and a great deal of nonsense, too, I've no doubt,' Libby answered acerbically. 'But there's always the chance it may not be, you know, and it would never do to take the risk.'

'Do you know, Libby, I'm beginning to think you're a romantic at heart,' he told her.

'Nonsense,' she said stoutly. 'No one can be a companion to a twitty old woman and stay romantic for long.' But she blushed as she spoke, and the blush did not go unnoticed by her escort.

'You may be right,' he said with mock-gravity, as if weighing up a singularly difficult metaphysical conundrum. 'On the other hand, it might be necessary to remain a romantic to keep one's sanity. ''Twitty old women'' can be very demoralising, I imagine. However, in view of Rupert's entirely uncalled-for remarks on my diplomatic ability, I undertake not to pass on to him your very flattering description of his grandmother.'

She laughed. 'I don't suppose he'd mind if you did,' she said, her self-possession returning. 'I'd rather you didn't, though; the family was both kind and generous to me, and it was churlish of me to describe the Dowager so.'

'But not inaccurate, I suspect. I don't recall there being a great deal of kindness and generosity once they knew I had offered for you and been accepted.'

'That was because it took them completely by surprise. You may not have been aware of it, but Lady Somerton was terrified you would make a play for Lady Selina. She didn't want you to, because you were quite unsuitable, but I think it was a little galling to discover that your attentions had been focused on the dowdy companion rather than the beauty of the family.'

He stopped and stared down at her. 'I don't think of you as dowdy at all,' he said.

Libby smiled wistfully. 'You're very kind, my lord, but I dare say you don't think of me as a raving beauty, either.'

'If I said I did you wouldn't believe me, but you must surely be aware that a woman does not have to be placed in a man's estimation at one end of the spectrum or at the other. You have good taste, and you wear your clothes with elegance. Once all this business is sorted out I shall take considerable pride in introducing you to Society.'

It was the greatest compliment Libby had ever been paid and, coming from that particular source, it made her heart swell with pride, even if she was not entirely able to discount the part tact might have played in its utterance. Still, it would never do to let him realise how much his words had meant to her, so she chuckled.

'I expect your pride will diminish quite rapidly if I behave as I did at the Dolphin.'

'You wouldn't dare,' he told her.

She fluttered her eyelashes at him. 'Ah, but can you be sure?' she said.

He stopped, and his hold on her arm tightened. 'I must warn you, Miss Barton, that if you start employing the tricks of a flirt—as you show a distressing tendency to do—I shall respond in kind.'

Libby looked up at him, her brown eyes wide and innocent. 'I'm not at all sure what you mean by that, my lord, but you make it sound like a threat.'

He gazed down at her for a few silent moments, an inscrutable expression in his grey eyes which made Libby's heart miss a beat, while for a fleeting moment she wondered whether they were playing to different rules. Before she had time to make up her mind, his mouth descended on hers in a kiss quite unlike any he had bestowed on her in the past. His lips were hard and forced her mouth open in an intimacy for which she was entirely unprepared, but to which, once the initial shock had subsided, she had no hesitation in responding with every instinct she possessed.

Sensing her response, he drew her body close to his own and, as they embraced with increasing abandon, Libby knew that their impending marriage need not be the passionless, convenient affair she had more than half expected—and dreaded.

They were lost in each other's arms for a few short minutes, and it was Miranda's nudging muzzle that brought them back to a sense of time and place. Lord Charlbury relaxed his hold. 'My apologies, Libby,' he said. 'I forgot myself. It was an unwarrantable betrayal of your trust.'

'Yes, I suppose it was,' she agreed. 'The point is, what are you apologising for? For having kissed me, or for having done so when you shouldn't?'

'The latter, of course,' he said, surprised.

'Then that's all right, isn't it?' she said in her matter-of-fact voice and then, seeing confusion in his eyes, she chuckled quietly. 'Oh, Marcus, do you really think I couldn't have let you know your advances were unwelcome, had I chosen to do so? And do you think I have any doubt you would immediately have stopped? You were, I think, teaching me a lesson.'

'But not, perhaps, the one I had in mind,' he said ruefully. 'Really, Libby, I can never be quite sure from one day to the next how you will react. I thought I could predict what women will do. You are fast destroying my complacency.'

'Then I'm unlikely to bore you in the future.' An unwelcome thought struck her. 'Unless you wanted to marry the invariably well-behaved and rather meek little companion,' she suggested.

'I have to confess that I did have something like that in mind initially,' he told her. 'If it's any comfort to you, my criteria are rapidly changing.'

Libby cast him a beaming smile. 'A very great comfort,' she said. 'You can have no idea how difficult it is to maintain a face that isn't really one's own.'

They remounted after that, and made their way slowly through the wood, each lost in his or her own thoughts and a little uncertain how best to break a silence that had arisen from a subtle and barely definable change in their relationship with each other.

The Viscount's thoughts were largely concerned with Libby's safety, which, as a result of Sir John's information, he now felt to be of paramount importance. It was he who broke the silence.

'I wondered whether you'd like to repair to Brighton for a change of scene,' he said. 'I could take a house for you. Or Bath, if you preferred,' he added, thinking that perhaps his betrothed would be ill at ease in the highly fashionable Sussex town.

'What an extraordinary suggestion from someone who is, on his own admission, on a prolonged repairing lease!' she replied. 'I'm sure Brighton is ludicrously expensive.'

'Oh, hideously,' he agreed. 'But perhaps you hadn't realised that my credit has risen considerably since my expectations of a suitable alliance—and consequently of inheriting Chase—are so very good.'

She laughed. 'Do you never forgo an opportunity of putting me down?' she asked.

'No, never, for I've not yet observed that any of my carefully constructed put-downs have had any more than a transient effect. Besides, you've usually goaded me into it by some remark which shows a quite astonishing degree of impropriety towards one's betrothed. You've not yet answered my question. Would you like me to take a house for you in Bath or Brighton for a few weeks?'

Libby regarded him gravely, wondering what lay behind this unexpected suggestion. Obviously he wanted her out of the way, but why? Did he find her company tedious, despite his protestations to the contrary? Or had Max, wittingly or unwittingly, struck the nail very precisely on the head? Did Marcus want her discreetly out of the way so that he could set up a new mistress or perhaps renew a connection with an old one?

'Well?' he asked.

Her heart sank at such a persistent wish to see her elsewhere. 'Why, Marcus?' she asked.

'I thought life here might be becoming a little tedious—that you might perhaps welcome a change of scene.'

The reason was plausible and emerged glibly enough, as if he had carefully worked out the phrasing of it beforehand, a fact which did nothing to raise her spirits. Libby considered acceding to his suggestion because it was clearly what he wanted, but all her instincts rebelled at so tamely relinquishing the field to another woman. No, forewarned was forearmed. It might be that their marriage would eventually prove so disastrous that she would welcome being in a separate establishment many miles away, but she had no intention of letting things get to that pass if she could possibly help it, and she certainly wasn't going meekly away now and losing the battle before she'd had a chance to enter the lists. So she smiled at him.

'Good gracious!' she said. 'What on earth can the excitements offered by Brighton be like, if life here is tedious? My marriage is stopped in the most melodramatic way imaginable, I'm attacked by an enraged bull which may or may not have escaped accidentally, and I eat luncheon with an extraordinary Frenchwoman who is clearly of the *haut monde*, yet masquerades as a governess. If this is tedium, my lord, I must forswear the excitements of Brighton or Bath!'

Her betrothed laughed ruefully. 'I must admit I hadn't realised the incongruity of my words in the circumstances. Perhaps I should recommend these resorts because they offer you a more peaceful existence!'

She looked at him steadily and, although she managed to keep her voice even, she was aware of her heart thumping with anxiety.

'Why do you wish to be rid of me?' she asked.

He looked down at her, the softest expression she had yet seen on his face.

'Is that what you believe? I wonder why you should imagine my reason is a desire to be rid of you? If that's what you really think, you must mistake the matter. To tell you the truth, the sooner we're married, the happier I shall be—and not only for the sake of Chase.'

Libby blushed furiously. His words were hardly a declaration of passion, but they indicated an attitude far removed from the cold calculation of her conformity to a dead man's requirements. They sounded sincere, too. Maybe that was just part of the Viscount's skilled charm, but perhaps not—perhaps he was beginning to enjoy her company. It was a little more puzzling to decide why, if he was anxious to marry her, he suggested her going away rather than an immediate wedding. After all, the banns had been read and the obstruction removed.

'I'm very happy at Chase,' she said. 'I'm well content to stay here, though I hope you'll not take offence if I admit that there have been occasions when I've been somewhat less than comfortable.'

Lord Charlbury chuckled appreciatively, and Libby wondered how far it was wise to seek a solution to her doubts. 'There's no reason to send me to Brighton or Bath—or anywhere else, for that matter,' she went on. 'At least, not for the reasons you've suggested.' She glanced up at him under the brim of her hat, unsure how specific she should be. 'Marcus, your reputation is well known. You have had mistresses in the past, and I suppose I must face the fact that you'll have others in

the future, but do you want me out of the way in order
to pursue an interest of that sort?'

His astonishment, followed closely by horror and
dismay, were so patently genuine that Libby felt immediately reassured.

'Good God, woman, what sort of a man do you think
I am?' he demanded. 'The past is the past and there's
nothing I can do to redress that, but a man doesn't plan
to take a wife and a mistress simultaneously!'

'Well, no, I imagine not. I suppose these things
happen, but a man who marries for convenience is likely
to feel the need of a mistress before long, don't you
think?'

'It's not a field in which I can claim much expertise,'
he said drily. 'I rather fancy most men in that situation
would at least endeavour to create a marriage which rendered mistresses superfluous. They might not succeed,
but surely one could expect it to be a few years before
they abandoned the attempt?'

'I suppose so,' Libby said doubtfully.

His voice softened. 'Is that something that's been
worrying you?' he asked. 'It need not. When I decided
to try for Chase on my uncle's terms, I also decided that
the woman who married me would not be the loser by
enabling me to get what I wanted. I made up my mind
that, once married, I would remain faithful.'

'I see.' Libby supposed she should feel much happier
about the situation, but it was in truth very deflating to
learn that, however noble his intentions, they had been
formed regardless of the identity of his future wife, and
therefore the increasing regard he seemed to have for her
played no part in his decision. She believed him, but was
no nearer knowing why he wanted her elsewhere.
'Marcus,' she ventured, 'do you want me gone for some
specific reason, or was it a suggestion made under the
impression that it was what *I* wanted?'

'There is a reason. I'm not sure I'm at liberty to dis-
close it, however.'

'Not even to your future wife?' They rode in silence
for a few minutes, during which Libby considered other

possibilities. 'Does it have anything to do with Max?' she asked at last.

Marcus didn't answer immediately, and when he did his voice was guarded and his words uninformative. 'What do you mean?'

'The attack on the road to Copthorne, the wedding, the bull, your brother's peculiar moods, Mademoiselle d'Angers—Max is the connection with all of them.'

'Is he, now? You've been busy putting two and two together, haven't you?'

'I'm not entirely stupid, Marcus,' she said with some asperity. 'Anyone could understand Max's not wanting you to marry me—or, indeed, anyone else for the time being. But if I'm right, he does seem to be prepared to go to quite extraordinary lengths.' She paused, wondering how he would take her final question. 'Marcus, is he mad?'

Lord Charlbury paused a long time before he answered. 'I don't think so. His behaviour is erratic and desperate, but I don't think he's insane. I'm fairly sure the cause of his erratic behaviour lies elsewhere, and I think I know to what it may be attributed, but I'd prefer to keep my own counsel about it until I'm sure one way or another. I do believe, however, that you may be in danger, and I'd be easier in my mind if you were elsewhere.'

Libby thought about that carefully before replying. 'If you insist, I'll go, but I'd much rather not. Marcus, if your brother is that desperate, it's much easier to arrange accidents elsewhere than it is here, where he can be watched and where it's easier to be on one's guard.'

He smiled at her. 'I suppose that's true. I hadn't thought of it like that. Common sense is certainly one of your strong points. Stay if you will, then, but be careful. Perhaps you should remove to Byfield, and Rupert and I come to Chase.'

'That would look most peculiar, and it would certainly make Max suspicious. No, I stay at Chase—but the more time you and Lord Wilcote can spend here the more comfortable I shall feel.' She paused for a long time and looked at the Viscount speculatively, wondering whether to put into words the thoughts that were forming in her mind. A suggestion had occurred to her which she thought would solve all their current problems at one stroke. Unfortunately it was a suggestion which would be extremely indelicate for any lady to put to any gentleman. If she put it to Lord Charlbury he would undoubtedly be extremely surprised, and he might very well be more than a little shocked. The Viscount might be a libertine of many years' standing, but Libby suspected that he was, at heart, a puritan. Nevertheless, she thought the solution was a good one. She was only puzzled that he hadn't suggested it himself but, since he hadn't, she had no choice but to do so herself.

'My lord,' she began, earning herself a quizzical look, for she rarely used the reverential form of address when they were alone these days, yet her tone on this occasion indicated that she was not indulging in irony. 'I think there is a solution, but it ill becomes me to mention it for fear of being branded pert and indelicate.'

He raised one eyebrow. 'You intrigue me. I think you'd better take the risk.'

'Why don't we present Max with a *fait accompli*? Why don't we marry quietly and soon, and then announce the fact? That surely would pre-empt any further plots on his part.'

'Dear me, whatever can have induced me to think you well-bred!' he exclaimed, recoiling in mock-horror. Then he became serious. 'My dear, I've already considered that—and rejected it. When I came back from Dover I took good care to obtain a special licence so that we can marry at any time and in any place, but I'm afraid that isn't the solution it appears to be. At the moment Max needs to get rid of one or other of us in order to prevent the marriage. It doesn't much matter whether he goes to the extreme of arranging a fatal accident, whether he succeeds in persuading you to cry off, or whether he can somehow arrange a postponement just long enough to extend beyond the necessary six months. However, if we marry, he must get rid of both of us. He can't inherit if I still live, naturally, but if he disposes only of me he runs the risk of my leaving an unborn heir. Now, it would undoubtedly be more difficult to get rid of us both, but the urgency to do so would be immediate. There is more at stake here than Chase. Quite apart from anything else, if he can prevent the marriage, neither of us is likely to remain here: you would leave anyway, and I would depart soon afterwards to find another suitable wife. If we marry quickly and quietly, we are both likely to remain at Chase for the foreseeable future—and that wouldn't suit him at all.'

'I don't see what difference that would make,' she said.

Briefly he told her about the magistrate's visit. 'It gives me no pleasure to tell you what sort of a family you're marrying into,' he concluded. 'If you don't cry off, you'll have a profligate rake-hell for a husband and a traitor for a brother-in-law.'

She appeared to consider the matter. 'The former sounds the more fun,' she said at last. 'And I must say I'm delighted to have confirmation of my suspicion that Mademoiselle d'Angers is up to no good, but what is her hold over Max? Is he the young man of property she intends to marry? The one whose brother stands in the way? I own, I thought that was all make-believe at the time, but it does fit. Or do you think he's in love with her, and that's why he's prepared to go to such lengths?'

Marcus shook his head. 'I wish I knew him well enough to speculate intelligently on that, but I don't. However, I have a feeling—a hunch, nothing more—that that isn't the explanation. I think she has a stronger hold over him than that, but, whatever it is, I'm determined that when you marry into this family it will once more carry an unsullied name.'

Libby had never seen him so serious. She understood the importance he attached to his family name, but she suspected his dismay might also be in part because he feared she would cry off at the prospect he had just painted. 'Oh, Marcus,' she said in a rallying tone. 'I do believe it's you who is becoming a romantic!'

He laughed reluctantly at that, but he didn't deny it. It was, Libby thought, the first time she had been allowed an unchallenged word—a fact which perhaps demonstrated more forcefully than anything else just how concerned he was.

CHAPTER ELEVEN

WHEN Max flounced out of the house after his unsatisfactory exchange with Libby, he did not, as she assumed, go either for a 'good gallop' or to attend to the
business of the estate. Instead, he made straight for the
little fishing-port of Lymington, leaving his exhausted
horse in the care of an ostler at one of the better hos-
telries before running in and demanding to see
Mademoiselle d'Angers.

The landlord's wife smiled indulgently. The Asthall
brothers were well known in the little town, and young
Mr Max's fondness for the dashing Frenchwoman had
become something of a byword. She must be a few years
his senior, and she seemed very much the lady, but with
foreigners you never could tell, so perhaps she wasn't.
It was generally held to be significant that he seemed to
be making no effort to introduce her to his family, a fact
which probably showed he had more sense than most
people gave him credit for. Still, Mademoiselle was
affable enough, she paid her bills on time, and Mrs
Lidstone saw no reason to interfere. Young Mr Max
lacked his brother's charm, and people didn't take to
him too well. But, by all accounts, he'd been shabbily
treated by some of his family and, if he was besotted
with the Frenchwoman, he'd probably grow out of it in
time and be none the worse for the experience. So Mrs
Lidstone smiled and nodded in the direction of the
private parlour Mademoiselle used when the inn didn't
need the space.

'You've timed it just right, Mr Asthall,' she told him.
'Mamzelle's been out for a walk, and she got back barely
quarter of an hour ago.'

Héloise looked up from the letter she was writing as
her visitor burst into the parlour, and slipped it un-

obtrusively into her writing-case. She raised her eyebrows.

'Such precipitation,' she remarked. She glanced at his face. 'And not in the best of tempers, I see.'

'No, I'm not, and it's all that confounded woman's fault. I've been trying to make her cry off, but she seems to be quite devoid of any of the finer feelings. Do you know, she told me she had a fancy to have a title and had every intention of going ahead with the marriage for that reason alone? Such vulgarity!'

Héloise, who privately thought it to be an eminently practical reason for marrying someone, shook her head disapprovingly. 'Some women are like that,' she said. 'One would have thought a man of your brother's experience would have seen through her.'

'I dare say he has. Why should he be bothered? All he wants is Chase. All they have to do is persuade the trustees she fulfils the Earl's requirements—and they're not going to have any difficulty doing that—and they're both home and dry. He has Chase, and she has her title.'

'What arguments did you use to encourage her to see the error of her ways?'

He frowned. 'It's odd, that. Until this morning, I'd have said she had quite a soft spot for him, that the convenience is largely one-sided. So I guessed the one thing she wouldn't be happy about was the idea of his setting up a mistress. He's bound to do so sooner or later, of course: leopards don't change their spots, after all, and even an admirer wouldn't call her a particularly interesting female, so I should think it's inevitable. I implied he had a mistress already, and that if he didn't he soon would have.'

'And her reaction?'

'She didn't seem unduly perturbed.'

'Perhaps she is one of those people who are good at disguising their feelings.'

He brightened perceptibly. 'Perhaps she is. I hope so, because time's running out, and if I can't persuade her to cry off—which will mean she packs her bags and Marcus has to go wife-hunting again—then I shall have to do something more drastic. I've got to get rid of them both.'

'They're certainly very much in the way at present,' Héloise agreed. 'Do you have any alternative suggestions for getting rid of them?'

Max shrugged. 'If she had a fancy to be a viscountess, she's not really going to be very happy for very long in the country. She's going to want to wave that title around in Society. I suppose it may suit her for the present to lie fairly low, but they *are* formally betrothed, which I imagine carries a certain cachet in some circles. Perhaps she could be persuaded that Bath would suit her better, or even Brighton. That would get her out of the way, and I wouldn't be surprised if Marcus accompanied her.'

Héloise nodded. 'And if an accident should befall them, no one would think of you, would they?'

Max's face lit up. 'I hadn't thought of that, but you're right.' Then the light faded and he slumped in his chair. 'I don't seem to have much success with accidents. It will suit me better all around if I can only persuade her to cry off—Marcus will never find another woman quite as suitable, not in the time he's got left, and I'd have killed two birds with one stone without actually killing either of them—if you know what I mean.'

'I think I follow the argument,' she said. 'It doesn't get us much further, does it?'

'You know, I could have sworn the thought of a mistress would have upset her,' he went on thoughtfully. 'Maybe it's worth a try.'

'And does he have a mistress, this brother of yours?'

'Lord, how should I know?' Max said, surprised. 'I'm fairly sure he hasn't got one at the moment, but that doesn't matter. All I need to do is to convince her that he has, and leave the rest to her.'

'And how do you propose to do that?'

'Simple. I plant the thought in her mind—and I've already prepared the ground, remember—and then arrange for her to see them together.'

'That should certainly do the trick if your assessment of her is correct. I should have thought it would be rather difficult to organise if he doesn't actually have a mistress.'

Max leaned forward in his chair and tapped the side of his nose. His eyes had narrowed and were bright with anticipation. 'I have a cunning plan,' he said, 'and, if my judgement of Libby Barton is right, it can't fail.'

'And if it isn't?'

He shrugged. 'We try something else. Are you with me?'

'You'd better tell me what you have in mind.'

'Very well,' he agreed, and drew his chair over, the better to sustain an air of confidentiality.

At dinner that evening Max was in a greatly improved frame of mind, though his remarks had a biting edge. Libby reflected that this was one area of similarity between the brothers though, whereas in Marcus's case the bite was wit, in Max's it was more likely to be purely sour. He particularly enjoyed himself on this occasion at Lord Wilcote's expense, but Lord Somerton's heir took the acid comments about his agricultural inexpertise with a bland politeness that Max found infinitely more irritating than a sharp set-down would have been because he could not be sure whether his shafts were getting home.

Lord Charlbury watched the interchange with cynical amusement. He knew Lord Wilcote well enough to know there was no malicious intent behind his placid acceptance of Max's gibes. Lord Wilcote always listened respectfully to the views of others, even when they were extreme and untenable, and the only time Lord Charlbury could recall his entering into an argument was when a fellow connoisseur had sought his opinion on an Indian jewelled hand ornament containing what purported to be a pigeon's egg ruby. Lord Wilcote had insisted against all opposition and amid much ridicule that it was a garnet. When the independent opinion of Messrs Rundell and Bridge had confirmed that of Lord Wilcote, he had been so far from revelling in having been proved right that he had apologised to the jewel's owner, knowing how deep must be the collector's disappointment.

However unprovocative Lord Wilcote might have intended to be, Max's sunny mood was rapidly clouding over, and Lord Charlbury wondered how long it would be before his brother turned his attention to Libby in the hope that she might rise more willingly to the bait. Max had long since learned not to goad his elder brother, but Marcus had a shrewd idea that Max still laboured under some preconceived notion of Libby's character. It was a notion he had himself formed when he first knew her, and was only recently learning that it was the veneer of subservience essential in a paid companion. If Max wasn't careful, he was about to learn that Miss Barton's demure exterior disguised the steel within.

Sure enough, Lord Wilcote was proving so unsatisfactory a target that Max turned his attention to the other guest.

'I'm surprised you choose to continue your stay here, Miss Barton,' he announced suddenly.

Libby looked mildly surprised that he should comment. 'Are you?' she said. 'I wasn't aware that a limit had been set upon my visit.'

'There isn't, of course. I just thought you must be bored to death.'

'Oh, no. Not *bored* to death,' she answered. 'I was nearly gored, of course, but I don't think anyone would regard that as boring, you know. Quite the reverse, in fact.'

He flushed. 'It was a figure of speech,' he said petulantly.

Libby smiled with honeyed sweetness. 'Not the most felicitous one you could have chosen in the circumstances,' she replied cheerfully. 'Still, your concern for my entertainment does you credit even though it's entirely unnecessary. I'm not in the least bored, and I'm enjoying myself enormously.'

Max ignored this assurance. 'Why don't you persuade Marcus to take you to Brighton? I'm sure he could raise

the money from the five-per-cents, and you'd find far
more going on there.'

Libby's glance flew across the table to the Viscount.
Almost imperceptibly, he shook his head. She turned
back to Max, who had been oblivious of this interchange.

'I don't imagine Brighton would suit me at all,' she
said. 'You must know I can hardly count myself one of
the *haut ton*.'

He looked her up and down in an insolent manner
that made Libby's hand itch. 'Then go to Bath,' he said
rudely. 'That's the place for dowds, I believe.'

'You're too kind,' Libby said, maintaining—with some
difficulty—the sweetness of her smile, while an infini-
tesimal movement of her hand arrested Lord Charlbury's
impending tongue-lashing. 'I really am very happy here,
and feel no need to go elsewhere for a change of scene.'

Max was becoming very agitated. 'You may not feel
the need,' he snapped, 'but Chase does. That turret
room, for example. The one you've appropriated for
yourself. It needs redecorating. If you went to Bath for
a good long visit, I could have it looking like new.'

'But part of its charm lies in the fact that it doesn't
look like new,' she replied, still outwardly unmoved by
his continuing rudeness. 'I shouldn't like it half so much
if it were to be refurbished. No, I prefer it as it is, just
as I prefer Chase to Bath.'

'You really are the most excessively unreasonable
female it has ever been my misfortune to meet!' Max
exploded, and his pale face blanched still further as Lord
Charlbury sprang to his feet, murder in his face and his
hand uplifted in an unmistakable signal of intent.

But before the Viscount's hand could descend across
his brother's face, Libby broke in, using the same calm
voice that had characterised her part in all the exchanges
of the evening.

'I confess that I am indeed unreasonable,' she said.
'I feel it only fair to point out to you that unreason-
ableness is generally held to be an essentially female
characteristic, and I'm afraid I'm far too old to change
now, you know.'

There was no disguising the fact that Max's temper had reached boiling point, but he was not yet sufficiently under its control to have forgotten the look on Marcus's face or the implication of the upraised hand. Besides, difficult as it might be to control his temper in the present circumstances, no useful purpose was likely to be served by losing it, and his purpose was very useful indeed. Libby had no intention of repairing to some provincial watering-place. Very well, he must take another tack.

He ate in silence for some time while a desultory conversation took place around him. When he was ready to speak, it must be without the tremor of anger.

'Are you busy tomorrow, Marcus?' he asked at last. 'I mean, could you put aside anything you've got planned?'

'I could,' the Viscount said cautiously. 'Why?'

'I wondered if you'd come into Lymington with me.'

'You're no stranger to Lymington. Why do you need my company all of a sudden?'

Max looked self-consciously vulnerable, almost boyish. 'There's a boat I've seen—nothing big, nothing grand, just a cutter—and it needs quite a lot of work done on it. I'd like your opinion of it.'

'Since when have you been interested in sailing?'

'I've been out a few times with Bill Benson. He reckons he can make a seaman of me by the time the cutter's seaworthy.'

'Does he now? And does the fact that Bill Benson's brother has a small boatyard have anything to do with this?'

Max grinned. 'It might. But it was the Bensons who taught you to sail.'

'True, but I never attained a proficiency that induced me to buy my own boat. Can you afford it?'

'I can afford this one—just. I wouldn't be able to if it were seaworthy.'

'But you can afford to make it so?'

'Over a period of time, yes.'

Marcus pondered his brother's words. He was more than half inclined to suspect that Max was working on a scheme to dispose of him, yet his request might be genuine. At the very least, he was going to have to produce an unseaworthy cutter at some stage, and Lord Charlbury found it hard to believe that the Bensons, for all their suspected smuggling links with the Continent, would countenance either treason or deliberate murder. Besides, he was already on his guard, and that was halfway to being safe. 'I think I could manage it,' he said. 'That is, assuming Libby doesn't need my company.'

Libby hastened to disclaim any interest in his presence the following day. 'After today's ride and yesterday's drive, I shall be very happy to stay at home tomorrow,' she said.

'I tell you what,' Lord Wilcote offered, 'I'll ride over so you'll have someone to talk to. If Marcus doesn't mind,' he added, realising that his offer could be misconstrued.

'Why should I mind?' Marcus replied. 'I think it's an excellent idea. I haven't been in a boatyard for years. I'll enjoy it.'

Lord Charlbury more than half expected his brother to raise some objection to Fratton's presence on the box, but Max made no comment, no suggestion that the groom was superfluous on this occasion. Which means, the Viscount thought, that an attack on the road is unlikely.

They reached Lymington without mishap, and Fratton saw to the horses while his employer accompanied Max to the Benson boatyard where they were obviously expected.

'It's been a long time since we've had the pleasure of your company, my lord,' Bill Benson said. 'Given up the sea, have you?'

'I'm afraid it was a young man's passing fancy,' Lord Charlbury told him. 'I seem to recall you were always bemoaning the fact that I didn't have seawater in my veins.'

The old seaman nodded. 'That's true enough. You never did much more than play at it. Still, we taught you a thing or two, I reckon.'

'You taught me that not every nasty situation can be resolved with money or a title.'

'Aye. Neither's much good in a storm, and that's a fact. Mind you, when I heard tell as how you was in difficulties, I did think we could do worse than cut you in, but it seems you're set fair to getting back on course again without our help.'

'Rumour seems to have been busy,' the Viscount commented without rancour. 'Now, what's all this about a cutter for Max?'

'Well, it seems your young brother's taken a sudden fancy to the sea. He's been out with us a couple of times, though he's still a lot to learn, but he caught sight of the *Elsie May* in Ned's yard here, and decided that was the thing for him. He reckons by the time she's sea-worthy again he'll have learned enough to be able to handle her, and maybe he's right. She's sound enough, my lord, and she's been a good little vessel in her day, and fast, but it's going to take a fair bit of time—and a fair bit of money, too—to put her back the way she was. I've told him he ought to think about it, my lord, but he always was more of a one to act on impulse than you ever was, my lord.'

'So the idea is something of an impulse, is it?' Marcus turned to his brother. 'What say you, Max? How much of an impulse is the *Elsie May*?'

Max coloured angrily. Marcus really shouldn't allow himself to be addressed with so much familiarity. If people kept their proper distance they wouldn't have the chance to gab. 'Having a boat isn't an impulse,' he said, trying not to sound sulky. 'Just having this one. I saw her yesterday and thought, just the thing. But I'd been thinking about it in general terms for a long time.'

'Well, from the look of her, it needs a lot more thought before you jump, but I dare say Ned Benson hasn't got buyers beating his door down to buy her. You and I need to have serious talk about the future, and I'm sure, if you really want the cutter, it will be found to be possible. Will that suit you?'

'It doesn't look as if I've much choice, does it?' Max said deliberately ungracefully, a carefully sullen pout disguising the smile that was trying to break through.

'Then we'll go and get something to eat, and see whether we can't find some common ground,' Marcus suggested. It began to look as if, on this occasion at least, his suspicions had been unfounded, and who was to know but that a new interest, such as the cutter undoubtedly was, might divert Max's interest from the less desirable activities in which he was currently participating?

As they made their way back along the quayside, Lord Charlbury's eye was drawn to the figure of an almost incongruously well-dressed female approaching them. No sooner had her elegance registered with him than he was dismayed to recognise Héloïse d'Angers. It was some consolation to observe that she was, if anything, even more taken aback than he. She glanced from one to the other, displaying an uncertainty that the Viscount, the first to recover from the surprise, found amusing.

'Mademoiselle...d'Angers, I believe?' he said, bowing.

It was Max's turn to be disconcerted. 'You know each other?' he demanded.

'It would be more accurate to say we have met,' Marcus told him, his eyes fixed on the Frenchwoman's face.

'I didn't know that. Why didn't you tell me you'd met my brother?' Max insisted.

Héloïse made a deprecating gesture. 'Because I was not aware I had done so,' she said. 'I don't believe anyone actually introduced us on that previous occasion.'

'I don't believe they did,' Marcus agreed. 'Perhaps because it was rather difficult to fit in the social niceties. Your servant, ma'am.'

As he spoke, his brain was working rapidly. The encounter had all the signs of being entirely fortuitous, but he had a deep-seated feeling that it was, on the contrary, contrived. He couldn't imagine why. He could think of no possible advantage to Max or his plans to bring his brother and his emigrée friend together.

'You, on the other hand, seem to have an acquaintance of some long standing,' he went on. 'Did you know of my brother's interest in boats?'

Héloïse looked surprised—genuinely, Marcus thought. 'I believe he has mentioned something about it,' she said. 'But whether it was a whim or a real interest, I did not enquire.'

'Perhaps I may once again invite you to join us for some refreshment,' Marcus suggested. 'I promise that this time you won't be subjected to quite as much cross-examination.'

He caught the uncertain glance she threw in Max's direction.

'Why not?' Max agreed. 'We were on our way to find something to eat, and I see no reason to change our plans, do you?' He put an undue emphasis on the last sentence, and Marcus had the odd impression the final question was directed, not at him, as would have been expected, but at Héloïse. It reinforced his feeling that the encounter had been contrived. It behoved him to tread warily.

The luncheon set for them in a private parlour was hearty rather than elegant, but neither gentleman minded that, and Mademoiselle d'Angers ate with the appetite of one who was delighted that someone else would be paying the bill. Conversation was general and largely uninteresting, as one would expect in such a group. Marcus was more and more puzzled. There seemed little point to this, yet Max seldom did anything pointlessly. Perhaps he was wrong. Perhaps it had all been one large coincidence.

Then Max made his excuses. 'Marcus, we're going to have to go back to Chase shortly. Would you be kind enough to entertain Mademoiselle d'Angers while I go back to the boatyard? There's something I need to confirm.'

'If Mademoiselle has no objection, I shall, of course, be delighted,' Marcus replied, though he would very much have preferred to go with his brother. However, good manners precluded his doing anything about it so, as the door closed behind Max, he turned to their guest. 'I seem to recall that you were awaiting the arrival of your brother,' he said. 'Has he come yet, or do you still wait?'

'My brother? Oh, yes, I still wait.' She glanced at the door as if anxious that someone would burst in. 'My lord, I am so glad to have the opportunity to speak with you alone. Mr Asthall is such a kind young man but not as much *au fait* with the world as you, and I have need of advice.'

'If I can be of assistance, you have only to ask,' he said politely.

'My problem is not a simple one, my lord. It is something...oh, so difficult to explain...*très compliqué*, you understand.'

'Then if you require my advice, I can only suggest you begin unravelling it,' he said.

She smiled perfunctorily and shook her head. 'There is no time, my lord. Mr Asthall is unlikely to be long. Dare I ask ... Would it be possible for me to have converse with you tomorrow? Could you perhaps return to Lymington? It is a great imposition, I know, but you would earn my undying gratitude.'

'I imagine I can be spared from Chase,' he admitted, wondering what lay behind this extraordinary request. 'Can you give me no idea what it concerns?'

She glanced at the door again and lowered her voice. 'It is a very personal matter, my lord, and not entirely unconnected with your brother.'

'I see,' he said, inaccurately. 'Then I shall wait upon you at noon.'

Max returned very shortly after that, downcast because the Bensons had gone out on the tide and he had been unable to verify whatever it had been that was exercising him.

When they drew up at Chase, Lord Charlbury learned that his betrothed had gone early to bed. No, Nurse assured him, there was nothing wrong with her that a good long rest wouldn't cure, and if he asked her opinion, which in all probability he wouldn't, she ought to stay there tomorrow, too.

'Then in that case, perhaps you'd be kind enough to wish Miss Barton well and tell her she need not expect me until tomorrow evening, when I hope she'll be sufficiently recovered to dine with me.'

Mrs Widford beamed and nodded. 'That you may depend upon, my lord,' she said.

Lord Charlbury drove back to Byfield Manor in thoughtful silence. 'I'm going back to Lymington tomorrow, Fratton,' he said as he handed over the horses.

'Very well, me lord,' the groom said impassively. 'I'll have them ready for you.'

'No, I rather fancy it's not very well at all. I've agreed to meet Mademoiselle d'Angers at noon for what I think she referred to as private converse.'

'Very interesting, me lord.'

'Possibly. Potentially dangerous, too, but I'm not sure to whom.'

'I'm not sure I follow, me lord.'

Lord Charlbury laughed. 'I'm not sure I do, either,' he said. 'Whatever it's about, she couldn't talk about it in front of Max, so I can't take him with me and thereby keep him out of harm's way.'

'Or Miss Barton's,' the groom suggested.

'Precisely. I don't suppose Lord Wilcote's interest in agriculture could keep him fully occupied again?'

'Not if what I heard about their last little outing is anything to go by, me lord.'

'That's my impression, too. So I go off leaving Miss Barton at Chase with Max. I can, of course, leave you to keep an eye on things, but on the other hand, if the purpose is to get me on my own, you're more use on the back of my carriage.'

'You don't think that there mamzelle just wants some advice?'

'No, Fratton, I don't. Oh, I've no doubt she'll find something to ask my advice about, but I'm quite sure there's something else behind this. My only uncertainty is whether it's directed at me or at Miss Barton.'

'With respect, me lord, aren't you forgetting Lord Wilcote?'

The Viscount sighed. 'No, I hadn't forgotten him, but I did hope I might be able to sort things out within the household. The stickier this gets, the less I want to embroil anyone else.'

'Understandable, me lord, but not very realistic, if you don't mind me speaking my mind. His lordship's been a very good friend to you over the years. You've every reason to trust him, and it's my guess he'd be deeply offended if he learned you weren't prepared to involve him. I'll go with you to Lymington because it'll look odd if I don't and even odder if I'm hanging around Chase when you're elsewhere. Lord Wilcote's been taking your place at Chase whenever you've been called away. Why should tomorrow be any different? No one will think anything of it.'

'You're right, of course. It's the only sensible thing to do.'

When Libby woke up the next morning she found she had benefited so much from having retired early the previous day that she no longer felt the need to spend a further day in bed, and once more ignored Nurse's protests and went down to breakfast. Max was in the breakfast-room toying with a cup of coffee, his meal obviously finished some time ago.

Her first impression had been one of restlessness, and there was no doubt Max brightened perceptibly when she came in. 'I'd heard you weren't getting up today,' he remarked as she crossed to the sideboard and helped herself to devilled kidneys and scrambled egg.

'I didn't intend to when I went to bed, but I feel so much better that it seemed a pity to waste a day.'

He smiled knowingly, as if he had fully expected a change of plans. 'I'm surprised you bothered. Marcus isn't coming over until this evening.'

Libby raised her eyebrows. 'Does that make a difference? Have you observed me to stay in my room except when he is expected?'

'No, as a matter of fact I was a bit surprised yesterday when you said you might not be down. It's gratifying to be proved right.'

'I'm glad it makes you happy, but I shouldn't have thought the point was sufficiently important to warrant your looking like the cat that's just eaten the cream.'

He laughed, surprisingly unoffended for one who was normally so touchy. 'Is that what I look like? Hardly surprising, in the circumstances. Far be it from me to gloat, but you see, that isn't the only thing I've been proved right about.'

He so obviously intended Libby to seek clarification, and he had such a smug expression on his face, that all her instincts told her to deprive him of whatever pleasure he was going to get out of it—and there must be some, to account for his attitude. So instead of asking him what he meant, she poured herself some coffee. 'Good,' she said. 'Today has obviously started off on the right foot for you. I hope it continues.'

'I have every confidence it will,' he smirked, and paused expectantly. When there was still no sign of interest on her part, he frowned. 'Aren't you going to ask what it is?'

Libby glanced up from her breakfast, carefully controlled surprise on her face. 'No. Why should I? I was always taught it was vulgar to enquire into other people's affairs.'

'And so it is, of course, only this isn't other people's affairs. Well, it is, I suppose, but there's no denying it affects you.'

'Then I shall find out about it in due course, don't you think?' she said repressively, becoming increasingly convinced that, because he was so keen to impart whatever information he had, it must be something she would probably rather not hear.

'Why wait until gossip distorts it out of all proportion?' he said.

Libby studied him. He was already metaphorically licking his lips in anticipation of her reaction, and he clearly had no intention of going away until he had told her whatever it was that he intended her to hear. Libby sighed. 'You're obviously determined to be the first to tell me,' she said, 'so I suppose I'd better humour you. What is this piece of news that proves you right?'

'I told you Marcus would take a mistress. I even told you there was a rumour he had already taken up with one since your betrothal was announced. Well, I now know it to be true. I saw them together yesterday while we were in Lymington.' He paused to watch the effect of his words.

Libby felt as if the floor had given way and she were falling into a bottomless abyss, but she knew Max well enough now to be able to dredge up enough self-control to school her features into complete unconcern. She kept her eyes on her cup and concentrated on stirring its contents.

'How extremely careless of him! Disappointing, too: I should have thought Lord Charlbury was sufficiently adroit in such matters to ensure absolute discretion.'

Max frowned. Did she really not care? Was he so bad a judge of character? 'A rather tall woman,' he told her. 'Extremely elegant. Not at all what one expects to see in Lymington. Not at all like you, either,' he went on.

'I imagine a man who takes a mistress is likely to pick one who differs from his legitimate companion, don't you?' she asked, deliberately ignoring his rudeness.

'What's more, I overheard them talking,' he went on. 'Well, not to put too fine a point on it, they'd gone into a private parlour and I listened at the keyhole. Reprehensible, I suppose, but understandable.'

'Oh, entirely,' Libby agreed.

'That's why he's cried off coming here today. She's got something important she wants to discuss with him, so he agreed to meet her there at noon.'

'Fascinating,' Libby said. She stopped stirring her coffee because the hand wielding the spoon was beginning to shake.

'I thought you'd be interested. It's a pity I'm going to be rather busy today, otherwise I'd happily drive you into Lymington to see for yourself.'

The effort to control herself was becoming increasingly difficult. 'I wouldn't dream of putting you to so much bother,' she said icily.

'Of course, Wilcote will be over later—we had a message from Byfield. He'll probably oblige quite happily.'

Libby said nothing and Max, his seeds sown, took his leave of her and went off to attend to whatever business was so pressing.

When he had gone, Libby pushed away the rest of her breakfast uneaten, her appetite suddenly dead. It was difficult to tell how much of Max's story was true, or whether it was something made up to distress her. She hoped she had at least deprived him of the satisfaction of knowing how well he had succeeded. It seemed improbable that Marcus, having taken a mistress, should have been so careless as to let his brother see them together, yet there was something in Max's manner that inclined her to the view that, while he may put the worst possible interpretation on what he saw, he was not actually lying. The simple solution was to wait until Marcus came over to Chase that evening and tackle him about it. Yet what did one say? And even if one found the right words, what man was likely to reply, 'Yes, as a matter of fact, I do have a mistress in Lymington and I was with her today'? Either way he would deny it, and she would be no wiser than she was now. There wasn't even any point in asking him if he had met this woman, for the same reason: if he denied it, she would still not know whether the denial were the truth. She reminded herself that one was supposed to trust the person one loved, but she wasn't sure if that theory still held good when the object of one's affections made no pretence of returning the emotion.

Only Max's final suggestion had any practical advantages. If she could get to Lymington by noon, she could at least ascertain whether Marcus met someone there or not. She despised herself for even considering it, especially since she guessed what Max's motive was. Well, he would be disappointed. Libby Barton had every intention of marrying Viscount Charlbury. But first she needed to know what she was up against. Knowing the truth might be painful. Knowing only rumour and gossip was bound to be destructive.

When Lord Wilcote arrived, he was more than a little surprised to be greeted by a Libby Barton clearly dressed for a drive and hovering at the top of the steps.

'Oh, you *did* drive,' she said. 'I was so afraid you'd ride over, but I took a chance.'

'The horses needed the exercise,' he explained. 'Not that driving to Chase and back does much to get rid of the fidgets.'

'But Lymington and back would,' she suggested.

'Certainly.' He looked her up and down. 'Is that why you're dressed as you are? I thought your last long drive tired you out?'

'I was a little fatigued afterwards,' Libby admitted. 'I'm quite recovered now, and I should very much like you to drive me there, if you'd be so kind.'

'Yes, of course. My pleasure. Pity you didn't let Marcus know you wanted to go—he'd have ... Well, no, perhaps not,' he finished lamely, recalling what the Viscount had told him of his errand. 'May I ask the purpose of this visit?' he added cautiously.

Libby had anticipated that question. 'I've been trying to think of some small gift to give Marcus to mark our betrothal,' she confided mendaciously. 'Nurse told me of just the thing in Lymington the other day, but I naturally couldn't do anything about it with Marcus beside me, now could I? So I needed another escort, and who better than you?'

'I suppose you're right,' Lord Wilcote said doubtfully. He frowned. 'She saw something in *Lymington*?' he asked.

'That's right.'

'For *Marcus*?'

'Yes.'

He shook his head in evident disbelief. 'We'd better be on our way, then,' he said. He wondered whether if would matter very much if she saw the Viscount in Lymington. It would probably be better to avoid him, because Marcus was bound to ask questions. It was a pity their destination wasn't Southampton. Much easier to miss someone there. He knew that the only message Lord Charlbury had left at Chase had been to the effect that he wouldn't be there until dinner, and he knew Libby was acquainted with Mademoiselle d'Angers and the fact that there was some connection between the Frenchwoman and Max. However, women were odd creatures, and although he knew Libby to be exceedingly sensible he placed no dependence at all on that good sense remaining in charge if she caught sight of her affianced husband in the company of any extremely attractive woman. Ways of avoiding that very eventuality occupied his mind during the drive. He was sufficiently socially adroit to disguise his preoccupation well enough to deceive his companion, but since Libby was grappling with her own problems it was unlikely she would have noticed even had he been completely silent.

Chief among them was that, although Max had told her the time of Marcus's assignation, he had made no mention of the precise place. Lymington was little more than a village, but it boasted a number of inns, and Libby had little desire to go from one to the other trying to find out where he and this woman were.

She guessed that Max knew, and it would no doubt have given him great pleasure to have told her, but she'd had no intention of asking him. She had no idea whether his story were true or false but, whichever it was, its purpose was to discomfit her and, if this did prove to be a wild-goose chase, at least he wouldn't have the satisfaction of knowing that his machinations had sent her on it. The smaller problem of the gift for Marcus was more easily resolved. She knew there was a small jeweller's in the town. Either what Nurse had seen was no longer there, or closer inspection would reveal it to be totally unsuitable after all—which, she thought wryly, won't surprise Lord Wilcote one bit.

The travellers therefore approached the small town with totally opposed goals, Libby being determined to find out whether Marcus was with this unnamed woman, and Lord Wilcote equally determined to prevent precisely that. Neither of them knew that Mademoiselle d'Angers was a third, very active protagonist who had every reason to wish to be seen.

When Lord Charlbury handed in his card at the inn where Héloïse was staying, he was not at all sorry that she joined him with her bonnet and pelisse on and the suggestions that it would be more *comme il faut* if they walked down to the quayside to talk, rather than be closeted alone in a private parlour. He offered her his arm, as courtesy demanded, and together they strolled down the cobbled street towards the little quay, the heart of the fishing-port.

'It is difficult,' Héloïse began. 'I need to speak to you of your brother. How I wish I had known who you were when we first met! May I speak frankly?'

'I think you'd better,' Lord Charlbury said drily, wondering what lay behind this interview that was so urgent.

'Max—Mr Asthall, I mean—is such a charming young man, but a little... erratic, don't you find?'

Marcus, who would not have described his brother as 'charming', refused to be drawn. 'In what way?' he asked.

Héloïse shrugged, and her gestures became Gallic. 'How can I explain? *Aux anges* one day, moody and irritable the next. You must have noticed.'

Lord Charlbury's face was carefully blank. 'I'm afraid I'm not terribly well-acquainted with my brother,' he said apologetically. 'There's a great disparity in our ages, you see. In fact, you appear to know him better than I, so I'm at a loss to see how I can be of any assistance at all in whatever problem you have.'

Héloïse sighed and gave one of her frequent glances behind her, as if to ascertain that they were not overheard. On this occasion she caught sight of a carriage, a gentleman's sporting vehicle, some way behind. She smiled to herself, and leaned more heavily on the Viscount's arm, her bonnet almost resting on his shoulder. Seen from behind, they presented a very intimate picture.

That, at least, was how it struck Libby. She saw the couple ahead, and the colour drained from her face. Marcus's form was unmistakable. Few men were as tall or as broad-shouldered as he, and none Libby had ever met wore his curly-brimmed beaver at quite that rakish angle. Rakish! A prophetically accurate word, if ever there was one, she thought. The woman, too, was familiar, but not immediately recognisable until one of those expressive gestures and something about the tilt of her head told Libby who she was.

Libby touched Lord Wilcote's arm. 'I don't think we need to go this way. From what Nurse said, it will be quicker up there.' And she pointed to a side-street barely wide enough for the curricle to get through.

Lord Wilcote glanced at her face and, seeing her eyes were not on the street she had indicated but fixed on something ahead, he followed the direction of her gaze, and groaned inwardly. There really was no mistaking Marcus's figure. Whatever had induced the man to stroll on the quay with Mademoiselle d'Angers no matter how innocent their encounter might be? He turned the carriage obediently into the street Libby had indicated, and for the next few minutes his attention was fully occupied in driving down it without scraping the paintwork. When they emerged into the wider street ahead and he was able to relax a little, he realised she was shaking.

He patted her hand. 'It's all right, you know. There's nothing in it.'

'You saw them?'

'Not as soon as you did, but I saw something had upset you, so I looked to see what it was.'

Libby shook her head. 'I can't believe it. I'm sure Marcus never met Mademoiselle d'Angers before we bumped into her in Southampton the other day.'

'He hadn't. Know what I think? I think you'd better let me take you back to Chase. We'll stop for some refreshment on the road because if we stop here you're bound to come face to face with Marcus, and I don't think that's a good idea. Tackle him about it at Chase. I'm sure he won't mind.'

'Of course not,' Libby retorted. 'You will have had time to warn him.'

'I'll drive you back to Chase and then stay there so that I've no opportunity to talk to him before you do. Will that suit you?'

She smiled waveringly through tears that hovered threateningly. 'You sound very sure,' she said.

'I am, but it's not for me to explain it to you.' His voice softened. 'Are you very upset, Libby?'

She nodded. 'I didn't want to believe Max, but I just had to see for myself, and now I wish I hadn't.'

'So Max is behind this, is he?' Lord Wilcote said, frowning. 'Don't forget to tell Marcus that. I think it may be relevant.'

The pretence of the gift tacitly acknowledged, they returned to Chase with no more delay than that occasioned by breaking for refreshment. Libby would have been happy to forgo this, but her escort insisted, rightly judging that, however brave a face she might be putting on, she had in the last few days undertaken far too much strenuous activity for one who had had so recent an encounter with Old Sidney.

It was a silent journey. Libby felt hurt and upset— and at least as annoyed with herself as she was with Marcus. She shouldn't have gone. She now realised that part of the reason she had done so was a desire to prove Max wrong, and, whereas she had thought nothing could be worse than not knowing, she now knew that ignorance would indeed have been relative bliss. She wondered whether she would have felt better or worse had the woman leaning so confidingly on Marcus's arm had been someone else. Mademoiselle d'Angers was beautiful and elegant and it was hardly surprising if he had decided it was an acquaintance he wished to pursue, though

he had disguised that interest very well when they had
first met her. The only thin straw of hope left to clutch
was that just because the woman *was* Héloise there might
be another explanation.

It was going to be difficult to ask Marcus about it,
simply because it would be impossible to do so without
revealing that she had, in effect, been spying on him.
She supposed she could stick to the story about a gift,
but if she did that she couldn't mention Max's part, and
Lord Wilcote had been quite insistent that she did so.
He knew more than he had been prepared to tell her,
but he was someone Libby was inclined to trust. It was
a pity she was going to have to live with this uncertainty
until dinnertime. The only thing that made the waiting
bearable was the depressing thought that what she would
then learn would confirm her worst fears.

In the event, she didn't have to wait quite that long.
Lord Charlbury drove straight to Chase on his return
from Lymington, and had Fratton stable the horses there.
He found Libby and Lord Wilcote in a small, pleasant
parlour at the back of the house. A tall window led on
to a flagged terrace which in turn led to the neatly scythed
lawns edged by the forest trees.

'A truly domestic scene,' he remarked as he entered.
'Rupert, it suits you. You must find yourself a wife.
Libby, will you receive me in my dirt? I've come straight
from Lymington, but if you prefer me to change I'll have
the horses put to and return to Byfield.'

'No...no, I've no objection,' Libby replied, so
obviously confused that Marcus looked enquiringly from
her to his friend.

Lord Wilcote stood up. 'Now you're back, I'll take a
turn in the garden,' he said. 'You'll not want me in the
way just now.'

He disappeared through the window, and Lord
Charlbury turned to Libby. 'What's going on?' he asked.
'Don't tell me Rupert's replaced me in your affections?'

Libby forced a tight smile. 'I think if he had he'd be
enough of a gentleman to stay with me while I told you.'

'True,' he agreed, and Libby wondered if it were her imagination that he seemed relieved. 'Rupert was never a coward. But there's something bothering you. Rupert knows what it is and has tactfully taken himself off. I think the sooner we sort ourselves out, the better, don't you? What is it?'

'Won't you sit down?' Libby asked him. 'It's very unnerving to have you towering over me like that.'

'Dear me, this begins to sound serious,' he commented, sounding both puzzled and amused, but he pulled up a chair so that he was sitting close to her, and took her hand. 'What is it, Libby?'

'First I have to tell you that Lord Wilcote took me to Lymington today.'

'Precisely my own destination, but Rupert knew that. I take it it was his idea?'

'No, it was mine. Marcus, we saw you there.'

'I'm not surprised—it's not a very big place. Where, exactly?'

'On the quayside.'

'And not alone?'

'No.'

'I take it you recognised my companion?'

'Mademoiselle d'Angers.'

'I see. May I enquire into your purpose in suddenly deciding to go to Lymington?'

'I told Lord Wilcote it was to buy you a betrothal gift.'

'In *Lymington*?'

Libby smiled sheepishly. 'That's what he said—and with an almost identical inflexion.'

'I imagine he might. Do I deduce that this was not the true reason?'

'I was spying on you.'

'You knew where I'd gone?'

'Max told me.' Libby hesitated. This was the part she had been dreading. 'He told me you'd taken a mistress, that he'd heard you make an assignation with her yesterday. He said she was beautiful and elegant and very different from me.'

'Which made it all the more probable, I take it?' he said. Libby nodded miserably. 'So,' he continued, 'like one of Bluebeard's wives, you had to find out for yourself?'

She nodded.

'When you saw who my mistress was, didn't it strike you as strange?'

'I didn't know what to make of it, but you seemed to be on such intimate terms that I just didn't know what to think.'

'Well, let me give you one piece of comforting information of which you may not be aware—never, I assume, having been anyone's mistress. When one meets a woman, no matter how desirable she may be, one is extremely unlikely to be on terms of any intimacy just four days later. I promise you, taking a mistress is not unlike catching butterflies: the fun is in the chase, which is often unsuccessful and rarely brief, and when it's over one frequently wonders whether it was worth all the effort.'

Libby looked at him with startled eyes. Of all the reactions she had been prepared for, none resembled this. 'You're laughing at me,' she said uncertainly.

He smiled and raised the hand he was holding to his lips. 'Just a little,' he admitted. 'I'm also touched that you cared enough to spy on me, as you put it, and courageous enough to tell me. That can't have been easy. I'm glad you did, however, because you've unwittingly supplied me with the missing piece of this particular puzzle.'

'I don't understand.'

'Max is both shrewder and more subtle than I gave him credit for. Yesterday I drove him into Lymington to look at a cutter he said he wanted to buy. It was perfectly obvious that any such desire was of extremely recent origin. Nothing odd about that—Max has always tended to act on impulse and be prone to short-lived but violent enthusiasms. However, we happened to bump into an acquaintance of his—none other than Mademoiselle d'Angers—and I formed the distinct impression that they

were both considerably put out to discover that the lady
and I had already met. If you recall, we didn't introduce
ourselves in Southampton. Mademoiselle seized an opportunity when Max was, by a happy coincidence, out
of the room, to ask me if she could seek my advice and
meet me today at noon. I agreed, as much out of curiosity as anything else. I was unsure whether the motive
was to have me ambushed on the way there—and, to
defeat that, I made sure I had Fratton with me—or
whether it was to leave you unprotected—and that was
why Rupert spent the day with you.'

'Did she ask your advice?'

'Oh, yes. She claimed Max had proposed to her, but
she was uncertain whether to accept because he was
so..."erratic" was her word. She wanted to know
whether it ran in the family.'

'What did you tell her?'

'I said the Asthalls were notoriously erratic, very unreliable, and are no longer received in the best circles.'

'Did she believe you?'

'I haven't the slightest idea. I don't think she cared
two hoots. I was surprised at the time that instead of
wishing to be closeted with me in a private parlour to
discuss such a personal matter she preferred a more
public walk on the quayside where we would naturally
be seen by almost anyone entering the town, and where
we could be very easily overheard. It seems that being
seen was precisely what she intended.'

Libby looked bemused. 'I'm not sure I follow you.'

'Max gets me to Lymington where an assignation is
arranged. He then sows the seed of doubt in your mind,
knowing that there's a good chance you'll persuade
Rupert to take you to Lymington or, alternatively, you
might have ridden there with a groom. If you don't rise
to the bait, nothing's lost. If you do, you see me with
an extremely beautiful woman—and, yes, she did
conduct herself in a way that would lead most observers
to assume an intimacy that was entirely lacking—and

you return to Chase seething with doubts and un-
certainties, and then one of two things happens. Either
you cry off, or you tackle me about it and I resent, very
loudly and very strongly, the interference in my private
life before we are even married; there's a tremendous
row and we agree that we're not really suited. It must
have come as a shock to both of them to realise that you
would recognise Héloise, but they wouldn't have had time
to concoct anything else because Max came home with
me and certainly had no time to talk to her. He couldn't
ride over to warn her today because he had first to plant
the idea in your mind.'

'He wouldn't need to if he was going to cancel the
whole thing,' Libby pointed out.

'You misjudge Max. He wouldn't want to forgo the
pleasure of needling you even if it was unlikely to lead
on to anything else.' He laughed. 'If I'd known all this
I shouldn't have hurried back,' he said.

'Why did you?'

'Because no attack had been made on me, and I was
anxious to see whether you were all right.'

It was the last answer Libby had expected, and her
eyes flew to his face. 'Really?' she asked.

'Yes, really,' he told her. 'Libby, your welfare is my
prime concern. When Max discovers there has been no
falling out, he will try something else and, remember,
we also know he needs to get us away from Chase. We
shall have to play things by ear. Libby, will you trust
me?'

'I'm ashamed that I haven't been doing so,' she said.

He lifted her hand and turned it palm upwards. Then
he kissed the palm gently, his grey eyes smiling at her
over her fingers. 'I shall be glad when all this is over,'
he said. 'In the meantime, I can only beg you to follow
my lead.'

Libby lowered her eyes and then glanced out shyly
from beneath their lashes. 'I shall endeavour to do so,
my lord,' she promised.

He grinned. 'Very demure. I wonder how long it will
last?'

* * *

Max came down to dinner in high good humour, but his eyes narrowed as he detected the undeniable warmth with which Marcus and Libby greeted each other.

'I hear Rupert took you for a drive,' he commented as Libby took her seat.

Libby gave him the benefit of a particularly radiant smile. 'Wasn't it kind of him? Do you know, I hadn't yet seen Lymington? Lord Wilcote didn't seem to think the drive would tire me too much, so he took me. You told me Marcus had gone there, if you remember, and Lord Wilcote thought there was a very good chance we should bump into him, and so it proved. And not only Marcus. We also bumped into someone we had met in Southampton. A very strange coincidence.'

Max's smile disappeared as he studied their faces and detected no sign of self-consciousness or apprehension on any of them. 'Yes, wasn't it?' he agreed grudgingly, and lapsed into a sullen silence which seemed to affect his previously keen appetite. He took no part in the ensuing conversation, which ranged superficially over such fascinating topics as Libby's comparison of Lord Charlbury's team with that of Lord Wilcote, whether the weather had been better when she went to Southampton, and the contrasting merits of various game-birds as items of food. Max's scowl deepened as it became apparent that his attempt to create a rift between Libby and his brother had been counter-productive, to put it mildly. Of course, they might have been play-acting, but he didn't think so; apart from anything else, there was no reason why they should. After all, Marcus had no way of knowing Héloise's real reason for meeting him, and Libby wasn't foolish enough to anger him by repeating what Max had told her. He thought he knew Marcus well enough to guess that it would have been he who cried off, Chase notwithstanding, if he learned that Libby had been spying on him. Very high in the instep, Marcus; one knocked his pride at one's own risk.

The plan clearly having failed, Max was going to have to devise some other scheme to get rid of guests who were fast becoming unwelcome. Time was running out, and it was hard to know what to do for the best. He was going to have to spend some time in Southampton soon, and life would be a great deal easier if he could see the Chase end of things tidied up before he did so. It would be one thing less to worry about.

'I was talking to Fencott today,' he began. Fencott was the estate's general handyman, one of those useful people who could turn his hand to almost any task and was kept fully employed doing just that. 'He says he could start doing over the turret rooms the day after tomorrow and then work through the house from there.' Max looked across at Libby. 'He asked if you'd mind choosing another room for the time being, and I said he needn't worry because you were going to Byfield.'

Marcus opened his mouth to speak, but Libby stopped him with a gesture. 'Now that was rather naughty, Max,' she said, speaking to him as if he were five years old. 'You know perfectly well we've discussed this before and, quite apart from the fact that I like the turret room as it is, I have no intention of removing to Byfield—which Marcus knows I don't like half as much as Chase—and, even if I were prepared to go, it would be a complete waste of time and—more importantly—money, because I've already formed very firm ideas about what I want to do to the house once I'm the Viscountess, and I don't suppose they coincide with your ideas at all.'

Lord Charlbury listened to this deplorable exchange with some satisfaction, and decided it was time to add fuel to the smouldering fire.

'I think we may safely leave any changes at Chase in Lady Charlbury's competent hands,' he said. 'Libby is probably too shy to mention it herself, but we've agreed to marry with the minimum of further delay, and we shall take up residence at Chase immediately after the ceremony.'

Libby, who had been under a precisely opposite impression, stared at him open-mouthed, but Lord Wilcote merely looked from one to the other of the three

protagonists without comment. Libby's expression of ·
surprise was not lost upon Max. He laughed shortly.

'I don't think shyness had much to do with it,' he
said. 'Judging by the expression on her face, she knew
nothing about it.'

'Not at all,' Libby butted in to retrieve her position.
'My surprise is due merely to the fact that I hadn't
realised the news was to be made public.' She turned to
Lord Charlbury, her dark eyes wide with appeal. 'I had
so wanted a quiet wedding, my lord,' she said
reproachfully.

'I should prefer it myself,' he replied blandly. 'But
when I'd given the matter more thought, I realised I'd
be doing you a grave disservice by making arrangements
which the uncharitable might castigate as hole-in-the-
corner. I'm not at all ashamed of you, you know,' he
added magnanimously. 'Indeed, I rather think we shall
deal well together.'

'You overwhelm me, my lord,' Libby retorted tartly,
but her lord continued unmoved, as if she hadn't spoken.

'I don't contemplate a *large* wedding,' he went on.
'Simply one to which most of our acquaintance may be
invited. I imagine a week from today will be too early
to have made all the arrangements, but a fortnight should
give us enough time, don't you think?'

'As you wish, my lord,' Libby replied meekly, maintaining the appearance of outward compliance while her
mind wrestled with this about-turn. It appeared Lord
Charlbury was now anxious to bring matters to a head,
to goad his brother into some sort of action. Which,
Libby thought indignantly, was all very well, but she
seemed to be the one most at risk and it would have been
pleasant to have been consulted.

'I suppose you expect me to get out of the house by
then?' Max said angrily.

'I've no desire to put you to the slightest inconvenience,' his brother replied. 'But I must admit that
Libby and I would rather like the place to ourselves for
a few weeks.'

'To make adjustments to our new situation, you know,' Libby added sweetly, at the same time casting a fulminating look upon her betrothed.

'Precisely,' he agreed, inclining his head slightly in accordance.

Max's manner became increasingly agitated. It was as if he was casting about wildly for an answer to a problem he alone comprehended. He had the unpleasant feeling that a situation over which he had previously had control was now running away from him. With an effort, he forced himself into a semblance of rational behaviour and good manners.

'You will realise this comes as a complete surprise,' he said. 'It leaves me little time to make my own arrangements. You'll have to forgive me, but I must go to Southampton tomorrow. I may be away for two or three days.'

'There's no need for you to make arrangements yourself. You're welcome to make Byfield your home until something more suitable can be found,' Lord Charlbury answered.

'Thank you, Marcus,' his brother said stiffly. 'I'd prefer not to be beholden. Excuse me.' And he rose to his feet.

'As you please.' Lord Charlbury's tone was off-hand, and his shrug underlined his seeming indifference.

There was silence for several minutes after the door closed behind the Honourable Max Asthall. It was broken by Lord Wilcote.

'Do I conclude that William Fratton will have business in Southampton for the next few days?' he asked.

'It seems probable,' answered his host. 'I must advise him to get a good night's rest, since I imagine he will need to make an early start, added to which I think he may not have a very comfortable time for a few days. Excuse me while I check the bedding-down of my horses.'

'An excuse which, among a wider audience, would cause instant suspicion,' Libby remarked. 'It's probably the first time he's done such a thing.'

'On the contrary,' Lord Wilcote contradicted her. 'It's one of those facets of Marcus's nature that never fails to surprise one, but he almost invariably does check his horses.'

'But not, I fancy, when he will shortly be driving them back home.'

'That point had, I admit, escaped me.'

When Lord Charlbury returned and found them still sitting at the dinner table, he expressed surprise that they had not withdrawn. Fratton, it seemed, would have business in Southampton on the morrow, and Lord Charlbury wondered whether Lord Wilcote's Connor would take over Fratton's equine duties for a day or two.

'I'm sure he will,' his friend said. 'And how do you propose to dispose of our time?'

'You may do as you please, Rupert. I shall return to Chase after breakfast. Libby, don't go anywhere without letting someone know where, how and by what route—preferably me or Rupert, but, failing us, Nurse or Mrs Chadlington. I think we can trust both of them. Above all, do, I pray you, be careful.'

'Oh, I shall,' she answered. 'Especially since I'm so soon to become a real Viscountess. I shall stay in my room and sew. That should be safe enough.'

He laughed. 'I was sorry to take you so much by surprise, but you retrieved your position admirably.' He put his fingers under her chin and raised her head so that he was looking down into her eyes. 'Make sure your needle isn't enchanted. Remember the fate of the Sleeping Beauty.'

'It was a spindle that caused all the upheaval, I believe, and I don't spin, so I should be safe enough. However, rest assured that in that event I shall depend upon you to be Prince Florimond.' She rose to leave the room, and found he had taken her hand. He raised it to his lips.

'The thought has certain charms,' he said softly, and accompanied her to the door. 'As I recollect, propriety—or the plot—did not oblige him to confine his attention to her hand.' Whereupon, ignoring the presence of Lord Wilcote, he kissed her full on the mouth.

Libby, blushing rosily, knew that propriety dictated that she should protest. 'I don't believe the story said anything about his having an opportunity to practise,' she said.

'Which is where I have the advantage,' he replied.

'Trying to force the issue, Marcus?' Lord Wilcote enquired when the door had closed behind her.

'Better than wondering what will happen next, and when.'

'Possibly—but potentially more dangerous, don't you think?'

'In that it excludes the remote possibility of a convenient but genuine Act of God, yes. On the other hand, it concentrates the activities into two weeks, and then this uncertainty will be done away with forever.'

'Why not tell Max what you know, and ship him abroad? We can find employment for him in India. Denmead would be happy to be of service in that respect.'

'What do we know? We have strong suspicions coupled with a great deal of corroborative evidence, but no positive proof. Besides, the Boshams tie in somewhere and I want to know where.'

'I thought you already had suspicions on that score?'

'I've suspicions as to why he goes to the Spliced Mainbrace, but they're not enough to account for the active role Tom Bosham has played. Somewhere there's a piece of the puzzle missing.' Lord Charlbury sat deep in thought for a long time. When he spoke again, his voice still held its speculative tone. 'Max was in the stables tonight,' he said.

'Checking his horses?' Lord Wilcote enquired. 'After all, you do.'

'He, however, does not.'

'Did he hear you talking to Fratton?'

'No. He came out of the tackroom as I arrived, and crossed to the house. Deep in the sulks, of course. He can't have failed to see me, but he chose not to speak. I thought he might be leaving instructions for the morning, but no one other than Fratton was there. He says Max muttered something about having left a whip behind. He was certainly carrying one when I saw him going back to the house.'

'I'd not have thought it a sufficiently important item to warrant fetching it at night.'

'Neither should I, but I can't think of any more sinister reason for going there, so I remind myself that Max's behaviour isn't always rational these days. Let's hope there's no more to it than that.'

Libby was nothing if not practical. When she went to bed that night, she locked the door, fastened the window-catch and, reflecting that this part of the house was far too recent to harbour secret passages or priest-holes, she nevertheless tapped on all four walls at various places to reinforce her confidence in her own judgement. Then she slept soundly. The maid who brought her chocolate in the morning was surprised that Miss Barton had to get out of bed to unlock the door, but too well trained to comment.

When she came down to the breakfast-parlour, it was obvious that Max had breakfasted and gone. The previous day's long drive and a night's deep sleep had given her a healthy appetite. Libby lifted the lids of the array of chafing dishes. The Dowager had often re-marked acidly on her unfeminine partiality for strongly spiced foods but, in a household which had for years catered exclusively for male tastes, Mrs Chadlington saw nothing amiss in her future mistress's preferences and always ensured there was something to take her fancy. This morning, Libby noted with pleasure, there were her favourite devilled kidneys as well as kedgeree, eggs and ham, and she was not the least influenced in her decision by the fact that, if devilled kidneys were provided, she had no hesitation in eating them as often as they appeared. She took a generous helping and a smaller one of mushrooms by way of a complement, and sat down to her meal with a pleasant degree of pleasurable anticipation.

Minutes later her body was seized with the most excruciating pains. Doubled over and retching wildly, she struggled to the bell.

By the time the bell had been answered and a terrified housemaid had fetched Mrs Chadlington and Nurse, Libby writhed, retching and vomiting, on the floor.

CHAPTER TWELVE

FRATTON arrived very early at Chase, ostensibly with a message for the housekeeper, and was therefore ideally situated to observe Max's departure. Since no one doubted his claim to be going to Southampton—for if he went elsewhere the whole chain of circumstances broke down—the groom made no particular haste to follow him. For much of the route he would be able to travel unseen through the forest, keeping a thickness of trees between himself and his quarry, but there were places which must be crossed and which afforded no cover so that anyone following would be clearly seen. So Fratton gave Max a good head-start, intending not to close the gap until Totton, at least, had been reached. Once they were among the heavy traffic heading towards Southampton, he could safely ride closer, but once they were within the confines of the city walls he would have to maintain a precarious balance: on the one hand he would need to stay close enough to Max not to lose him in the crowds; on the other, he must be sufficiently far from him to obviate the risk of being seen.

Anyone who was only superficially acquainted with William Fratton would have dismissed him as phlegmatic and stolid, a reliable and loyal servant but an unimaginative one, and this was, indeed, the face he normally chose to present to the world. It was deceptive. Fratton was capable of making rapid decisions and acting on them promptly, as well as with discretion and subtlety. His interests were those of his employer, and that gentleman knew he could repose full confidence in his groom.

A man in the stews of Southampton might very probably be robbed, but a man on horseback, while he would be safer, would also draw unwarranted attention to himself. Fratton expected Max to leave his horse at the Dolphin, and was surprised when they passed that hostelry without his doing so. Instead, he rode into the yard of a much meaner establishment, soon afterwards emerging on foot.

This put Fratton in a predicament. He must follow Max, and on foot; if he returned to the Dolphin he might well lose him, but if he baited his horse here he risked the certainty of Max's recognising it when he came to fetch his own horse—a risk far greater than at the Dolphin, where bloodstock was a normal sight and there the stabling was on such a scale as to make any one animal less noticeable.

As he hesitated momentarily, an urchin tugged at his stirrup.

"Old yer 'oss, sir?' he said.

Fratton tossed him a sixpence. 'You take him to the Dolphin and hand him over to the ostler,' he said. 'Stay there till I come for him and there'll be another shilling in it.' The ostler would recognise one of Lord Charlbury's cattle, and the promised shilling would ensure the urchin's honesty.

The boy, who saw himself earning in a few easy hours enough to keep him in the lap of his sort of luxury for a week—not to mention any largesse that might come his way while he waited at the Dolphin—accepted the task with alacrity and counted himself lucky.

Max was some way ahead by now, but Fratton was able to catch a glimpse of his hat just before it turned down a back alley, and he hastened to follow it. In these winding lanes and alleys it was difficult to keep his object in sight without being close enough to be spotted himself. Many of the backways were unfrequented, and Fratton feared his footsteps would be heard. But Max trod swiftly through the noisome stews, oblivious to all but his own concerns.

At last he turned from a narrow passage into a relatively open and busy street, and Fratton saw that the Spliced Mainbrace stood ahead. He was not at all sur-

prised to see Max enter its insalubrious portals, but he
did not immediately follow him.

The last time he had been here, the tavern had been
crowded and he had been able to slip both in and out
unobserved. Had he known at that time that the landlady
at the Mainbrace was a former Byfield servant, he might
not have taken that risk. Now he did know it, and knew,
moreover, that his visit was likely to be a long one. Nor
could he expect the tavern to be so crowded at this hour
in the morning. There was a very slight chance that Milly
Radlett would not recognise him when he ordered, but
not to order would be certain, except in very crowded
conditions, to draw a very close scrutiny upon himself.

Pulling his hat down over his eyes and turning up his
coat collar, Fratton opened the door cautiously. The
tavern was better patronised, despite the hour, than he
had anticipated, but it was by no means full. Of Milly
there was no sign. It was Tom Bosham who stood behind
the bar. There seemed to be no other serving staff. There
was no sign of the Honourable Max Asthall, either. There
was an outside chance Bosham would recognise him as
the groom at the church, though it was unlikely he had
seen enough of him from the back of the church to
identify him now and in a place where his presence was
not expected. The risk was sufficiently small to be worth
taking. Fratton entered and sat down on a settle beside
the smoking fire. From this position he was secluded
and had no view of the entrance to the alehouse, but he
could see the door beyond the bar quite clearly. It was
the only other door off the taproom. If Max was not in
the taproom, then that was where he had gone.

Tom Bosham bought his ordered tankard of oyster
stout and pocketed the coppers without comment or
interest. So far, so good. Fratton made himself
comfortable in the corner of the settle to observe events.
He was likely to be here for a long time.

Between the smoke from the fire, which seemed to
waft across the room more often than it escaped up the
chimney, and the pall of tobacco smoke that hung across
the taproom, he found himself trying to see through a

bluish haze which hurt the eyes and made him realise that, while it aided his own inconspicuousness, it necessitated great alertness if he were not to miss anything. The strangeness of the atmosphere was enhanced by the sound-dampening effect of sawdust on the floor, which deadened footsteps, and by the same strange, sweet, sickly smell that he had caught before.

Suddenly, that particular part of the atmosphere increased as the door behind the bar opened and Milly Radlett—as Fratton still thought of her—came out. She whispered something to her husband, who screwed his face into a grimace of annoyance before disappearing through the door, leaving Milly in charge. Fratton lowered his head and rested it, thoughtfully, upon his hand which, more effectively than his hat, shaded the upper part of his face from such light as was thrown by the flames that struggled through the smoke.

He had only a short time to wait before the door opened again and Max emerged reluctantly, propelled by Tom Bosham towards the outer door. Just behind Fratton's settle, and therefore where he could not see, he guessed Max to have turned intransigent and refused to go on, for they stopped there and Max, in a voice so low that the listening groom could barely identify it, said something he couldn't make out. The tone, however, was urgent, and the relative clarity of Tom Bosham's reply suggested he was less reluctant to be heard than his guest.

'You owes me money, Mr Honourable Asthall, and there's naught in the back room for them as don't pay their dues,' the landlord said, and his tone was menacing.

Max's nerves were stretched to such a pitch that he found it hard to control his voice, with the result that he became increasingly easy to hear.

'It's only a matter of time, Bosham. You know that,' he said. 'My chances of inheriting the estate increase with every day that passes. In fact,' he added, 'I've good reason to believe they're better at this precise moment than they have been at any time since the old man died.'

'Oh, yes, and what makes you so certain sure?'

'Never you mind. You know too much already. But think you, even if I don't get the estate, there's always the other matter. That will pay well. Not as well as the inheritance, I grant you, but well enough to clear my debts to you, and more.'

'I don't doubt it,' replied Bosham. 'But it hasn't come off yet, and a hundred things could stop it. It's a chancy do at best. What's more, we won't know when it will come off, do we? Could be next week, could be next month, and it wouldn't surprise me if it was next year— or never.'

Max became more agitated. Fratton, unable to see him, nevertheless received the impression he might be looking furtively around, for there was a pause before he spoke.

'Not long now,' Max whispered, barely audible, and Fratton had to strain every nerve to catch his next words. 'The tides and the moon are both right next week.'

'Next week!' the landlord exclaimed. 'But there's a houseful of people up at Chase! How can the matter go ahead while they're there?'

'They'll be gone, I promise you. One way or another I shall be rid of them in time.' Max's voice took on a renewed urgency. 'Let me into your back room, Bosham. I'm in no fit state to ride, you can see that. It was hard enough getting here. I wish to God I could be shot of the damned stuff. Let me in, Bosham. I've got to get to Lymington to say that all's in train. Do you want to risk it now for the sake of a couple of guineas?'

Tom Bosham looked him up and down. The Honourable Max Asthall was certainly in an increasingly unfit state to do anything, and it was in everyone's interests to keep him more or less competent. He led him back to the room behind the bar and once again, as the door opened and shut, the smoke-laden atmosphere subtly shifted and sweetened.

William Fratton stayed a while longer, turning over in his mind what he had heard. It looked as if he had found out Bosham's hold over young Mr Asthall: plain, old-fashioned debt. He debated whether to stay in the tavern and follow Max to Lymington, but since that must

mean he would be seeing that Frenchwoman, and since
Lord Charlbury had wanted the full strength of the
Bosham link explained, not the one with Mademoiselle
d'Angers, which he said he knew, Fratton decided there
was little point in risking discovery by staying. In any
case, it would be much more difficult to remain incon-
spicuous in Lymington. Accordingly, he drained his
tankard and departed, discharged his debt to the urchin,
and returned to Chase.

A servant dispatched to Byfield interrupted Lord
Charlbury at his breakfast and brought him hotfoot to
Chase. He had barely had time to throw off his caped
greatcoat and toss his beaver and gloves to Mrs
Chadlington before Dr Kennet followed him into the
house.

'What has happened?' Lord Charlbury demanded.
'What's the matter with Miss Barton? Where is she? In
her room, I assume?' And he started up the stairs, the
physician on his heels.

'Oh, no, my lord,' the housekeeper called after him.
'In the breakfast-room. We tried to get her back to her
room, but she was too bad. Nurse is with her.'

'Make sure there's a reliable groom standing by with
a horse,' the doctor demanded. 'He must be ready to
go to the apothecary as soon as I say.'

Mrs Chadlington hurried out to convey this order to
the stables, and the doctor followed Lord Charlbury into
the breakfast-room.

The smell that greeted them sent the Viscount striding
over to fling up every window in the room despite Mrs
Widford's protests.

'Rubbish!' he said. 'I can't imagine this stench is
healthier than some fresh air.'

Dr Kennet knelt over Libby's prostrate form while
Nurse hovered anxiously and a scullery-maid scuttled
about, evidently under instructions to do what she could
to clear up the successive bouts of vomiting and purging
through which Libby had passed.

Libby herself lay on the floor, a death-like pallor on
her face, her body still racked by agonising spasms,

though her stomach contractions brought nothing more up.

'Thank God she has vomited,' the doctor said. 'Quickly, Nurse. Dissolve a tablespoon of salt in a glass of water and bring it here.'

Nurse did as she was bid. Dr Kennet raised Libby's head and poured the fluid down. Almost immediately she retched and vomited, and the doctor repeated the process.

Eventually he sat back. 'I can do no more,' he said. 'Get her to her room, put her to bed and keep her warm. Persuade her to drink a little warm milk or gruel from time to time, and pray we've been in time.' He looked around the room. 'Have any of the breakfast things been cleared away?' he asked.

Mrs Chadlington had returned by now and was profuse in her apologies, but explained that they had been so concerned over Miss Barton that clearing away hadn't seemed of prime importance. It would be done immediately, she assured him, and to make good her word she nodded towards the skivvy to start clearing away.

Happily for that poor girl, who was terrified at the thought of performing any task above stairs and particularly one which provided ample opportunity to drop things, the doctor stepped in.

'No, no,' he said. 'I intended no criticism, Mrs Chadlington. Once Miss Barton is more comfortably disposed, I wish to examine the remains of the meal. Pray leave everything as it is. My lord,' he added, turning to the Viscount, 'we must move Miss Barton to her room without further delay.'

Lord Charlbury immediately picked Libby up in his arms and carried her up to her room, preceded by Nurse, who opened the door and turned back the bedclothes.

'Do you lay her down here, my lord,' she instructed him, 'and I'll undress her and make her comfortable. Mrs Chadlington,' she went on, addressing the housekeeper who had arrived at the door, 'do you get someone to make up the fire in here without more ado, and let me have a pitcher of hot water and a hot brick for Miss

Barton's feet. Off with you, my lord. There's naught you can do here, and we'll have her as right as a trivet in no time. I'll send down to the doctor when she's settled.' And she hustled him out of the room and closed the door behind him.

Lord Charlbury returned to the breakfast-room, where he found the doctor lifting the lids of the chafing dishes.

'Who would have breakfasted here, my lord?'

'Only Miss Barton and my brother.'

'As I thought. The kedgeree doesn't seem to have been touched, but the toasted ham, the eggs, the mushrooms and the kidneys have all been sampled.' He sniffed each dish in turn and then tasted small amounts. The ham, the eggs and the mushrooms provoked no comment, but the kedgeree produced a pronounced grimace and so did the devilled kidneys. 'Is Miss Barton partial to devilled kidneys, do you know, my lord?'

'Since I don't yet have the pleasure of breakfasting with the lady, I can't say, but I have observed her to like highly spiced foods in general.'

'No matter, the housekeeper will know. It's an unusual choice for a woman, but since the kedgeree is untouched it must be the kidneys.'

'If those kidneys were devilled to disguise the fact that they were no longer fresh,' Lord Charlbury exclaimed angrily, 'the cook will be dismissed forthwith with neither references nor testimonials.'

The doctor looked grave. 'Don't be in too much of a hurry to dismiss the cook, my lord. This isn't a matter of bad offal.' He paused. 'My lord, Miss Barton has been poisoned.'

Lord Charlbury stared at him, thunderstruck.

'Arsenic, my lord. Both the kidneys and the kedgeree are heavily laced with it, one presumes in anticipation that the spice will disguise the taste.'

'You seem to be implying that the arsenic was a deliberate addition.'

'It's hardly something which any cook would be likely to pick up accidentally in mistake for something else.'

There could be no disputing the doctor's logic.

'Your brother doesn't appear to have eaten the affected food. If he had, he would hardly have been in a condition to leave the premises, and he is certainly not on them. Either he didn't eat the tainted dishes or the poison was added later. Have any of the Chase servants cause to wish Miss Barton—or, indeed, your brother—ill?'

'I should hardly have thought so,' the Viscount replied, having his own ideas on the subject—ideas which he had no intention of sharing with the doctor. 'I suppose one can never be entirely certain.'

'Quite so. Forgive me, my lord, for referring to something which I would not normally consider to be any of my concern, but the terms of your uncle's Will are well known locally.'

Lord Charlbury turned to look at the doctor. That gentleman caught his eye and held it. Their understanding was mutual—and tacit.

'Tell me, my lord; would I be right to assume that arsenic is kept in the stables at Chase?'

Lord Charlbury stared at him. 'Almost certainly, I should think. The Byfield stables are never without it and neither, I imagine, are any other well-run stables in the country. It is, after all, the standard physic for poor doers.'

'Precisely, my lord. Shall you check?'

'Naturally. I feel bound to point out, however, that its mere presence will not tell me whether the level is lower than it was yesterday, and its absence will not necessarily mean it wasn't there yesterday.'

'Quite so. These matters, however, become of considerable importance if Miss Barton should die.'

Lord Charlbury was startled. 'You believe her to be that badly affected?'

'I dare not overlook the possibility. Fortunately, so much arsenic was added that I doubt if she could have tolerated more than one mouthful—a very bungling, amateur job, if I may say so—but she has swallowed enough to give grave cause for concern. She's by no means out of the wood yet, and it will be some time before I'll be able to pronounce myself happy about her.'

'If at all, it would appear.'

'If at all, my lord.'

Dr Kennet visited his patient once more before taking leave of the Viscount and promising to return that evening unless his attendance was deemed necessary before then, in which case he undertook to return as soon as he was summoned.

His departure left Lord Charlbury deep in thought. There was no doubt in his mind that it was Max who had attempted to poison Libby—and who might yet succeed. He recalled his brother's unwonted visit to the stables the previous night—to the harness-room where medicaments as well as tack were stored. That the doctor tacitly shared his suspicions, he had no doubt. Proof of Max's guilt was another thing altogether, and his brother's odd temper was such that it was unlikely that, faced with such evidence as he had, he would do anything other than laugh the accusations to scorn and be on his guard thenceforth because he would know he was suspected.

No, Max could not be confronted until there was absolute proof—or unless Libby died, in which case he would have to voice his suspicions. On the contrary, care must be taken to give Max no cause to think his actions were in any way suspect. For the time being the blame must be placed fair and square on the kidneys, unjust as it was to a very good cook. Fortunately the cook had served the late Earl—who had had an unfashionably high opinion of the merits of female domestic staff at all levels—for many years and, while she would be deeply offended at the slur on the care with which she selected meat, was unlikely to serve notice or take herself off in a huff.

Cook's professional sensitivities notwithstanding, he must ensure that no one but Nurse handled any food which was intended for Libby, at any level of its preparation, until she was sufficiently recovered to be removed to Byfield.

If, indeed, she recovered at all. Now that he faced that thought alone, without the need to present a confident,

assured demeanour to the world, he found it an unexpectedly bleak prospect, and it had nothing to do with
losing Chase. He had proposed to Libby because she
had conveniently fitted all his uncle's criteria and, in
addition, he had found her to be a restful woman with
whom he judged it would be no great penance to be
united and, if her company proved to pall, he would
always be able to find some pretext to be gone for a few
days. Doubtless a married Viscount Charlbury would
have very little more difficulty in finding alternative
company than the single one would have done. That had
been the frame of mind in which he had proposed to
her. He had been surprised to find himself quite shocked
by the discovery that she had not dismissed out of hand
Max's malicious story that he had already taken a
mistress. He supposed he should regard it as flattering
that she had not accepted that situation with equanimity, but when he had driven back to Byfield he had
been very angry that she should have been put in a situation which caused her distress. He had told himself
that this was because Libby had done nothing to deserve
such a deliberate attempt to make her unhappy, and that
reason had been perfectly satisfactory—yesterday. Today,
suddenly, he realised that, while his anger was still on
Libby's behalf, it was for the more subjective reason that
he didn't want her hurt than for the objective one of
whether or not she deserved it.

He had come to know Libby very well indeed during
the last few weeks, and had learnt that there was far
more to her than simply a restful woman who had the
necessary qualities to win him Chase. Above all, she had
the ability to make him smile, even at his own expense,
and she never took herself too seriously; she was forth-
right—sometimes uncomfortably so—and her practical
common sense was allied to a certain innocence that he
had no wish to see destroyed. And now he stood to lose
her. He had lost Maria-Giulietta all those years ago. He
had been young and distraught and had wished the world
would come to an end, taking him with it. As the years
had passed, he had pushed those memories to the outside

corners of his mind, only bringing them forward when he measured another woman against his recollections of Maria-Giulietta and found the new one wanting. Libby, he suddenly realised, was the first woman he had met with whom he had not made that comparison. He supposed the reason was that he had never imagined himself in love with her or even accepted the possibility. He had taken her for herself; at no time had he ever felt for her anything remotely resembling the grand passion he had felt for his wife, yet, if Libby died now, he knew he would grieve as much for her as he ever had for that Italian beauty.

And if she lived? What then? Several people had expressed the opinion that she had fallen in love with him. She had said as much herself but, if she had, she disguised it well. His experience of women who fancied themselves in love was one of sighs and languishing glances, of fluttering eyelashes and a limpet-like tendency to cling. Libby did none of these things. No, that wasn't quite true. She sometimes fluttered her eyelashes, but they both knew it was consciously deliberate and designed to mock. Only when he had kissed her had he sensed that those who knew her might be right, and he now cursed the conventions that limited the opportunities by which an honourable man could further his more intimate acquaintance with his future wife. It was, he thought bitterly, a singularly stupid convention—after all, with what woman was it more important to become intimately acquainted? If Libby recovered—— No, he corrected himself, *when* Libby recovered he must endeavour to discover the extent of her true feelings for him and persuade her that he no longer regarded their marriage as one of convenience. He rather thought the latter task would be the more difficult, if only because Libby would be quite sure that his motive was to make her feel better about it.

He turned from the window. Enough of this. Soul-searching was an enervating pastime and a luxury in which he could not afford to indulge. There was too much to be done. He dispatched a groom to Byfield with a message for Lord Wilcote, informing his guest that he would be staying at Chase for the rest of the day and inviting him to join him if he were so inclined. He found he had no appetite for the light repast prepared by the cook for luncheon, and shortly afterwards he betook himself upstairs, and tapped on Libby's door.

Nurse opened it and, her finger to her lips to enjoin him to silence, gestured for him to enter. Libby slept, her features no longer distorted by pain but her face still deathly pale. He looked his question at his old nurse.

'I think she'll do, my lord,' she whispered. 'But it'll be a close-run thing. What was the cause, do you think?'

'The devilled kidneys, I imagine,' he replied truthfully.

Mrs Widford looked at him in silence for a few seconds before commenting. 'It do be strange how a person can suddenly develop an aversion to something they've always enjoyed.'

'It is, indeed,' he replied. That's it! he thought. A sudden aversion would answer the case without offending the cook. God bless Nurse!

'Miss Barton does seem prone to accidents,' that worthy woman went on.

'She certainly does,' he agreed. 'We must take greater care of her. As soon as you and Dr Kennet think she's well enough to travel, we will move her to Byfield.'

'A very good idea, my lord. It had already crossed my mind to suggest it. And shall you tell Mr Max of your intention? Or simply about her sudden aversion?'

'Just the latter for the time being, Nurse. After all, we don't yet know whether Miss Barton will recover, do we?'

'That we do not, my lord.'

Lord Wilcote rode over to Chase during the afternoon, and listened in silence while his friend related the events of the morning. Having heard the whole, he agreed that Libby must be moved away from Max's sphere of activity as soon as possible.

When William Fratton returned from Southampton, Lord Wilcote was still with Lord Charlbury in the study and the groom was instructed to wait upon his employer there. When he saw Lord Wilcote, he paused on the threshold, uncertain of the extent to which that young man was in his friend's confidence.

'Come in, man,' the Viscount urged. 'You may speak quite freely in front of Lord Wilcote. He knows where you've been and why.'

Fratton told him in meticulous detail what he had seen and heard, not forgetting to explain why he had returned rather than follow Mr Asthall to Lymington.

Lord Charlbury nodded. 'You judged correctly,' he said. 'That link seems clear. I should perhaps tell you that Miss Barton was taken very ill shortly after breakfast. It's being put about that she has suddenly developed an aversion to kidneys.'

The groom's face was expressionless. 'If you say so, me lord,' he said. 'It's none of my business, of course, me lord, but would I be right in thinking that you yourself are of a different mind?'

'As you say, William, it's none of your business,' the Viscount answered amiably. 'I should, however, be most grateful if you'd check whether there's arsenic in the harness-room.'

'Don't need to, me lord. There is. That peacocky bay of Mr Max's is a dreadful bad doer. His groom sprinkles some on his mash most days. Swears that's the only way he keeps any body on him at all.'

'See whether or not it's still there. If it is, try to find out whether there's less than there should be.'

'Yes, me lord. The first will be easy done. The second's impossible, as like as not. I doubt if Mr Max's groom keeps that close an eye.'

'I'm sure you're right, but see what you can find out, all the same—and thank you for your excellent work today. Where would I be without you?'

'To tell you the truth, me lord, I've often wondered that meself.'

The Viscount laughed as the door closed behind his groom. Lord Wilcote looked concerned.

'You give that man too much licence, Marcus,' he said. 'He's too dashed familiar. My grandmother says if we

don't keep them in their place we'll be having a revolution of our own—tumbrils and all that, you know.'

'Do you share the Dowager's views? Many do.'

'No, I don't. More significantly, neither does my
father, and he's usually right. But that don't alter the
fact that Fratton's a dashed sight too familiar. I've
observed it before.'

'Of course he is, and a more loyal servant I'd go a
long way to find. He taught me to ride and he's helped
me out of innumerable scrapes ever since I was a child.
Indeed, it looks as if he's still trying to do so. He takes
a sort of proprietorial interest in my well-being and yes,
sometimes he oversteps the mark. But he knows when
he's done so, and it's a very small price to pay for such
loyalty. In this instance I think he really has brought us
the last pieces of the puzzle.'

'How do you now see the final picture?'

'Something like this. Max, for what reasons I know
not, has developed a taste for opium. There are dens in
any maritime port, and Southampton's no exception.
Why he ever took it up in the first place we shall probably
never know. Surely he didn't find life so intolerable that
the dreams induced by the drug were preferable?
Whatever the reason, his addiction explains his strange
moods as well as his frequent visits to Southampton. I
almost feel I'd prefer his moods to be due to madness.'

'No, you wouldn't,' his friend said bluntly. 'You'd
always have the fear that the insanity might run in the
family. Opium won't.'

'Thank you, Rupert—the voice of down-to-earth
sanity, if ever I heard it. I'll bear your comment in mind.'
He laughed, but it was a laugh of relief rather than
humour, and Lord Wilcote didn't join in.

'So Max has become addicted and must pay for his
addiction,' Lord Charlbury continued. 'I've no idea to
what extent they've fleeced him, but his own income is
very small. It's perhaps his misfortune that the den he
frequents belongs to someone in a position to know what
his expectations may be. One can live very well upon
expectations,' he added wryly.

'For a time, at least,' his companion commented.

'As you so rightly say, Rupert, for a time, at least. Max hoped to be left Chase if he could persuade the Earl he was a fitting heir, and he worked hard to that end. Perhaps he convinced the Boshams it was a certainty.' Lord Charlbury paused. 'I wonder if he borrowed money from them as well as owing them for the drug? No matter. It's enough that he owes them money at all. Then he meets a dashing Frenchwoman—whether fortuitously or whether the Boshams, knowing Mademoiselle's requirements, point her in his direction, I don't know, though I'm disinclined to set too much store by coincidence. There's money available—and possibly the favours of Mademoiselle—to anyone who aids the Corsican in his plans. Max now has two possible sources of income—the estate, and Bonaparte. When the Will is read he realises that Chase may slip out of his hands—and Chase is what he really wants. His immediate course of action is to have me waylaid on the road to Copthorne. Had that been successful, his worries would have been over. I wonder if he would then have dropped the treason?'

The Viscount lapsed briefly into silence while he turned this futile speculation over in his mind. Rupert said nothing. The Asthalls could live down opium addiction, even insanity. Treason was another matter.

'I don't imagine he realised I would so quickly find a woman who fitted the Earl's requirements,' Lord Charlbury went on. 'I have to admit I was surprised myself. Max had to stop the marriage or at the very least delay it until the six months had elapsed. I presume he took the Boshams into his confidence. Milly remembered the gossip. They didn't know exactly what had happened to my wife, but that didn't matter. If she was alive, I couldn't marry. If she had died abroad I would find it impossible to prove in the present state of hostilities, and if I hadn't actually married her at all I should have had some difficulty proving I hadn't. In other words, there was a very good chance of stopping it altogether. When it seemed possible I was going to be able to overset the odds, a clumsy attempt was made to eliminate Libby. Now a more drastic attempt has been made, and will, I most desperately hope, fail.'

'You forced his hand, Marcus.'

'Yes, I did. I confess if I'd realised how suddenly and how drastically he would move, I might have handled it differently. I'd hoped merely to push him to Southampton and, by having him followed, find out precisely how involved he was. I hope Libby may be induced to forgive me,' he added.

'I think you need have no fear on that score,' Rupert assured him. 'Libby has depths of resolution that never fail to surprise me. Ten to one she'll think it capital sport.'

Lord Charlbury laughed. 'I question your odds, Rupert, but I've no doubt she will own herself quite diverted by the whole affair.'

'What will you do now?'

'That's the problem. First, Libby must be removed from Chase. Then I must tackle Max. If there is any way whereby I can scotch his involvement in this invasion scheme, I must do so. If I fail, I have no choice but to place all I know before Sir John Bere and pray for his discretion.'

When Lord Charlbury looked in on Libby later, he was pleased to see her sleeping peacefully, though still paler than she should have been, and when Dr Kennet paid his promised visit he confirmed that the patient was progressing better than he had anticipated and that if she continued to go on well he would no longer fear for her life.

'Keep her on bland food—the milk and gruel are ideal,' he said. 'I've every expectation that she will make a full recovery now. She is, after all, a strong, healthy young woman not given, I imagine, to dwelling upon ill-health. She'll pull herself through, given proper nursing. I've no doubt that Mrs Widford will see that she gets exactly that.'

'You may depend upon it,' Nurse answered, curtsying respectfully.

Dr Kennet had barely left the premises when a clatter of hoofs on the gravelled driveway announced the return of the Honourable Max Asthall. He came into the house in high, good spirits, his normally pallid cheeks almost flushed. He flung his gloves and beaver on to a side-table, and tossed his cape beside them.

'Was that old Dr Kennet I saw riding away?' he asked.

His brother confirmed that it was.

'What did he want? Nothing amiss, is there? Lord knows I'm ravenous. I'll be glad to eat.'

'Dr Kennet came to attend to Libby.'

'Libby? What's happened to Libby?' Max laughed. 'Let me guess—she's dropped dead on you, Marcus, and left you without a wife to gain you the inheritance. Poetic justice if ever I saw it.' He laughed again, a wild glint in his eye.

His brother looked at him, unsmiling. 'I really don't feel the entrance is the place for this conversation,' he commented crushingly. 'I suggest we retire to the study.' He led the way upstairs. The door closed behind them, and Max took a chair opposite Lord Wilcote, who acknowledged his arrival but appeared otherwise enthralled in a book. Good manners should have dictated his removal elsewhere, but he knew that, at least initially, Marcus would like him there: Max's reactions these days were often open to more than one interpretation.

'I don't know whether your comment about Miss Barton was intended as a joke,' Lord Charlbury said stonily. 'If so, then it was in execrable taste. She is extremely ill.'

When he answered, Max's voice was all solicitude, but the gleam in his eye did not escape his brother's notice. 'Extremely ill, you say? How extreme? Not dangerously so, I hope.'

'Dr Kennet isn't sure. We must await events,' Lord Charlbury equivocated.

'What's the matter with her? It must have been very sudden. I didn't see her before I left, but she was in perfectly good health yesterday, dashing about the countryside with Rupert and deciding to change everything at Chase, as I recall.'

'Dear me! Do you know, I'd formed the distinct impression that it was you who were planning alterations—to the turret room in particular, I seem to remember. Wasn't there something about suggesting I should take Libby to Brighton—or was it Bath—while the work was executed? That suggests rather extensive alterations. Your memory appears to be a shade unreliable, Max.'

It struck Lord Charlbury that his deliberate failure to answer Max's question had left his brother a trifle on edge. Certainly the high spirits with which he had entered the house were fast evaporating.

'Are you avoiding the issue, Marcus?' he asked. 'What *is* the matter with Miss Barton?'

'Why should I avoid the issue? I merely sought to establish the facts. One should always endeavour to do so, you know.'

'All right, all right,' Max snapped tetchily. 'What about Miss Barton? What seems to be the matter?'

'I'm sure your concern will be most comforting to her,' Lord Charlbury said. 'As to what ails her, it's hard to be precise, but Dr Kennet is of the opinion that she seems to have acquired an aversion to devilled kidneys.'

'Devilled kidneys? What had devilled kidneys to do with it? There was nothing wrong with them this morning. I had them myself.'

'Did you, now? How interesting. So gratifying that you're able to be so emphatic. Cook will, I'm sure, be relieved to learn there was nothing wrong with the kidneys. It suggests Dr Kennet is correct and Libby has inexplicably developed an aversion to them.'

'Is she bad?'

'She certainly was at the time. If she makes the recovery we hope for I shall certainly take your advice and remove her to Bath—properly chaperoned, of course.'

'Of course,' Max replied absently, his mind apparently grappling with considerations which had not been mentioned.

Lord Wilcote caught his friend's eye, put his book down and rose to his feet, begging his hosts to forgive him but, although he knew they wouldn't mind his dining in country clothes, he really must make some adjustments if he were not to look as if he had just that minute ridden in.

Max looked suspiciously after him. 'Why should he need to "make adjustments"?' he asked. 'Byfield isn't so far, after all. I don't recall his ever having bothered about it before.'

'But then,' his brother reminded him gently, 'you didn't recall that it was you who planned to refurbish the turret room. And that was only the other day.'

Max flushed, and let the matter drop. The two brothers sat in silence for a few minutes, and Lord Charlbury noticed the agitated manner in which Max's fingers played with the signet ring he wore.

'Do you have any problems, Max?' he asked bluntly.

'Problems? No. Why should I have problems?'

'Most people do, of one sort or another. Take me, for example. If I'm to inherit Chase I must marry very soon, but it does seem as though every time I make definite plans something occurs to frustrate them. I'd call that a problem, wouldn't you?'

Max laughed harshly. 'You can hardly expect me to sympathise with that particular problem,' he said. 'After all, I've no reason to want you to inherit.'

'Very true. It is, however, one thing not to want me to inherit and quite another to take active steps to prevent it.'

'What do you mean?'

'Nothing. It was merely an observation and irrelevant to the point at issue, which is simply that I rather think you do have problems just now. If that's so, I'd like to help.'

'You can help me best by breaking your neck in a fall.'

'A true expression of fraternal affection,' Lord Charlbury commented. 'Max, if it's money, I have every intention to seeing you comfortably established.'

'As your pensioner? No, thank you.'

'Don't be a fool, Max. I mean to settle a substantial amount on you and in addition to settle any debts you choose to declare to me. After that, you're on your own—I'll not bail you out of any further difficulties.'

'If you pursue the same life after you inherit as you have done to date, I doubt if you'll be in a position to bail me out,' Max snapped.

'Quite so. All the more reason for letting me know how you're situated now, so that I can help you while I'm still in a position to do so.'

'Except that until you inherit you're not actually in such a position, and you've not yet inherited.'

'True enough, but make no mistake, Max—I intend to do so, come what may. The difference in our ages— our circumstances, too—is such that perhaps neither of us knows the other as well as we might. Perhaps that has been a mistake, but it's probably too late to alter it now. Take my word for it that I *shall* inherit and put out of your mind any lingering hope that I shall not. Bet on the certainty. I'm willing to have a settlement drawn up tomorrow which will be binding on me when I inherit. Your debts will be paid and you'll have an easy competence thenceforth. Come, Max, surely you can see this is the only sensible solution?'

For some moments it looked as if Max was wavering in his dislike and jealousy of his elder brother and would see the sense of the Viscount's suggestion, which even his opium-befuddled reasoning recognised as generous. But habit was too strong.

'Damn you, Marcus,' he said. 'Don't patronise me. You're not the only Asthall with determination. The game isn't over yet!' And he stormed out of the room, slamming the door behind him.

Lord Charlbury remained in his chair, staring into the fire, and was still sitting thus when Lord Wilcote returned, having heard Max storm into his own room and slam that door, too. Lord Charlbury looked across at his friend as the latter resumed his seat.

'I've lost him, Rupert,' he said, and there was only sadness in his voice.

CHAPTER THIRTEEN

WHEN Libby awoke she was weak and exhausted. She felt as if she had neither bones nor muscles and that if she tried to move she would simply flop like the old stuff doll she had had as a child. She smiled weakly up at Nurse, who had come to her side as soon as her eyes had fluttered open.

'What happened?' Libby whispered. 'I feel . . . feeble. And sore,' she added, putting her hand on her stomach and finding she had bone and muscle after all.

'You've been very ill, my duck,' said Nurse. 'And it's not to be wondered at that your belly hurts, for there's next to nothing left in it, and you got rid of what there was right forcefully. You may well laugh, miss,' she added, noting Libby's weak smile. 'But it weren't funny for the rest of us, I can tell you. Real worried, you had us.'

'I'm sorry. I do seem to be a nuisance to you all.'

'Never you bother your head about that. Truth to tell, it gives me something to do and there's little enough scope, else, since Master Max grew up. Now you just lie still while I fetch you some warm milk to set you to rights. You had some a few hours ago and kept it down, but I don't suppose you remember that. You were barely awake and you dropped straight off again afterwards.'

She bustled from the room, and Libby was too weak and drowsy to notice that she locked the door behind her.

She slept on and off for most of the day, gradually regaining strength on the prescribed diet, and when Dr Kennet came to see her that afternoon he pronounced himself very satisfied with her progress. This was so satisfactory, he later confided to the Viscount, that it led him to the conclusion that the future Lady Charlbury had the constitution of an ox, if his lordship would forgive the comparison. He recommended several more days in bed but, in the circumstances, agreed that she might be moved to Byfield the following day provided she was kept warm and the short journey was accomplished with as little discomfort as possible.

Since he had returned to find Libby ill, Lord Charlbury had not gone back to Byfield, but a note delivered by Fratton to Lord Wilcote and thence to the housekeeper ensured that all would be in readiness for her, and so, as soon as Nurse declared Libby fit to receive visitors after breakfast, he went to apprise her of her imminent removal.

'I don't particularly want to go to Byfield,' she protested weakly.

'But I particularly wish you to do so,' he replied. 'I think you'll make a speedier recovery there, so please be so kind as to oblige me in this.'

Libby frowned, trying to understand why Marcus was so insistent. 'But Byfield is so near,' she said. 'I can't imagine why I should be expected to make a speedier recovery there, especially since I so much prefer Chase.'

'I'm sure the change of scene will be of benefit.'

Libby looked at him. 'What happened this time? Why was I so ill?'

'Dr Kennet and I have agreed that you've developed an aversion to devilled kidneys.'

'So Nurse said. I don't believe it. I might, if it hadn't been preceded by other incidents. Marcus, was I poisoned?'

He sighed heavily. 'I sometimes wonder whether I wouldn't have been better advised to select a hen-witted female as the future Viscountess Charlbury.'

'A hen-witted female would not have fulfilled the conditions of your uncle's Will,' she replied with as much asperity as she could raise.

'And would probably have become a dead bore in a very few weeks,' he laughed. 'Something which I feel sure you, my dear, will never do.'

'You're evading the question, Marcus. Was I poisoned?'

He glanced round and noticed that Nurse had tactfully withdrawn. He took her hand between his and held it gently captive.

'We think it quite possible—and that the kidneys were the vehicle.'

'I see. So Byfield might well be a safer place in which to make a recovery.'

'Precisely. And then I shall send you to Bath as soon as you're well enough to make the journey.'

'Oh, no, you won't!' she exclaimed with some force. 'I'll go to Byfield, but I haven't forgotten that there's something else going on here. Something which involves Mademoiselle d'Angers. If I'm well enough to travel to Bath, I'm well enough to stay here and see this thing— whatever it may be—through to the end.'

He laughed and raised her captive hand to his lips. 'So be it,' he said. 'I see before me a lifetime of compromise. I wonder if I shall ever get used to it?'

The day was well advanced before Libby had been conveyed to Byfield and established comfortably in a large, south-facing room. She had never liked Byfield as much as Chase, but felt bound to admit that this low-ceilinged room with a log fire blazing heartily in the grate went a long way towards dispelling her dislike. Lord Charlbury's instructions had been followed very thoroughly by the small staff he had managed to afford to retain. If the future Lady Charlbury could be persuaded to like the Manor, who knew but that the couple might spend a greater part of their time there than the Viscount, alone, ever had?

Lord Charlbury stayed long enough to see Libby installed and comfortable, and then rode over alone to the home of Sir John Bere—huntsman, magistrate, landowner and, Lord Charlbury suspected, slightly dark horse.

Sir John was at home, and Lord Charlbury was shown into him with no delay. The magistrate rose to his feet immediately, and offered his visitor a glass of Madeira.

'Thank you, Sir John, but no. My business with you is urgent and—for me—extremely unwelcome.'

'Not, however, so urgent that you won't be seated, I hope,' replied Sir John, casting a shrewd glance at the Viscount's face which, ever austerely at odds with his reputation, was now set in hard, uncompromising lines. 'So far as I can, I shall treat anything you tell me as a confidence. If I'm unable to keep the information entirely to myself, rest assured I shall be as discreet as possible.'

'The matter involves my brother. Were it not that it also involves our country's safety, I'd handle it myself— I am naturally reluctant to bring opprobrium upon my family.'

'Naturally.'

'You were correct about Max's involvement in an invasion scheme. I've established why he had become caught up in it and that, too, reflects no honour upon my brother or, through him, our family, but I think there's no need to explain those reasons. Let me just say that the invasion is more imminent than you had thought. It will be next week, when there's no moon and the tides are right.'

'Go on.'

'I took an observant ride, as you suggested. The turret room at Chase can be aligned with the last stack of the Needles. A light in that room would be as good a guide as a lighthouse upon the stack itself.'

'Have you reason to believe a light would be available?'

'Until very recently, when I unwittingly removed it, there was an oil-lamp in that room. It seemed out of keeping with such a pleasant apartment. If an expeditionary force landed to the west of such a light, they would make landfall under the sandy bluffs along the Chase shore.'

'Precisely so. Will this landing take place while there is a visitor at Chase?'

'The visitor has gone. The reasons need not concern you, but Miss Barton and Mrs Widford are now at

Byfield. Word is that they will shortly remove to Bath with Lord Wilcote and myself as escort.'

'"Word is"—I take that to mean that the word will differ from the fact.'

'You take it exactly. It means that those remaining at Chase will be confident of having the estate to themselves.'

Sir John rose from his chair and paced the floor, thinking hard. 'I appreciate the difficulties of your position, Charlbury,' he said at last. 'Tell me frankly; having informed me that the invasion is decided for next week, do you now wish to know no more about what is to happen, or do you wish to play a part?'

Lord Charlbury laughed reluctantly. 'I wish I could indeed wash my hands of the matter, but it involves my brother and if, by playing a part, I may mitigate his treason, then I will do so. Besides,' he added, a gleam in his eye, 'it sounds as if it might be fun, and life in the country can be a tedious bore!'

'I rather fancy "fun" is not quite the most apposite word,' Sir John remarked drily. 'However, let us not quibble over semantics. I fear your tedium may not prove to be very much relieved. All I ask for the present is this: arrange for there to be as few people at Chase as possible; lie very low at Byfield, and give me permission to deploy men at will over Byfield and Chase lands. Finally, keep all this from the Byfield household.'

'The first I've no control over: Max runs Chase until I inherit. I've already removed all those over whom I have influence. However, since the late Earl kept only a small staff, mainly of women, in the house, and fewer estate workers than Max felt desirable, you will find fewer people there than would otherwise be expected on a place of that size. I can promise you to lie low at Byfield, though it will irk me to amuse myself around the house. You may deploy whom you will, as you will, at Byfield and—so far as it concerns me—at Chase, but remember Chase is Max's province for the time being. Byfield, as I'm sure you're already aware, has even fewer staff than Chase, due to my own improvidence. Those there are, are loyal. I'll endeavour to keep them in ignorance of all this, but should anything of it leak out, I've no doubt I can depend upon their silence.'

Sir John was thoughtful. 'Let us hope we can maintain secrecy,' he said. 'Tell me, does Tipper's Wood not divide both estates from the coast inland?'

'I'm sure you know it does. Most of it belongs to Chase.'

'But not all. With your permission we shall camp in the Byfield section of the wood where the cover is excellent due to your reprehensible neglect of coppicing over the years—very bad husbandry, if you'll forgive my mentioning it, though I own in this case it can be turned to good account. At night we may well stray a little.'

'Enough. The less I know, the less I can let slip. I must, however, inform Lord Wilcote and Miss Barton, both of whom have become more intimately involved in this affair than I would have liked, but who cannot now be kept in ignorance.'

'Lord Charlbury, I rely as much upon your discretion as you do upon mine. I hope neither of us will be disappointed. Now, forgive me, but I've work to do. May I suggest you ride quietly home through the forest? So much less observable than the tracks, don't you think?' With that, he pulled the bell.

The manservant who answered it was not surprised to see his rubicund employer jovially pumping the Viscount's arm and inviting him to hunt with the Buckhounds. 'Damn good sport, Charlbury,' his bluff voice bellowed. 'Lay odds you'd enjoy it.'

'I'm sure I should, Sir John,' Marcus answered, appreciatively noticing the magistrate's return to the character of the hearty squire. A man of many parts, Sir John Bere, he thought. I wonder exactly what role he played in the Americas?

Lord Charlbury's ride home was leisurely, and to a casual observer he would have appeared sunk in thought. But there were no casual observers, for he followed Sir John's advice and, although he had a great deal to occupy his mind, it was not so fully occupied as to prevent his noting just how empty of human life the forest was.

He sought out Libby as soon as he returned and found her resting on a day-bed in her room. She had been surprised to find herself so weak after such a relatively short journey, and it had taken little persuasion on Nurse's part to keep her in her room.

Lord Charlbury paused on the threshold and surveyed with some appreciation the scene before him. 'You look most charmingly, Libby,' he said.

Libby smiled ruefully. 'You're very kind, sir,' she replied. 'But my mirror tells me I look sadly hagged. I thought I was stronger than to be set back so easily.'

'You're lucky to be alive at all, and most women of my acquaintance would have taken to their beds indefinitely after the sort of experience you have just had. Harebell-blue becomes you,' he added, and Libby, involuntarily smoothing the fabric of the morning-gown to which he was referring, made a mental resolve to include more of it in her wardrobe. 'Are you well enough to listen to a story?' he went on. 'If you are, I'm here to entertain you.'

Libby looked at him curiously. 'It doesn't sound quite your style, Marcus, to be entertaining invalids with stories.'

'A great deal depends upon the identity of the invalid,' he told her. 'And I have to confess that if there were more than one in the house I should probably make sure I was elsewhere. Mind you, my style—as you put it—seems to be changing in more than one direction. May I sit beside you, or would you prefer me to draw up a chair?'

Libby blushed. 'As you will, my lord.'

'Very demure,' he commented drily, and seated himself on one side of her couch, possessing himself—almost absent-mindedly, it seemed to Libby—of one of her hands. He told her, simply and straightforwardly, all that had happened so far, both known and conjectured, and of his visit to Sir John Bere together with its outcome.

When he had finished, Libby spent several minutes thinking over what she had learnt.

'There's one thing that puzzles me, Marcus,' she said. 'Surely they would choose to come during a full moon? How else will they be sure of landing safely?'

'On a moonlit night they will be clearly visible from the Isle of Wight and at any point along the coast for a considerable distance. This is why they need a signal from Chase to direct them away from the Needles, and if anyone else spotted the light they'd think nothing of it.'

'I see. So life at Chase bids fair to becoming very exciting in the next little while. Dear me, what a pity I'm no longer there. I think I'd have enjoyed it. Must I truly stay here and "lie low"?'

'You must—truly,' he replied, laughing. 'For one thing, if you were to return to Chase, one of two things must happen: either the invasion would have to be postponed, or you would have to be removed. In either event you would miss the excitement. By staying at Byfield, you will at least learn about it afterwards. As I will,' he added as an afterthought.

'I believe you'd rather enjoy it, too!' Libby exclaimed.

'I believe I should,' he agreed. 'So let us both take comfort in the fact that absenting ourselves from Chase and forgoing the excitement constitutes our duty in the present circumstances. Irksome though that duty may be,' he added ruefully.

Over the next few days, Libby's strength increased rapidly. She explored the old house and decided that it had its charms even though it somehow, and despite its age, lacked the atmosphere of Chase. It wasn't long before she felt well enough to walk in the gardens with Nurse's support. Mindful of her instructions to 'lie low', she made no attempt to venture far—and privately acknowledged herself to be still unfit to do so—but it seemed to her that there were rather more labourers in the fields than she would have expected, even in high summer. She made no mention of this to Nurse, thinking that, despite what Marcus had told her, she might well be mistaken. She was therefore surprised when Nurse accosted a young labourer who was half-heartedly cutting and inexpertly laying a hedge that bordered the further boundary of the garden.

'Jem Stamshaw!' that good woman exclaimed. 'What are you doing here? You haven't ever worked at Byfield, and it's clear as makes no matter you don't know what you're doing, for I could make a better job of it, leaving aside that it's a funny time of year for laying hedges.'

The young man looked embarrassed and flustered. He assured 'Mrs Widford', as he respectfully called her, that he had come back home for good, and his lordship, being a kind man, had given him work.

'His lordship a kind man? Rubbish!' she snapped, and then, realising this was a somewhat infelicitous remark to make in front of Libby, she became herself so covered in confusion that Jem Stamshaw was allowed to get on with his work.

Nurse's confusion did not, however, prevent her from grumbling on. It seemed that Jem had been the local ne'er-do-well who had taken the King's shilling years ago and hadn't been seen since—until now. It was Nurse's opinion that he had deserted, since it stood to good reason that the King would not release a fit young soldier in the middle of a war, and what could his lordship be thinking of?

Libby had her own thoughts on the matter, and mentioned them to Marcus, who confirmed her suspicions that there were now a number of estate workers who, very recently, had been wearing regimentals. He must ask Sir John to keep them further from the house.

It seemed to Libby that both Lord Charlbury and Lord Wilcote looked a little fatigued these days. She was not aware that every night they took it in turns to stay awake in case events should warrant their presence.

When William Fratton, who kept his ear well tuned to local gossip, reported to his master that a French filly had set up residence at Chase, neither Lord Charlbury nor Lord Wilcote interpreted the rumour as meaning that Max was intending to breed bloodstock. The words in which Lord Charlbury passed the information on to Libby were rather more carefully chosen.

She looked up at him thoughtfully. 'That must be Mademoiselle d'Angers.'

'Almost certainly, I should think.'

'Which suggests the landing is very soon to take place.'

'Precisely. Let us now hope it will soon be upon us and done with, so that we may return to normal.'

'Do you know, Marcus, I'm no longer at all certain what "normal" is. Since I accepted your offer, back at Copthorne, what I always thought of as normality has been quite foreign to my experience.'

'Poor thing!' he laughed, slipping a sympathetic arm around her waist. 'This must have been the coldest courtship and the oddest betrothal to which any woman has been subjected.' His grey eyes looked down into her brown ones. 'None of this is what I planned, and I sincerely hope your life as Viscountess Charlbury will be tedious by comparison. It has had one useful outcome, however.'

Libby, who raised no objection to her waist being held, even though she knew decorum required her to withdraw unobtrusively from his clasp, considered the matter and could think of nothing. 'In what way?' she asked.

'I think we know each other better,' he told her. 'Would you believe me if I told you I'm quite looking forward to our marriage?'

It was not the most hyperbolic of compliments, but it was so unexpected that Libby felt herself blush and was covered in confusion. She rallied sufficiently to keep her voice steady. 'I'm glad to hear it, my lord,' she said.

He chuckled and, turning her face towards him, kissed her briefly, but far from gently, full on the mouth. 'I don't often succeed in bringing confusion to your countenance,' he remarked. 'I assure you it becomes you well.'

Libby's blushes deepened, and not only at his words, but she spoke with renewed asperity. 'Let me inform you, my lord, that it doesn't become you, as a gentleman, to

remark upon the fact—or to take such unfair advantage
of the absence of a chaperon.'

He bowed. 'I'm indebted to you for the lesson,' he
said. 'I'll refrain from pointing out that you, as a lady,
would be on firmer moral ground had you done anything to dissuade me.' And as she opened her mouth to
utter an indignant protest, his closed upon it in a kiss
compared with which its predecessor was a fraternal
greeting.

'Let that be a lesson to you,' he said, grinning, and
was gone before she could think of a suitable retort.

CHAPTER FOURTEEN

LIBBY sat up in bed. Something wasn't right. A nightmare? No, she thought not. What, then? The room was in total darkness; not even an ember glowed faintly in the hearth. It must have been the tail-end of a nightmare, she decided. That settled, Libby prepared to snuggle down again under the bedclothes.

Her head had hardly touched the pillow when she heard the unmistakable sound of someone thumping on the heavy oaken front door. That was it. That was the sound which had woken her up. She was fully conscious this time, and her eyes quickly adjusted to a dark which had so recently seemed absolute. She reached for the wrap which lay across the end of the bed, and threw it round her shoulders. She reached towards the tinder-box that lay by her candle and then had second thoughts, though she was unsure why. Holding her wrap around her, she tiptoed to the door of her room and quietly turned the handle. She looked in both directions along the landing to see if anyone was about. A slight glow came from the direction of the stairs, and she walked towards it. As she made her way cautiously towards the stairs, the insistent thumping stopped. She paused when she reached the stairwell, and peered carefully round the corner of the wall. She could hear the sound of bolts being drawn back, and as she looked over, down into the hall, she could see the shape of Lord Wilcote outlined by the glow from a single candle. He was fully dressed and had clearly not been to bed that night. It was he who was pulling back the bolts and, as she watched, turned the heavy key in the lock.

Suddenly a hand slipped round her waist while another simultaneously covered her mouth. She started violently, and cast terrified eyes over her shoulder. Lord Charlbury, also fully dressed, had her in an iron grip. As soon as she recognised him, his hold eased; he smiled and put one finger to his lips and, when she nodded, released her immediately.

By this time Lord Wilcote had the door open and his candle held up, casting a flickering light that somehow managed not to expire completely upon whomsoever had come calling at this extraordinary hour. It revealed and distorted the features of a young man in a uniform which conveyed nothing to Libby and, more dimly, other faces peering out of the dark behind him. Lord Charlbury's hold on Libby's arm tightened to a grip.

'My God!' he breathed in her ear. 'They've mistaken the house!'

The uniformed young man made no attempt to step into the house. He bowed, and enquired of Lord Wilcote if he had the honour of addressing the Honourable Mr Max Asthall. His voice was pleasant, his English accurate—and his accent unmistakable.

Before his friend could answer, Lord Charlbury came out of the shadows at the top of the stairs and proceeded down towards his visitor.

'I'm Max Asthall,' he said. 'I rather imagine we've been expecting you.'

The young Frenchman looked at him doubtfully. 'Forgive me, but I had been given to understand that you were a much younger man.'

'You flatter me, *monsieur*.'

The Frenchman flushed under the ironic gaze cast upon him, and murmured something about reports not always being reliable since people saw things differently. Lord Charlbury did nothing to ease his discomfiture. He simply let him flounder and then closed the discussion with 'precisely', having elicited the information that his visitor was a Captain Ramballe.

The Viscount was thinking rapidly. He had no way of knowing how detailed were any plans that had been made nor how large a part he, in his role as his younger brother, was supposed to know about them. He didn't even know how large or small this expeditionary force might be, and was, in any case, uncertain what best to do with them until help could be summoned. Help, however, was nearer than he thought.

An impeccable French voice came from behind him. 'Ah, Capitaine Ramballe,' Libby said as she descended the stairs. 'At last. We are so relieved you have arrived safely.' She paused. 'You *have* arrived safely, I presume? No one saw you?'

The captain bowed and raised her proffered hand to his lips, gallantly overlooking her déshabillé. 'It went smoothly, *mademoiselle*. The guiding light shone clear and no one saw us. Forgive me, *mademoiselle*, but you are Mademoiselle d'Angers?'

'Who else?' she replied.

'Of course. *Mademoiselle*, you will appreciate we must change into our disguises as soon as possible. We must not be seen in uniform.'

'Your disguises are available—but well hidden,' she replied, improvising wildly and wishing Lord Charlbury and Lord Wilcote would come to her aid. The latter was watching her with a look of mild amazement on his face. The former was plainly amused. 'I'm surprised,' she went on, 'that it was not considered wise to issue them before you set sail so that you might have landed ready-disguised. Surely that would have been less conspicuous?'

'Certainly, *mademoiselle*, but had we been caught— and there was a suspicion the plan had leaked out—we would have been treated as spies. In uniform we would be prisoners of war. And now, *mademoiselle*——' his voice became urgent '—we should get under cover. We must not be seen here in uniform like this.'

'Of course, Captain. How thoughtless of me. The kitchens, I think, don't you?' And she led the way into the nether regions of the house.

Lord Charlbury and his friend stood aside as the French soldiers trooped into the house. Fifty of them. Hardly an invasion force such as Sir John had envisaged, but a very useful scouting party to prepare the way for something larger. All seasoned campaigners, too, by the look of them. Even the Captain, though young,

was no raw graduate from the military academy at St
Cyr. No, each of these men had been hand-picked for
the job required, and each would be able to give very
good account of himself.

Fortunately, in view of the number of Frenchmen who
had arrived, there were two kitchens at Byfield, adjacent
to one another. Both were low-ceilinged, as befitted a
house of such age, and both were huge. One contained
the bread ovens and the copper, the other the huge open
fire with its accompanying ironmongery of spits and
hooks. Libby turned to Captain Ramballe.

'Do you set your men to rekindling the fire,' she said,
'and we can make coffee. There's water in the kettle if
they will but swing it over the heat. Ale might be more
to their taste,' she added, 'but I've no expertise at tapping
a barrel.' At that point she looked defiantly at Lord
Charlbury.

Recognising appreciatively a master-stroke returning
the ball neatly into his court, Lord Charlbury expressed
a willingness to tap barrels.

'But later,' he said. 'There are more important matters
to deal with first. Your disguises are hidden in Tipper's
Wood. My groom—who is entirely to be trusted—will
fetch them.' He turned to Lord Wilcote. 'Rupert, be so
kind as to summon Fratton while I—er—tap a barrel.'

Captain Ramballe spun round, a suspicious light in
his eye. 'Forgive me, Monsieur Asthall, but who is this
man—and who is your groom? We were assured that
only yourself and Mademoiselle d'Angers would be here.'

'Then you were assured incorrectly, my dear captain.
Do you imagine there are no servants here? It's true we
operate with a minimum of staff, but, I assure you, to
have dismissed them or have given them all leave of absence at the same time would have caused the very
speculation we seek to avert. Their quarters are in a far
wing, and I pray God they didn't hear you knocking.
Of Fratton's loyalty to me there can be no doubt. As to
this gentleman, he is Lord Wilcote, whose maternal
pedigree is entirely French. He is here on the very highest
authority. Indeed, I've long suspected him to be the

master mind behind this plan. He had been ordered here to see it to fruition.'

Lord Wilcote appeared at this moment to be taking an inordinate interest in the shine of his boots, and Libby couldn't help thinking how very unlike a master traitor he looked.

It didn't seem to strike Captain Ramballe as at all odd that this master planner should be expected to summon the groom and, since it didn't strike Lord Wilcote as at all unexpected either, he was able to slip out to the harness-room where Fratton had been sleeping for several nights past.

When Lord Wilcote returned, the Viscount suggested that Mademoiselle d'Angers might be more comfortable if she took advantage of the necessary wait to get dressed.

Libby obediently went upstairs, and checked that no one else in the house had so far woken up. Then she dressed quickly and returned to the kitchens where fifty cramped Frenchmen refreshed themselves with good English ale while they awaited the arrival of their disguises. Where these were to come from, Libby had no idea, but neither Lord Charlbury nor Lord Wilcote seemed unduly anxious, so she could only await events.

Since Libby had privately considered the whole question of the availability of disguises to be one big bluff, she was genuinely astonished when William Fratton appeared at the kitchen door with two huge bundles. These he brought into the kitchen, untied them, and emptied the contents into two heaps on the floor. There were rustic smocks, rough shirts and trousers and misshapen hats of felt or wool.

'No boots,' he said tersely. 'But if you wears your boots under these trousers and ties the trousers below the knee, it's odds no one will notice. Especially if you takes care to get them good and grimy.'

The invaders fell upon the clothes, sorting out in silence those which were a rough fit, and it seemed to Libby that it might be more expedient to take herself quietly elsewhere while the transformation from Imperial soldier to English rustic took place.

Suddenly she recollected that it was in Tipper's Wood that Sir John Bere had established his encampment—and his militia had been disguised as farm-workers. This, then, must have been the cache of disguises to which Lord Charlbury had referred. If Fratton had brought them from Sir John's men, it followed that the alarm had been raised and it was a reasonable supposition that the magistrate and his men would soon be here.

Libby had got thus far in her deductions when Marcus emerged from the kitchen and joined her. 'Go to your room, Libby, and stay there,' he instructed. 'Sir John will soon be here.'

'How like a man!' she answered acidly. 'I take the initiative, coop them up in the kitchen and am then told to go away and be a good girl because it's going to become exciting.'

'Exciting, yes—and almost certainly dangerous as well.' He put his hands on her shoulders and looked down into her eyes. The only thought in Libby's mind at that moment was how desperately she wanted him to encircle her in those arms and hold her tight. She knew the time, the place and the circumstances rendered it an impossible dream, so she smiled instead. Marcus smiled back. 'I know,' he said cryptically, 'a much more satisfactory way of passing the time, and one day—soon—we won't have to bother about all these other people. In the meantime I don't want any more harm to come to you. I dare not let you take the risk. A stray musket-ball could succeed where Max has failed.'

'And that would never do,' she said cheerfully, 'because then you'd have to seek out another sensible, well-bred woman, versed in habits of economy.' She had had the disconcerting impression that he had known exactly what was in her mind, so she took refuge in her vaunted practicality. 'You're overlooking something, however. *We* know it may be dangerous. They do not. How very odd it will look to them if I now take to my room! I can't imagine they expect me to retire so tamely from the lists. I'm sure Mademoiselle d'Angers wouldn't consider her part played out yet.'

He looked at her thoughtfully. 'You have a point,' he conceded. 'Thus be it—but Libby——' and he caught her arm as she turned back towards the kitchens '—take care—for God's sake, take care!'

'And for yours, my lord,' she answered over her shoulder, smiling. His concern had suddenly made her happier than she had been for a long time.

When she re-entered the kitchens it was to find them bursting at the seams with English yokels, and she couldn't completely suppress the giggle that bubbled up. Captain Ramballe noticed it and commented that it was indeed sad to see fine soldiers this reduced, but owned that he, too, could see the amusing side.

'If you will now direct us to the barns where we are to stay,' he said, 'we will settle ourselves down before the servants are about.'

Lord Charlbury agreed that this should now be accomplished without too much delay. 'But can you be sure, Captain, that there will be no sound at all until tomorrow night, when we move you? I realise your men are tired and sleep will come easily, but you must appreciate that we can't have snoring emanating from the barns and hay-lofts.'

Captain Ramballe looked surprised. 'Tomorrow night?' he queried. 'Forgive me, Monsieur Asthall, but I was under the distinct impression that we were to remain hidden here until the moon was again sufficiently full to light our route.'

Libby threw a startled look at Lord Charlbury. It was going to be impossible to carry this thing through. They had reached this far on a mixed basis of rumour, conjecture and coincidence, but they had no way of knowing just how detailed were the plans that had been made, nor how much of that detail was known to Max and Héloise, though she suspected the latter might know more than the unstable Max. She wondered how Marcus would talk them out of this present inconsistency.

In the event, it was not he but Lord Wilcote who thought the fastest.

'That was, of course, the plan,' he began, 'but I've had to change it. Rumour has got about that some landing such as yours is planned, and the militia is alerted. However, since it is common sense that no one would attempt such a thing when there is no moon, especially so close to the Needles, the militia won't be looking for you except when the moon is once more waxing. I therefore decided we must move you during the darkest time. It's too late tonight, of course, and, as you so accurately noted, the servants will soon be about. You will therefore spend today in the old tithe barn which no one should have cause to visit, and as soon as it's fully dark a guide will lead you on your way.'

Both Lord Charlbury and Libby stared at Lord Wilcote in amazement. Neither had ever heard him make such a long speech in all their acquaintance with him. Lord Charlbury's amazement was tinged with perturbation: the French were supposed to be at Chase, which, being a secular foundation, had no tithe barn. Byfield, on the site of a nunnery, did possess such an architectural feature. It was to be hoped that Captain Ramballe was not too familiar with the finer points of the Dissolution of the Monasteries.

He was not. Captain Ramballe found nothing but good sense in Lord Wilcote's suggestion.

Suddenly the door to the yard burst open and two uniformed men with muskets at the ready stood there. Simultaneously, windows were broken in both kitchens by musket-butts and the weapons pointed inwards. The two men at the door moved slowly sideways, into the room, and were followed by others until the French expeditionary force was surrounded, if not outnumbered. Their own weapons had been carefully stacked against the wall while they had changed into their disguises. There was no possibility of their overwhelming the far less experienced militia.

Sir John Bere entered, bowed to Libby, and shook hands with Lord Charlbury. 'Well done, my lord,' he said. 'What a beautifully neat job this has turned out to be! I'd envisaged any number of problems chasing disguised Frenchmen through the forest, and look what we have—a neat rounding-up, no bloodshed, no local alarums. Lovely job.' He turned to Captain Ramballe. 'I shall need to borrow your uniforms for much the same reason that you have borrowed our own disguises. This isn't the house at which you were expected to arrive, and we must send an appropriate force there to bring this matter to a satisfactory conclusion. One wouldn't wish to leave loose ends, you know.'

'The wrong house?' queried the captain. 'How can this be? Surely this is Chase?'

'No, Captain,' Lord Charlbury interposed quietly. 'This is Byfield Manor. Chase is further along the coast to the east.'

'But we had a signal—a light. If we steered west of it we should avoid the rocks and land in the right place.'

'As indeed you did—from our point of view. The light you were looking for will have been in the tower room at Chase. By sheer coincidence—and I assure you, Captain, it was sheer coincidence—Lord Wilcote here was sitting in the library tonight without closing the shutters or drawing the curtains. You spotted that light, which can also be seen at sea, but a great deal further to the west than Chase. I imagine your ship, to be safe from the rocks, steered too far to the west and then the light from Chase would have been cut off by the belt of woodland that separates the two estates.'

'The ship's captain was extremely anxious to give your Needles a very wide berth.'

'Very wise of him, I assure you. So here you are, safe and sound—which you might not have been had he had been less cautious.'

Captain Ramballe's chagrin was obvious. He was young and ambitious and this expedition, had it succeeded, would have earned him his majority. He must salvage what he could from the wreck.

'Our uniforms are there,' he said. 'We are soldiers, not spies.'

Sir John bowed. 'Agreed, Captain. Permit me the loan of your uniforms and you have my word they will be returned to you before you're marched to the prison at Portchester. Your men will empty their pockets of tinders and flints and you will all spend the night under guard in the tithe barn. In the morning your uniforms will be returned and you will proceed under guard to Portchester.'

'Portchester is for the prisoners of war only, I think.'

'It is.'

'And I have your word we will have our uniforms back and be treated as such?'

'You have.'

'Very well. I have no option.'

'My good captain,' Lord Charlbury's ironic voice broke in. 'You would have no option even if Sir John marched you to the convicts' hulks in Portsmouth. Sir John merely seeks to preserve the outward appearance of chivalry.'

The French soldiers in their smocks were marched out and over to the barn in which they would spend the remainder of the night. Their place was taken by Sir John's militia, and this time when Libby left the room while they transformed themselves into French soldiers it was with the firm intention of retiring to her bed.

Lord Charlbury followed her out. 'Can I persuade you to go to bed this time, Libby?' he asked.

'That was my intention,' she replied. 'I fancy my part in this charade is over.'

'It would seem so, and I'm grateful for the part you played so willingly—and the initiative you displayed.'

'To tell the truth, I quite enjoyed it.' She sighed. 'Life has certainly not been boring since you proposed to me.'

'It's strange you should mention that. It's something I observed myself, and I find myself wondering whether my illustrious uncle realised that such a lack of tedium accompanied betrothal to a female such as he prescribed. I'm sure you will own that the description he gave sounded most tedious.'

'In general, I believe we are held to be so. Perhaps that's why most women try so hard not to appear sensible—or thrifty.'

He laughed gently and his eyes softened, but there was a touch of irony in his voice when he spoke. 'Is that the reason?' he said. 'I'd never have thought it! Go to bed, Libby, and get some sleep. I must ride to Chase with Bere and Rupert.'

'Must you? You will be careful: I fancy it may not prove as bloodless as this night's work.'

'I must. I can't allow Max's arrest to take place without its being clearly demonstrated that at least one Asthall is true to the Crown. And I will be careful,' he added, drawing her to him. 'Not least because you wish it.'

He slipped his arm round her waist in a manner which Libby found as delightful as it was reprehensible. She knew that a truly sensible woman would now remind him of the social conventions and require him to remove his arm from such an indecorous position. But Libby did not feel the least bit sensible and the last thing she wanted just now was to have him remove his arm. Indeed, she was not at all averse to his tightening it, and when his free hand tilted her chin so that he was looking down into her eyes she found herself doing nothing more sensible than blush. He kissed her gently.

'Are you so surprised I should take heed of your wishes?' he asked. 'I assure you, it was never my intention to be an insensitive husband.'

Libby looked up at him under her lashes in a way that, had she but known it, was not only quite flirtatiously minx-like but very nearly deflected him from his intention of continuing to Chase. 'I'm delighted to hear it, my lord,' she purred. 'Being a sensible woman, I should otherwise have to think twice before allying myself to a man who was *not* prepared to pander to my every whim.'

He pulled his head back then, and Libby had the satisfaction of knowing she had disconcerted him. 'I don't recollect making any promise quite as rash as that,' he said. 'Furthermore, I'm fairly certain I didn't mean to be taken quite so literally.'

'Then you should choose your words with greater care,' Libby replied, unabashed. 'If you don't, you could land yourself in goodness knows what sort of predicament.'

'I seem to have landed myself in quite a predicament now,' he answered teasingly. 'Formally betrothed as I am to a woman who insists on a literal interpretation to everything I say.'

'If you feel very strongly about it, I could always cry off,' Libby suggested.

'And lose Chase? Never!' he exclaimed. But the materialism of his words was more than a little mitigated by the further tightening of his embrace. He kissed her again, and this time there was no chaste brushing of lips, no lover-like tenderness. His mouth was hard and passionate against hers, as if in tacit acknowledgement of the fact that the night's affairs were not yet over and success was not yet assured. Libby sensed all this just as she sensed within her betrothed that same surge of feeling within herself that was, for her, so new an emotion. All the same, the intensity of his embrace startled her even as it gladdened her heart. Perhaps, she thought, perhaps it was just possible her dreams might be answered. Perhaps there was something more than convenience on his side.

'Goodnight, Libby,' he said at last, his voice an endearment in itself. 'I'll look to see you tomorrow.'

She smiled up at him. 'Later today, I think,' she corrected him.

'Of course. How sensible!' But there was no gibe in his voice, and, although Libby was soon in bed, it was a long time before she was sufficiently composed for sleep to take over.

CHAPTER FIFTEEN

SIR JOHN BERE cast anxious glances at the sky. Thank God it was still pitch dark. Even so, dawn couldn't be very far off, and their arrival at Chase would lack credibility if light was already touching the horizon. He could suggest they had lost their way, but who would believe that with the guiding light in the turret window? The journey between the two houses was one quickly accomplished by carriage and both short and quick on horseback, travelling across country. But on foot and in darkness it was a different matter.

Lord Charlbury led the way by the shortest route he knew, which lay through Tipper's Wood. On roads or decent tracks a steady jog-march would have eaten up the distance, but this was out of the question when unseen roots lay in wait to trip men up, while unsuspected branches slashed across their eyes, temporarily blinding them. Lord Charlbury, too, wondered whether dawn would overtake them.

At last the contingent reached the edge of the wood and assembled silently within the fringe of trees. There must be nothing to lead those at Chase to suspect that anything might be wrong, and therefore it was vital that the men should approach the house from the south, the only direction from which they would have been able to see that guiding light. It was fortunate that no fixed day had been set for the landing: anyone keeping a vigil at Chase would, by now, be dismissing the possibility of landing this night and would therefore be slightly off-guard.

Accordingly, the men slipped southwards through the trees for a quarter of a mile, and Lord Charlbury sought Sir John Bere and led him to a position from which the lamp in the turret window could be seen. As they looked, they could make out a figure that stood for a moment beside it, apparently looking out. Then it moved away. It wasn't possible to identify it, but it appeared to be a man.

'We can't approach from here,' said Sir John. 'No officer would send men in such conspicuous uniforms across such a large and open space.'

'I can see that it would be better to approach obliquely,' Lord Charlbury agreed. 'But there's no cover now. Does it really matter if we're seen? We're only expecting there to be Mademoiselle d'Angers and Max, surely?'

'To say nothing of whoever will be guiding the disguised invaders to Southampton and possibly whoever has provided the disguises—for I can't imagine your brother will have been able to accumulate so many, if only because it would have occasioned so much local comment. Nor, I may add, have I any desire to be intercepted by patriotic yokels who might catch sight of us on their way to milk their cows.'

Lord Charlbury laughed softly. 'Of course. The workings of the military mind.'

'Nothing of the sort. Mere common sense, I assure you. Come, we must waste no more time.' He whispered orders to his men.

The party advanced slowly and split into two as it approached the house. One group slipped silently round by the stables to the kitchen entrance while the others went to the front. It was unlikely that the main door would have been left unlocked, though the possibility couldn't be overlooked since it had been to the front door of Byfield that the genuine invaders had presented themselves.

Suspicion proved correct. The kitchen entrance was unlocked, but that party didn't enter unobserved: Max's groom saw them from the window of the harness-room where he had fallen asleep that night. He saw them slip into the kitchen, and he saw another group come quietly round from the front of the house at a signal and join them. He reached for an old pistol that lay ready to accompany a coachman on any long journey. He knew it was kept primed and loaded since it had more than once seen action against poachers.

It had been agreed that, once inside the house, Lord
Charlbury must remain out of sight. Sir John, too, was
a figure familiar to Max Asthall, if not to his French
guest. The task of alerting Max and Héloise to the arrival of their expected visitors was given to a keen young
lieutenant.

'For the sake of this mission do not, under any circumstances, forget you're French,' Sir John empha-
sised. 'Don't attempt to speak French unless you're
fluent. Speak English as a courtesy to Mr Asthall, and
make sure you speak it with a strong accent. And try to
avoid saying anything at all if you possibly can.'

The lieutenant grinned in acceptance of this impossible task, and followed the directions Lord Charlbury
had given him which were likely to lead to Max—the
Viscount and the magistrate meanwhile positioning
themselves in the coldly tiled game-larder.

Lord Charlbury's directions proved superfluous, for
Max's voice could be heard greeting the young officer
almost as soon as that young man had stepped through
the baize door. The soldiers had not been as quiet as
they had hoped, or perhaps it was because Max and his
house-guest had been more than half expecting their arrival. Whatever the reason, he had heard their boots on
the flagged floor of the kitchen and, with Mademoiselle
d'Angers behind him and a pistol in his hand, had come
to see whether the slight noise was that of his expected
guests or of unwelcome visitors.

His pale face smiled as he saw the uniforms in front
of him, but his eyes glanced nervously this way and that,
and more than one of the soldiers noticed the tremor in
his gun-hand and vowed to keep a wary distance should
that weapon be raised. It was Mademoiselle d'Angers
who took charge of the gathering, doing so—understandably enough—in French, a circumstance which
caused no little consternation among the militiamen, who
had no idea what she was saying. Fortunately Max unwittingly came to their rescue.

'Not French,' he snapped petulantly. 'You know I
can't concentrate on the details unless you speak English.
Besides, they have to pass themselves off as Englishmen,
so they may well get used to it.'

So Héloïse obligingly reverted to English. She explained that disguises had, with great difficulty, been obtained for them and were now hidden; that they would hide in a barn on the edge of the estate until the moon was waxing once more, and they would then be led to Southampton.

Lord Charlbury, listening to this from his cold hiding-place, found it a disconcerting experience to have the events of the night repeating themselves in an almost uncanny way. The lieutenant, in a monstrously heavy accent, enquired whether their guide, whom he presumed would be a local man, could be trusted.

'Of course he can,' exploded Max. 'I shall be leading you myself. I know the forest between Chase and Southampton as well as any man. Do you dare to suggest that I can't be trusted when I've done so much already?'

Before the lieutenant could form a diplomatic answer, Lord Charlbury, closely followed by Sir John, stepped out of the larder.

'It seems to me, Max,' he said icily, 'that trust is the one thing that can't be reposed in you. Be so good as to hand me that gun.'

Unnerved by the appearance of his brother, and quite unable to work out what had happened or why these Frenchmen made no move to capture either the Viscount or the magistrate, Max made as if to hand his pistol over. He had hardly lifted if a few inches, however, when a loud report and a cry of anguish rent the room.

At first everyone present, including Max, thought the pistol must have exploded and the ball hit some one. It soon became apparent that this was not so, but no one had had time to speculate upon what exactly had occurred before the outer door burst open and Max's groom stood there, a smoking pistol in his hand.

''Tis the French, Mr Asthall, sir!' he shouted. 'I got one on 'em, but I rackons I ought to ride for the magistrate.' Then he realised he had walked into a veritable nest of Frenchmen and his face blanched.

But he had unwittingly caused just the distraction Max needed, and the door to the outside now stood open. While everyone else was assimilating this latest development, Max leaped for the open door, and was through it before the others realised what was happening.

Realisation dawned first upon Lord Charlbury, and in very little more time than it had taken Max to assess the situation's possibilities he followed his brother out, passing almost without noticing him the soldier who had been shot by Max's patriotic groom. The young lieutenant made as if to follow him, but was restrained by his commander's hand.

'Leave it,' he said. 'Let Lord Charlbury deal with him. I fancy we shan't regret it. You would do better to arrange an escort for this lady. *Mademoiselle*, you will almost certainly be charged with espionage. These men will take you to Byfield village and procure a cart which will convey you to a place where you will be held. I doubt if you'll find it pleasant, but that is what one must expect if one abuses the hospitality of another country.' He turned to the lieutenant. 'Tie her hands,' he said, 'and don't be misled by pretty words. The lady has been suspected of spying for a long time. She's clever. Don't allow yourself to be outwitted.'

The young man gave his solemn assurances and, together with an escort, marched Héloïse back to Byfield Manor, where they resumed their normal uniforms before taking her on to the village. Sir John sat down to await Lord Charlbury's return.

That gentleman had no difficulty in keeping up with his brother, whose stamina, like his nerve, had been sapped by opium; but Lord Charlbury was unarmed, and he kept a respectful eye on the pistol still being held by Max. He recognised it. It was one of the matched pair of duelling pistols owned by the late Earl, and it had a hair trigger. Not the safest weapon to carry on a cross-county run.

At last it seemed to him that Max was faltering. He called to him to stop. They were entering woodland now, and this made both escape and pursuit more difficult, for the canopy of leaves held back the gradual approach of the dawn which would otherwise have illuminated the way. Again Lord Charlbury called to his brother to stop. Max was about a hundred yards ahead of him now, and at this second call he turned and raised the pistol in his unsteady hand, pointing it at his brother.

'Damn you, Marcus!' he shrieked. 'You shan't have Chase! You shan't! If it's the last thing I do, you shan't have it!'

But even as he spoke, his brother continued to advance, and Max correspondingly backed. He felt something behind his ankle and half turned to see what it was, his pistol-hand correspondingly turning away from the Viscount. But Max was too late. In the very act of turning, he tripped and fell, his finger unconsciously tightening on that hair trigger.

When Lord Charlbury reached him, he was dead.

Lord Charlbury might have intended to see Libby again later that day, but the formalities necessarily attendant upon Max's sudden death in somewhat unusual circumstances took up so much of it that he didn't even attempt to go back to Byfield for dinner. Consequently, it was the next day before he returned and suggested to her that they should ride out together.

Libby was glad that the overture to do so had come from him. She had been both hurt and upset that he hadn't returned the previous night, even though her common sense told her that he must be very tired and would have a great deal of business to attend to. Word of Max's death had been quick to reach Byfield, and, while she did not think the bond between the brothers had been a particularly close one, yet she couldn't imagine that the death of the younger man would leave the elder unmoved. She had heard a necessarily garbled account of the early morning's work from Nurse and was anxious to hear the full story, while at the same time concerned not to add to Lord Charlbury's distress.

When he sought her out after breakfast, she expressed her regrets at Max's untimely death.

'Word certainly travels fast,' Marcus said bitterly. 'Yes, he's dead. I'm trying to convince myself that it was inevitable and that the manner of it, given the circumstances, was possibly for the best. So far I've not been very successful.' He changed the subject abruptly then, asking Libby whether she had slept well, and she took her cue from him. If he wished to talk about it, it would be for him to re-introduce it, though as they clattered out of the yard she wondered whether it might not be better if he were obliged to face the issue.

In the event, the decision to raise the matter wasn't hers. They rode southwards in silence, and Lord Charlbury drew rein at the top of the low sandstone bluff which stood between the beach and Byfield, just as it separated Chase from the sea further along. He turned in his saddle and looked back the way they had come. Byfield was largely hidden by slightly rising ground. Only its roof and chimneys were visible at one end of the building where the land in front of it dipped sufficiently to reveal a part of the first floor.

'Do you know,' he said as if to himself, 'I've never noticed that before. We had assumed that the French force had mistaken a light in Byfield for the signal from Chase because it was the only explanation for their mistake which made sense, but I didn't really believe Byfield could be seen. That room on the end is the library. Rupert and I were sitting there and the lights were on. No wonder they mistook it.'

Libby followed his eye and then surveyed the dark hump of the Tipper's Wood that lay before them. 'So the wood really does cut off Chase,' she commented. 'But out at sea surely Chase would be clearly visible—or, indeed, both lights?'

'Only that from Chase. From far out in the Channel, Byfield would be invisible—it lies too low to be seen. But if they were guided by the Chase light, and steered rather too much to the west in their understandable desire to avoid the Needles, there would come a time when the wood cut off Chase's light, and as they came closer they'd see the Byfield one. It was sheer coincidence that there was a light from Byfield at all—normally Rupert and I would have been sitting in the small study. It just so happened that Rupert decided to examine some Moghul miniatures the old Earl once gave me, and they're kept in the library.'

They rode along the beach until they had left Byfield land and stood on that of Chase. With Tipper's Wood behind them to their left, they could see the great house clearly.

'Poor Max,' Lord Charlbury said, yet without a great deal of warmth in his voice. 'He wanted all this so much.'

'So did you,' Libby pointed out gently.

'Yes, I did, but I can't imagine ever stooping to his depths to get it,' he replied. 'I feel partially responsible for his death. If I hadn't chased him, he wouldn't have tripped and fallen and killed himself.'

'From what I hear, if he hadn't done so at the moment, he might well have shot you.'

'He might. He would certainly have tried, but I doubt if his hand was steady enough.' He sat in silence, absent-mindedly stroking his horse's neck. 'I also wonder what life would have held for Max. The opium seems already to have affected his ability to reason. I wonder if the old Earl knew of it—or suspected it. That might explain why he made such a strange Will. At the time, I thought he was trying to bring me to heel, and I still think there was an element of that in it; but I wonder now whether there was more on his mind than saving me from total ruin.'

'If Max is dead, who will inherit if you fail to comply with the Earl's conditions?'

He looked at her. 'I'm not sure. That possibility wasn't covered. I suppose I do, though the new Earl might also be able to claim. I rather fancy it might be a matter for the lawyers to settle.'

Libby thought about that. 'So you may very well not need to marry me to inherit Chase?' she said in a small voice.

He looked like a man struck by a sudden revelation. 'I may very well not need to do so, indeed!' he exclaimed. 'How wise my uncle was in stipulating common sense as one of the virtues to be sought! Without your excellent common sense, dear Libby, it might have escaped my notice that I need no longer marry you in order to inherit.'

Libby said nothing, but stared down at her gloved hand on the reins. Her heart beat terrifyingly hard in an unaccustomed place—her throat, it seemed—and she felt as if she would choke on it. She loved this man so much, and had done so since she had first met him; she had so nearly been his and now, because of her confounded common sense, to say nothing of her ill-judged tongue, she was about to lose him. Suddenly her inside had become an agonising, aching void. She could no longer envisage an existence without him, and even the prospect of such an eventuality made her feel physically ill.

So absorbed was Libby in these tumultuous and unwelcome reflections that she was totally unaware that Lord Charlbury was observing her closely, an appreciative gleam in his eye and a sympathetic smile on his normally sardonic lips.

'On the other hand,' he went on in the tone of one dispassionately weighing up pros and cons, 'I might lose an inheritance case and, even if I didn't, they take years to settle, create a great deal of thoroughly undesirable scandal, and often eat up most of the inheritance in the process. If, in accordance with my uncle's wishes, I marry you, I make quite certain of Chase. Quite certain,' he added, and then, when she made no answer, his tone became unexpectedly peremptory. 'Dismount,' he ordered, doing so himself as he spoke.

Libby lifted her right leg over the horn and disengaged her other foot from its stirrup. Lord Charlbury's arms were held up towards her, and it was the most natural thing in the world to lean into them and let him lift her to the ground. Once she was there, he did not let her go but retained his hold on her waist and looked down, laughing, into her eyes.

'My little love,' he said, and his voice was tender as she had never known it before. 'Can you really believe that I only wish to marry you in order to make sure of Chase?'

She looked up at him doubtfully. 'It was the reason you sought me out at Copthorne and the reason you sought my hand.'

'It was, but it has been a long time since I put the convenience of the marriage from my mind and admitted to myself that I loved you.'

'Don't tease, Marcus,' Libby begged, the entreaty in her eyes underlining her words. 'I would infinitely prefer you to say it was a marriage of convenience than to pretend to a love you do not—cannot—feel.'

'Cannot?'

'Oh, Marcus, with the life you've led, the wealth of experience you've had, a wife you loved to distraction— with all this, how can you love me?' she replied with a little of her old asperity but with an undertone of despair he did not miss.

'With the life I have led—about which you, my love, as a woman of breeding, are supposed to know nothing— I'm in a better position than I might otherwise be to know not only that I love you, but just how deep that love is. I can't pretend to have loved you since I first set eyes on you. You once said I took as much notice of you as I had of the wallpaper, and you were right—and if I tried to pretend otherwise you wouldn't believe me. Nor do I know when I began to love you. All I can say is that it seems incomprehensible to me now that there was ever a time when I knew you without doing so. Nor can I pretend you're the first woman I've ever loved. My love for Maria-Giulietta will never be forgotten. I had thought it could never be replaced, but I was wrong. Libby, you know you're not the first woman with whom I have ever wanted to spend the rest of my life, but I vow you will be the last. Of course,' he added lightly, 'if you would rather I insisted it was purely a matter of convenience, I'll do so if that would make you happier.'

'Of course it wouldn't!' she laughed. 'I love you so much, Marcus. Your love may have crept up on you gradually, but mine for you has been something which struck me like a thunderbolt the first time you visited Copthorne. I wasn't surprised that you regarded me as if I were part of the furnishings: I was so afraid of drawing unfavourable attention to myself that I deliberately became as unobtrusive as I could. Oh, I dreamed that you would notice me and love me in spite of it, but even as I dreamed I knew I was being silly. It never crossed my mind that I would one day receive an offer from you, and I accepted because I loved you and it was one way—perhaps the only way—I could help you to get your heart's desire. Nothing could possibly make me happier than the knowledge that you have indeed come to love me.'

He pulled her to him and kissed her with the undiluted passion he had kept in check for so long. Libby felt herself soften in his arms in response to the strong tide of feeling that both had kept suppressed, and as their mouths and bodies moved closer she knew her dreams were dreams no longer. When his lips at least released hers, his eyes looked down with a warmth she hoped would never die.

'Will you marry me, Libby?'

She chuckled. 'I thought that was what this was all about,' she said.

'And I was beginning to think you were a romantic!'

'Not at all! Common sense is my forte, as well you know.'

'I do know it, but I've observed that it sometimes manifests itself in very romantic disguises. Libby, this proposal is not like the previous one. That was a matter of convenience. This is a matter of the heart. Will you marry me?'

'Yes.'

'When?'

'How soon is it possible? You can hardly marry while you're in mourning for Max.'

His face darkened. 'Max seeks to separate us even from his grave. I'll not give him that satisfaction. If you have your heart set on a grand affair, we must, of course, wait, but we can make Max's death the excuse for marrying quietly. Will tomorrow be too soon?'

'Tomorrow!' She was startled. 'Marcus, surely that isn't possible?'

'Why not?' He patted his pocket. 'I've not travelled anywhere these past weeks without that special licence. Tomorrow?'

'Tomorrow,' she agreed and, hand in hand, the horses following quietly, they walked across the lawns towards the house that had so dramatically changed their lives forever.

BATTLEFIELD OF HEARTS

Joanna Makepeace

Coerced into marriage? Never!

Rather than be forced by her widowed stepmother to marry Thomas Stoodley, Aleyne escaped, hoping to find protection of her cousin. But in this year of 1471, Warwick the Kingmaker had fomented trouble, and the armies of Edward IV and Queen Margaret were set to battle at Tewkesbury.

Sir Dominick Allard, Richard of Gloucester's man, found he couldn't abandon Aleyne on the road, but Richard's solution was also marriage! Swept up in the turmoil, Aleyne had little choice but to accept Dominick . . .

TWO
HISTORICAL ROMANCES

Masquerade historical romance bring the past alive with splendou excitement and romance. We wil send you a cuddly teddy bear an a special MYSTERY GIFT. Then, i you choose, you can go on to enjoy more exciting Masquerades every tw months, for just £1.99 each! Sen the coupon below at once to – Reade Service, FREEPOST, PO Box 236 Croydon, Surrey CR9 9EL.

&

TWO
FREE GIFTS!

NO STAMP REQUIRED ──→

Yes! Please rush me my 2 Free Masquerade Romances and 2 Free Gifts! Please also reserve me a Reader Service Subscription. If I decide to subscribe, I can look forward to receiving 4 Masquerade Romances every two months for just £7.96, delivered direct to my door. Post and packing is free, and there's a free Newsletter. If I choose not to subscribe I shall write to you within 10 days - I can keep the books and gifts whatever I decide. I can cancel or suspend my subscription at any time. I am over 18.

Mrs/Miss/Ms/Mr _____ EP04N

Address _____

_____ Postcode _____

Signature _____